Praise for Without th

Anne has always, and unfairly, been t
her work considered less important than ~~that of her sibling~~
even threatened with suppression by her own sister, Charlotte, author of
Jane Eyre, who wrote to her publisher:

*Wildfell Hall it hardly appears to me desirable to preserve. The choice of
subject in that work is a mistake, it was too little consonant with the character,
tastes and ideas of the gentle, retiring, inexperienced writer.*

Inexperienced? Hardly, as DM Denton's meticulously researched and
beautifully written account of Anne's life so acutely delineates. Now, of
course, we recognize *The Tenant of Wildfell Hall*, Anne's second and final
novel, as being far ahead of its time in its close study of a woman's
determination to escape her abusive marriage.

Without the Veil Between catches both the triumph and the tragedy of
Anne's short but quietly courageous and determined life. Her
disappointments and heartbreak patiently borne; her originality of
thought in opposition to contemporary mores; her searing and
unflinching insights into the experiences of women and the need for
resistance and positive action that we now call feminism.

This is no cozy account of three sisters living in harmony in their
parsonage home while happily creating their masterpieces for posterity.
DM Denton convincingly explores the tensions that existed between the
sisters as well as their mutual love and support; and the security and
emotional comfort Anne found within her family juxtaposed with the
need to separate herself in some way. This is perfectly captured in the
author's precise description of both Charlotte and Anne being "torn
between the calling to leave and the longing to stay". Here, also, we see
the author's careful and measured examination of the different
personalities at work within the Brontë family: Charlotte is driven to
venture out more by "curiosity and enterprise", while Anne's purpose is
a serious and morally driven desire to develop character and endurance,
and demonstrate what she is capable of. And, indeed, it is she of all the
sisters who does endure for longest in the world of work: five years as a
governess before she resigned, probably due to the ignominy of her
brother Branwell's disastrous liaison with her pupils' mother.

DM Denton skillfully captures Anne's distinctive personality and
strength of character while poignantly contrasting this with her frail
constitution, blighted by asthma and then the tuberculosis that killed her
at such a young age. The final pages of the book leading to Anne's
inevitable demise are written with a simplicity and restraint that is
intensely moving and wholly convincing.

Above all, DM Denton reveals the Anne that Charlotte could not – or would not – see. This book gives us Anne. Not Anne, the 'less gifted' sister of Charlotte and Emily (although we meet them too as convincingly drawn individuals); nor the Anne who 'also wrote two novels', but Anne herself, courageous, committed, daring and fiercely individual: a writer of remarkable insight, prescience and moral courage whose work can still astonish us today.

~ Deborah Bennison, bennisonbooks.com

Early in Diane Denton's book the young curate, William Weightman, says to Anne Brontë: "You must find such satisfaction in being able to capture those moments the rest of us let slip away and sometimes aren't aware of to begin with." This is an essential part of Denton's own gift. With this ability she is able to enter the world of a shy artist who lived in the shadows of her father, brother, and sisters, and in the light of a determined and insightful intellect. Anne Brontë set herself a more difficult task than her famous sisters, Charlotte and Emily. She was on a course of an artist whose subject was her life. Making this even more difficult, she sought to achieve emotional and mental stability.

Denton shows us the tensions in the austere home of the Reverend Brontë, the hopes for and disappointment in his drunken son, Branwell, and the longings of the three sisters for a more fulfilling life. The sisters' books are populated with people who live large lives, with secret loves, deception, greed, passion, and loyalty. In this setting, quiet Anne makes her own way, exploring human relationships with a keen sense of morality and ethics. As a governess she has to be with people all day, at their beck and call, and can barely aspire to more. But as a true Brontë, she does aspire. Brief moments with the young curate open her heart to the possibility of love. And she dreams of opening a school with her sisters, and being in charge of her own life. William's sudden death from cholera plunges her into depression, but she concentrates on duty and endurance, and calls on her faith.

On return to her father's home, Anne witnesses Branwell's descent into drugs, sexual escapades, and fantasy. Denton writes, "To reside within the dissolution of principles and proper behavior without being party to it meant that constant vigilance was required, which left little time or inclination for make-believe." Anne realizes she will never be comfortable at home, able to escape into her writing as Emily has. She believes she will never be useful in society or at home unless she pursues a "well-cultivated mind and well-disposed heart," and "have the strength to help others be strong." Denton indicates these are the real-world issues she explores in her writing.

Denton builds the story of Anne's young life gradually, taking us through her thoughts and experiences as she matures. The tempo steps up with the three sisters together again at Haworth, after having been separated for a few years. Charlotte has an idea for a book of poetry featuring all of them. Emily balks, and Anne mediates between the two, securing Emily's participation. I found this one of the most fascinating parts of the book. The dynamics among these three gifted women sizzles on the page. Descriptions of Charlotte and Emily are haunting in their excellence. Each woman changed literature and the way in which women were viewed in society. Anne's *The Tenant of Wildfell Hall* has been called one of the first feminist novels.

The book roars through the tragedies of Branwell's and Emily's deaths from consumption. Through all of this Anne faces reality with determination. She has come to believe she was meant to be "an observer, and given … a quiet skill to extract lessons from what she saw. There was truth to be told, warnings to be issued, patience and prudence to instill in young women." She depicted people and society with realism, not romanticism. This book made me wonder what Anne Brontë's influence would have been had she lived to reach full maturity. Sadly, she died soon after her sister, Emily.

In *Without the Veil Between*, Denton's writing has reached its maturity as well. I kept copying excerpts and pasting them in a file for me to read, enjoy, and think about later. Whole passages are beautifully written: meticulous, poetic, luminous, and powerful. The ending, echoing the title, is especially brilliant. I can't think of anyone better suited to bring us into the world and the life of the sensitive, creative, and quietly courageous Anne Brontë.

~Mary Clark, author of *Tally: An Intuitive Life* and *Miami Morning*

Diane Denton's new novel, *Without the Veil Between*, should be read in a place where time, inside and outside the reader, is suspended, where today and tomorrow are not absolutes, but songs faintly heard as the sun descends into the horizon of a shining sea. The story of the Brontë family told through the senses of Anne Brontë, the sister who did not become the powerful force in English literature her sisters, Charlotte and Emily, did, explores how genius interplays with the everyday frustrations, sensations, and tragedies of life, transmuting the imagination and observations of three brilliant sisters into the tapestry of stories and poetry that is still relevant to our contemporary lives.

What the story of the Brontë's has always had at its core is a question, how did literary genius flower in three of the women of a Victorian family from the English village of Haworth and the landscape of the

English Moors when the mother died so young and the father was a clergyman in a small village? After all, in the years she served as a governess the idealistic Anne had a status that was only a little better than the servants in the stratified society of the England of that time.

Denton's novel provides at least a hint of how the three sisters turned the societal and domestic constraints in which they lived into characters and stories and poetry that have stood the test of time. Anne was, at least to the modern sensibility, a great novelist in spite of her contemporary reputation, and as she weaves her gentle spirit into dealing with the dissolution of her brother, her father's loving distraction, and her two sisters' determination to overcome the limitations of their sex in Victorian society, the reader gets a sense of how genius rose out of the tensions, love, and straining within the family itself.

This was not a flowering from wealth and status, but sparks engendered out of living in a certain time and place where meals were prepared and eaten, long walks in foreboding weather were gloried in, and conversation helped spur what would seem to have been at the time literary efforts without much chance of bearing fruit.

What Denton has achieved is a portrait placed in a time very different from the jangling present, but that resonates in a way that suspends years and centuries and lets us feel the joys and sadness of a writer whose unflinching look at life, especially in her novels, rings with the authenticity of who, inside, she really was.

~ Thomas Davis, Author of *The Weirding Storm*

DM Denton's historical novel, *Without the Veil Between /Anne Brontë: A Fine and Subtle Spirit,* is the story of the Brontë family from the point of view of Charlotte and Emily's younger sister. The title comes from a line in one of Anne's poems, *In Memory of a Happy Day in February.* The last stanza of the poem is quoted in the afterword of Denton's novel.

As was the case with many nineteenth century families, the Brontës suffered loss. Anne was born in 1820. Her mother died in 1821 and two of her sisters, Maria and Elizabeth, died in 1825. This left the father, Patrick Brontë, an Anglican priest, to raise the three sisters and one son alone. Denton's emphasis on the thoughts and desires of the youngest Brontë sister brings color and life to the pages of her novel. She expresses Anne's concerns in lavish prose that matches the 19th century Brontë style. *Without the Veil Between* isn't simply a biographical novel; it is a journey back into the day to day lives of one of history's most famous literary families.

Anne's brother, Branwell, was a primary focus of her thoughts due to his troubled lifestyle. He often returned home after his habits left him no alternative.

"Branwell also had the refuge of home for career disasters, but nowhere but drink and opium for those of the heart."

Early in the novel, Anne desired a relationship with William Weightman, an assistant to her father and a good friend of Branwell's. Her feelings for the young curate were a mixture of her own interest and respect for the effect William had on her troubled brother.

"Branwell had even confided to her that 'Willie' was the best friend he'd ever had – with a wink that caused Anne to wonder if William had admitted something, too. She knew she shouldn't think so. Nevertheless, before she closed her eyes on that day she would be tempted to hold and look at one of her most treasured possessions: a Valentine..."

Of course, the role writing played in Anne's and her sisters' lives is the most interesting of their concerns.

"Writing and talking about their writing inspired them, and defined them, at least to each other."

It was, as it is for most writers, a means of escape and a way of dealing with life's frustrations.

"Anne found writing a most natural and constant way to seek relief. Her reason became another's, a naively optimistic, determined, almost invisible young woman named Agnes, who composed musings out of sorrows or anxieties to acknowledge in a resilient way all those powerful feelings that could never be wholly crushed and for which solace from any living creature shouldn't be sought or expected. Anne hoped Agnes' story would mark her own passage from a woman of mere occupation to one of true vocation."

The works of Charlotte and Emily, *Jane Eyre* and *Wuthering Heights*, are the two Brontë novels most well known today, but Anne's novels *Agnes Grey* and *The Tenant of Wildfell Hall* are still taught in schools around the world. *The Tenant of Wildfell Hall* was successful enough during Anne's life to earn a second edition.

~ Steve Lindahl, author of *Hopatcong Vision Quest*, *White Horse Regressions*, and *Motherless Soul*.

Without the Veil Between

Anne Brontë: A Fine and Subtle Spirit

DM Denton

ALL THINGS
THAT MATTER
PRESS

In the spirit of the intense love Anne Brontë had for her Flossy,
I dedicate this novel to my brother cats, Gabriel and Darcy,
who passed from this world during the writing of it

A fine and subtle spirit dwells
In every little flower,
Each one its own sweet feeling breathes
With more or less of power.

~From *The Bluebell* by Anne Brontë

Brontë Parsonage
Haworth

PART ONE

"What a fool you must be," said my head to my heart, or my sterner to my softer self.

~ Anne Brontë, *Agnes Grey*

CHAPTER ONE

Scarborough, July 1842

The sea made the world vast. Anne must have known this before she traveled to the North Yorkshire coast—any coast—for the first time two summers ago, her pencil sketch *Sunrise Over the Sea* born three years earlier while she was at Blake Hall.

Emily assumed the drawing was conceived of Gondal imaginings.

Anne kept it in a leather envelope folder along with other artwork and a sketching block. She liked to look at it as a reminder of her early courage and optimism, which posed a young woman on a rocky precipice, her arm lifted and shielding her eyes to a brightening outlook.

The seagulls were real now, as were the ships as light on the waves as wisps of clouds hung from the heavens. Anne was once again in Scarborough with the Robinsons, well-situated on St. Nicholas Cliff in lodgings she appreciated, not because of their elegance and prestige, proximity to the Spa, Gothic saloon, an excellent library and pleasant walkways, but for the magnificent view of the shimmering South Bay. Looking away from the harbor, arcades, and finery, over a stretch of shore little disturbed except by the tides, beyond swelling, spraying waves to where the sea calmed to meet the sky, she could think of only one way she might be happier.

"Doesn't Miss Brontë look different?"

Anne didn't mean for anyone to notice, not outside of Haworth and there only by a certain acquaintance if he was wishing as she was. She pretended not to hear Elizabeth's question or Lydia's snippy reply.

"Yes. I see how she hopes to improve her looks with a slightly altered hairstyle and dress a mere five years out-of-date."

Earlier that year it had been difficult for Anne to give up the chance to stay at home. She might have used the excuse of her sisters going to school in Brussels, an ironic turn of events considering Emily's anger when Anne accepted a position forty miles from Haworth. "You won't come back for months. We'll end up hardly knowing each other."

How would a longer distanced, lengthier separation affect their bond? Especially as Emily rarely corresponded.

The previous Christmas, Anne was resolved to permanently leave Thorpe Green and not look for another position while Charlotte and Emily were abroad. Charlotte claimed her youngest sister wasn't up to helping young Martha with household chores and caring for their father like sturdier Emily was, and took credit for Anne's change of plan. Anne was actually swayed by a letter from the Robinsons declaring how much they valued her, imploring her to return to them.

***

Lydia, Elizabeth, and Mary were, like Anne and her sisters, close in age. They were obsessed with growing up and outdoing each other, unlike the Brontë girls, who had their scribbles of stories, poems, and letters to the future to keep them childlike, and hopes for a school of their own to encourage collaboration over competition.

Anne watched her pupils with thoughts they would never guess she had, accepting they related to her as a necessary part of growing up advantaged. She wasn't averse to being friends with them, but didn't forget the true purpose of her employment. Although never as intolerably bad as the Inghams, the Robinson siblings did, at times, test Anne's resolve to educate and care for them like a gardener nurturing and protecting tender plants.

Anne didn't know where Edmund Jr. was that afternoon, not sorry for his absence; there was nothing peaceable or teachable about him. He wasn't always the youngest. When Anne first took up her post, Georgina Jane, at just over two, wasn't ready for schooling, but now and then Anne would relieve Nanny in the nursery and know a few cheerier hours in the Thorpe Green household.

"Can Mary go for a donkey ride?"

"May Mary," Elizabeth was corrected by her youngest sister. "May I, Miss Brontë?" Mary's expectant eyes and heart-shaped lips reminded Anne of Georgina's.

Anne hesitated to decide, thinking how she might be refreshed by a walk along the strand and amused by a donkey that jingled merrily and loved having its neck rubbed. She wished she could go by herself or only with Mary, who, away from the bickering of her sisters, could be quiet, curious, and sympathetic. Anne knew she couldn't take one without the others, but hoped Edmund wouldn't come. She had been worse than embarrassed by him digging his heels into the donkey's flanks, pulling its ears, and kicking sand at the gypsy boy who ordered him off. Edmund's behavior made him little better than the spoiled Ingham boy who removed baby birds from their nests to torture them.

Anne didn't give up on anyone easily, especially children who hardly knew better than their pampered lives and parents' neglect or ineffectiveness afforded them. It was odd she should feel more fortunate than they. Both the Inghams and Robinsons lacked the cohesion of family, the kind of affection rivalry couldn't overturn, and the companionship of kindred spirits no matter differences in desires and temperaments. She couldn't help but try to convince poor privileged youngsters to be glad of their siblings in a world of sorrows, stumblings, and, especially, strangers. She didn't dare hope they would ever share the intense collaboration of spirit and creativity the Brontë brood did.

"Well, have you thought about it long enough?" Lydia's insolence was effortless.

"I agree as long as your mother does, it's not too hot, and you all promise to behave like the ladies you were born to be."

The girls fetched their lightest and, therefore, prettiest bonnets while Anne did the same and went to look for their mother, only to be told she had gone to bed with a headache. Anne Marshall, Mrs. Robinson's personal maid and Anne's only friend amongst the Thorpe Green staff, added her mistress had been quite well before an argument with Mr. Robinson, the younger Edmund being the cause of it.

The Robinson girls applauded when they heard their brother had been ordered to stay indoors.

It was a breezy walk along Cliff Bridge, summer bonnets flattering except when gusty winds forced unladylike gesturing to prevent them flying off with seagulls that swooped, nearly collided, and screamed hysterically. Due to the threat of their skirts billowing wider and higher than several starched, flounced petticoats intended, the girls were contortionists reaching upwards and downwards to hold onto their hats and dignities. Halfway across, Anne directed the girls to one side of the bridge and suggested they turn back and spend what was left of the afternoon in the museum instead. They had to press against the railing to let the increasing foot traffic move past.

"Oh, come on, Miss Brontë. You'd rather study sea foam than fuddy-duddy fossils."

"I hate museums." Elizabeth pouted.

"And what is your opinion, Miss Mary?" Anne used her teaching voice. "It doesn't have to be the same as your sisters."

"I don't always agree with them." Mary played with the bright yellow bow behind her right ear. "I would rather go down to the beach and see Daisy."

"Childish things are for children." Sixteen-year-old Lydia stuck out her tongue and escaped in the direction, for the moment, she intended to go.

"We'll never find her," Mary whined and took Anne's hand.

Overprotected by her own family, Anne relished the responsibility of offering reassurance to young women. "I'm sure she'll look for us. Eventually."

What really consoled them was the cluster of colorfully bridled donkeys near the backwash just north of where the beach curved and narrowed. Creamy, gray-speckled Daisy was there with her nose stuck in a feed bag, her ears swaying at the sound of Mary's voice and her tail lifting in a less pleasant greeting. The barefooted boy nearby made no attempt to warn Mary.

Anne laughed. "Watch your step."

Despite her obvious delight at being reunited with Daisy, Mary wasn't as eager to ride her. Elizabeth had no qualms haggling with the donkey's young raggedy handler about the charge, the deal sealed when she decided the red-checked bandana around his neck needed adjusting, almost kissing his cheek as she re-tied it. Elizabeth's favorite companions at home were the stable lads she allowed to call her Bessie. She could easily ride sidesaddle but straddled her horse whenever she thought she might impress them.

Surprisingly compliant to Anne's request, Elizabeth helped Mary mount Daisy in a ladylike fashion and keep upright and balanced.

"Fifteen minutes only," the donkey handler demanded, no doubt because of all the excited children lining up.

"Stay with her, Miss Elizabeth," Anne was quieter with her command.

The farther Anne went from the donkeys, huts, bathers, and concerns for her giggling, argumentative charges, the sand was less and less disturbed and eventually almost perfectly smooth so her footprints were the first that day, for many days, or, as she might pretend, ever. To the east was somewhere foreign and, therefore, appealing. Her gaze and steps traveled over low mossy rocks around rippling pools, and followed little streams down to the dazzling, daring expanse of the North Sea.

As indecisive as it seemed, the surf was coming closer, offering to wash her feet.

Anne should have scolded her girls if they had wetted just the hems of their skirts and petticoats. It would have been indefensible to allow them to remove their shoes and stockings and lift their dresses, let alone show them how to sink into the sand and feel it and slithery seaweed between their toes. What missteps they would all have taken if, on impulse, Anne led them further into the cold, frothy, toing and froing water.

The indecency of baring her lower calves along with the sensation of the sea's salty shallowness drawing her in deeper should have caused Anne shame if anyone saw her. Sharp stones contradicted liquid caresses, and, as she might be imagining, fish nibbled her legs and feet. Eventually, she heard the faint sound of her charges, possibly even Lydia, summoning her.

Anne wanted to delay resuming that part of her life a little longer.

Something was coming to her. It wasn't an idea for a painting or poem, but a story that could be hers after all. It began from its ending, a happy one in the passages of an individual. Coming out of nowhere and everywhere, a figure was on the beach: "A gentleman with a little dark speck of a dog running after him," a sentence she repeated a few times out loud so she wouldn't forget it before she had a chance to write it down.

CHAPTER TWO

The small rocking chair in a corner near the fireplace was Anne's usual place in the dining room that also served as a parlor. She liked to prop her stockinged feet on the hearth's fender, a habit from childhood.

That evening it wasn't Aunt Elizabeth looking in that had Anne scrambling to put on her shoes. Her own reserve created the potential embarrassment, also of what was in plain view on the pedestal table. Company hadn't been expected. Anne was happy for it, but wished she had been warned in time to clear away any confidences and have the evening paper on display instead.

William stood a while by the open window, commenting on the scent of honeysuckle also pervading his lodging now. "Finally, it's warm enough to let the outside in. Not always with such pleasant effect."

Branwell picked up her writing desk. "I don't think you meant to leave this here."

Anne took it from him, not sure if he was being devilish or thoughtful.

"Ah. The letters ladies send to one another. Ever intriguing."

"And best left so to us, Willie."

"I think I can handle knowing a little more of their thoughts."

Anne patiently persuaded the cat Tiger off the sofa to encourage William to sit, thinking she might mask her appreciation of her father's curate with gratefulness for her brother having such a good companion.

Anne wasn't surprised to find Branwell at home when she arrived for a few weeks respite from Thorpe Green. Charlotte had written to her of his dismissal from Luddendenfoot Station and Anne had prepared herself for his worst reaction. His latest career disaster was almost forgotten in William's cheerful company, something of Branwell's boyish charms and outlook revived by the warmth and mischievousness of the young man their father had wisely chosen as an assistant a few years earlier. Branwell had even confided to her that "Willie" was the best friend he'd ever had—with a wink that caused Anne to wonder if William had admitted something, too.

She knew she shouldn't think so. Nevertheless, before she closed her eyes on that day she would be tempted to hold and look at one of her most treasured possessions: a Valentine, a pretty thing of lace paper, satin ribbon, and embossed flowers with a little bird in an egg-filled nest,

Anne, dear, sweet, Anne quickly written but not yet slowly spoken.

It was *unto her spirit given*. She rocked with her portable desk on her lap as Branwell sat at the table, got up, walked around it and sat again, picking at his sidebars and rubbing the bridge of his nose where his spectacles pinched. He probably wasn't listening as intently as she was to William talking about his visits earlier in the day to ailing folk in the village, some "far on their way to where none return, cholera taking such a toll."

Branwell turned his back on William's glistening eyes, softening mouth, hands folding and unfolding, right leg jumping once and then again, and how the young curate glanced in Anne's direction.

"I weigh the conversation down. I'm already missing both your smiles."

Anne immediately relaxed without looking at William directly, her thoughts not for speaking. *The lightest heart I have ever known, the kindest I shall ever know.*

"Good thing the Major isn't here. She wouldn't oblige you. I don't think there's the possibility of smiling in her."

"The blooming heather would disagree with you, Branny," Anne said meekly but fully in defense of her sister Emily.

"Now, now. Where's your shy pleasure gone? Perhaps it will return if you know I've spoken to Branwell about your idea."

William mentioning her shyness embarrassed her, but any specific awareness he had of her did. "Thank you," she could say to him for one reason if not another.

"And will there be posh holidays in Scarborough for me, too?" Branwell rose and went over to Anne. Despite her protests, he put her desk on the sofa next to William and, as slim and agile as ever, lifted her into his arms for waltzing in place.

William applauded the exercise.

"You're next, Miss Celia Amelia." Branwell let go of Anne to dance with William, all three laughing.

Anne was becoming even fonder of the bright curls and rosy cheeks that gave Curate Weightman his nickname.

How could she not feel tender towards a man who realized unlucky even misguided choices must be forgiven for progress to be made? William was the best influence her brother could have. He knew how to enjoy Branwell's immaturity without pandering to his moodiness and self-pitying, and encouraged him to be wiser and steadier without wanting him to change too much. He found pleasure in Branwell's company through cerebral conversations, robust explorations of the moors—taking a gun but, as Emily ribbed, rarely a victim, so only hopes for roasted grouse were shot—and proving a couple of pints were more companionable than a dozen.

William was not the deceptive flirt Charlotte made him out to be, but a congenial irresistible fellow who paid attention to many so he would not slight any. He was a respectable servant to the parish and reliable friend to her family, a tonic for the disheartened, a shoulder for the uncertain, an envoy of charity and tolerance. He was good but not at all sanctimonious. Rather unclerical, as Charlotte accused, he provided happy company never to be regretted, not even by Anne's piqued older sister who initially had been among the number who hoped to become his one and only.

Despite being the youngest, a restrained nature, and the designation of "Waiting Boy" in the Glasstown Confederacy, Anne never accepted her place in line meant she was out of contention. Not that she would obviously compete for anything, certainly not William's affection. She wished to savor her consciousness of loving, not tempted to hurry because of misgivings or time passing. Surely physical parting was only injurious to love when accompanied by doubt, a test necessary to true believing. Faith had so far sustained her, it was her salvation on earth as it would be in heaven.

Faith was certainly needed in setting Branwell on a steadier course. Anne relished the opportunity to join hers with William's, which, in being convincing and effective, had the advantage of his gender.

It was promising Branwell had been dissuaded from joining up and his habit of staying out half the night was almost broken.

Her brother was even willing to play the organ again at Sunday service. With Aunt Branwell restricting her interest to the church service and folds of her black skirt, there was no one to assume the interpretation of soft sighs or furtive glances, telling quietness or downcast eyes as Anne and "the young reverence" — yet another nickname assigned to William, by Charlotte's friend Ellen Nussey — sat on opposite sides of the aisle and surely thought of nothing more or less than being grateful for that day the Lord had given them.

Anne was also glad of the new dress she had sewn in between her governess duties from eight yards of gray silk the eldest Robinson daughter decided she didn't want. Anne's appreciation of the quality fabric and its achromatic color was an influence of her aunt's refined, if sober, style. Miss Lydia asked nothing for it until she needed Anne to turn a blind eye to something she didn't want her mother to know. Another part of the pact was the loan of one of Lydia's gowns to make a pattern from.

"Too inhibiting for me, but proper for you. I'd outright give you the frock, but it's one Mama wants me to wear to church. You'd have to alter it anyway."

It was a suitable dress for Sunday service, colorless, and compatible with Anne's small form. Squeezed in next to her aunt, sitting upright with her hands folded around the hymnal on her lap, Anne was overly-conscious of proving she was content to be a vicar's daughter. And prepared to be a curate's wife?

William's surveillance changed direction as often as Charlotte claimed his flirtations did. Anne would rather attribute his shifting attention to amiability than fickleness.

There were many men who could at first and, for a while, please and astonish others, but eventually they would reveal their weak characters, insincerity, even dishonor, until their eyes, hair, form, and words were finer than their appeal. Anne wouldn't deny William was independent and mischievous, but only as he liked to encourage pluck and cheerfulness in others. It was clear he always meant to do what was right and just, over and over proving his good nature through the tireless kindness he showed everyone, especially those whom circumstance had been most unkind to. At once prepossessing, to some suspiciously so, the longer Anne knew William the more she trusted how she felt about him, especially as he held dear those she did.

His arm around her brother's shoulder, assuring Branwell his return to the organ wasn't spoiled by him losing his place in the processional hymn *All Praise to Our Redeeming Lord* and struggling with uncertain pedaling and clumsy fingering in *Love Divine, All Loves Excelling*, was an embrace of her, too.

"In the end, my friend, you found your way," William's cheeks were almost crimson, little streaks of sweat on them, "with *Hark, I Hear the Harps Eternal*."

William moved to follow the stragglers out of the church. Branwell couldn't avoid escorting Aunt Elizabeth home. Her large old-fashioned cap and forelock curls accentuated her head shaking, but her nephew bore her slightly scolding opinion of his performance with gratefulness for the forbearance she also showed him.

"Well, if I don't find new employment, Aunt," his arm hooked hers under the shawl she wouldn't be without, even on such a warm day, "I will have more time to practice."

Her small stride forced him to slow down. "I can't deny it is good to have you home."

Anne was left behind, slipping up and down the pews, tidying prayer books and hymnals. She stepped up to the top of the triple-decker pulpit to gather her father's papers in anticipation of supporting the excellent words and deeds of a husband intent on spreading the "peace of God which passeth understanding."

William would eventually become adept at transforming the apathy and lethargy of so-called worshippers, which necessitated Sexton John Brown walking up and down the aisles poking drowsy adults with his long staff and verbally intimidating fidgety children. Even Reverend Brontë couldn't convince everyone he was worth paying attention to. Ellen Nussey had once described the change that came over many when he began his sermon, how "a rustic, untaught intelligence gleamed in their faces", more pronounced if he offered a parable from the gospels, going over it word by word and explaining it in the simplest manner. Anne knew her father did so to speak to their straightforwardness and not to show superiority, his parishioners' understanding more important to his sense of achievement than oratory skills.

Anne could hear William's lively chatter just outside the church, reminding he was gregarious, generous with his time and joyousness, and happiest when he was lifting others out of sighing and sadness. She chided herself for minding he didn't observe her passing by, his occupation requiring him to be available to everyone, even silly young ladies who shouldn't be denied a little of his sparkling company.

Anne wasn't prepared for him walking beside her before she caught up with her aunt and brother.

"What will you do with the rest of your day?" he asked, sliding his hands down his long white cravat and folding them around its ends against the front of his heavily-buttoned frock coat.

She looked up for the sunshine that might yet peek through the dark and light clouds, a skylark singing frantically and flying as if looking for a way through them in the opposite direction the sun was. William was patient while she considered what to say, one answer in her heart and another in her head, someone else calling his name with an urgency she doubted she could ever express. The perfect afternoon activity would be a walk beyond Penistone Hill, across the high-ground, gray-green heath where curlews, golden plover peregrines, and merlins nested and by now would have some young. Even unintentional intruders might flush a few grouse out of the bracken and delight at them taking off to glide over the hair grass, cotton sedge, fern, and heather. There was always time to dally for such sights and talk to curly-horned sheep crowding for scraps of bread before continuing to the top of a steep slope, catching a glimmer here and there of the stream in the gully below. As the journey neared its end, hands would clasp to carefully descend the uneven stone steps to the waterfall weakened but its appeal not diminished by early summer. Emily's chair would offer rest; other large stones also shaped, if not quite so perfectly, for sitting. What a pleasant diversion if the rain held off, invigorating if the wind was brisk, and respectable if Branwell came along, leaving little doubt how, as avowed in Psalm 104:24, the Lord had given them an earth full of riches.

"I hope you will excuse me." William barely breathed and was gone.

***

Anne took a low wooden stool from the kitchen, her desk box, and art folder outside, managing to carry them all at once across the lawn to settle within the shade of some currant bushes Emily called their bit of a fruit garden. After half an hour, Anne felt chilled and relocated away from the high stone wall and elder and lilac shrubs that divided the parsonage yard from the church's. At first, she couldn't write or draw, trying to restrict herself to practical thoughts. The little flower patches of lupines and cornflowers underneath the house's front windows were ready for weeding again. She even saw diversions that weren't there, like the Sicilian sweet peas, which should have shown some attachment to a trellis by the front door and would have needed tying up if Martha hadn't forgotten to plant the seeds Emily had collected from last year's blooms. Anne wondered if it was too late.

Anne worked on a drawing begun some months before. Little Ouseburn Church was most picturesque viewed from the other side of Ouse Gill Beck, its chancel encased by shrubby trees, a grassy bank inclined towards the stream, the mausoleum just out of sight. The Robinsons' bonneted phaeton was commandeered every Sunday to transport the family nearly two miles to the church, immediately afterwards waiting to take them back to the Hall for dinner by half-past noon. Anne was included in and yet irrelevant to the Sunday ritual, the latter demonstrated by no one questioning her folder tucked under her arm or even thinking to refuse her request to stay behind to draw a while before returning on foot.

"You may do what you please, Miss Brontë," Mrs. Robinson was mimicked by her children for saying.

"Aren't you afraid to walk back alone?" Mary wondered before her mother insisted she get into the carriage.

Anne was relieved she didn't have to answer, for any explanation of her need for bucolic solitude would have implied dissatisfaction with her indoor life at Thorpe Green. Her bedroom was small and gloomy, the subdued light through the only window waking her very early but, by late afternoon or in the evening, providing inadequate illumination for reading, writing, or artwork. She took whatever time she could to be on her own out-of-doors, freed from capricious children and their equally variable parents, the dissatisfaction of servants and repetitive duties, and, especially, the dreariness of back stairs and dark corridors. In contrast, it was easy to put up with feeling too warm in the sun and too cool in the shade, watch for rain, hold her paper from curling in the wind, and wave away midges. She welcomed the distractions of birdsong and any of the creatures she could hear but not see or see without seeing, like the fish making little whirlpools of bubbles in the stream between her and the church.

Months later, resorting to memory and imagination, she attempted to finally finish her impression of the Little Ouseburn Church scene.

Anne had her head down for over an hour, the shade chilling her again, St. Michael's and All Angels' bell tower, her dry mouth and stomach telling her it was time for tea. Her aunt and father often preferred to take late afternoon refreshment in their bedroom or study respectively. In that case, the kitchen, although too warm with the range stoked for heating water, was an agreeable substitution, along with Martha and her chitchat, much of it about the residents of Haworth and more unseemly than Anne would otherwise ever hear and was too prudent to comment on. If Branwell joined them, he wouldn't hesitate to express his cynical opinion and even add some tavern gossip.

"Yes, it is that time, isn't it? I'm taking tea with the Browns. They complain I'm rarely with them although I live and work amongst them."

Anne wasn't so much startled by William as embarrassed by him witnessing her graceless act of picking up her seat while she held onto her desk and sketchpad. She left the stool on the ground and stood straight to see him sitting on the edge of a horizontal gravestone nearly as high as the churchyard wall he was leaning over.

"May I see? I don't wish to burden you with any sort of critique. I hardly have the qualification for that."

"It's not a burden to show you, just to do the drawing in the first place."

"Surely not." William was already looking at her work and not just her imitation of Little Ouseburn Church, but flipping through sketches and watercolors of landscapes, animal studies, and portraits. "You must find such satisfaction in being able to capture those moments the rest of us let slip away and sometimes aren't aware of to begin with."

"I can't easily enjoy them as others do, always troubling myself with whether I can really reproduce what I see, what I feel, especially of nature's beauty. I fear vanity and a weak spirit urge me to try to do so."

William carefully closed the folder, standing and hesitating before giving it up. "Well, even if you haven't satisfied yourself, you've succeeded in impressing and delighting another."

"Hey, you two," Branwell called down from an open window on the second floor of the parsonage. "What scheme are you leaving me out of?"

William hopped over the wall, picked up the stool, and followed Anne to the house, putting it just inside the front door she slowly opened. With her back to him she was afraid he must think her cold, dull, awkward, even ill-tempered, not at all a possibility for his happiness let alone her own.

It was his hand that turned her around, lightly but sincerely pressing the fingertips of her left one with a wordless promise of *trust me.*

CHAPTER THREE

Thorpe Green Hall, three months later, September 1842

School was on the first floor below Anne's bedroom. Uninspiring with its old cotton-warp and wool filled drugget and drearier hearth rug, mahogany chest against one wall, glass-fronted book case filling another, and small frayed divan, it was the center of her world ten and a half months out of the year. During the week, her morning and afternoon meals were taken there on an abused Pembroke-style table, one or both of its leaves up or down depending on whether or not her students ate with her.

Most outings happened because the Robinson siblings wanted to ride their pony or horses, run with the dogs, or do any frivolous thing rather than improve their intellect, discover the joys of art or music, study the science of things, or cultivate sensitivity in their hearts. For them, being out-of-doors wasn't slowly and quietly walking so as not to disturb what was crouched in long grass and perched in glistening trees. Exercise books were forgotten, although brought along in long-strapped satchels, only Anne making notes about the Vale of York's fertile meadows, easy woods, unkempt hedgerows, and canopied lanes. She was unable to convince her students to notice the sky, no matter how she poeticized the shapes of clouds and golden breaks in between, or the rolling in of more rain.

Her pupils stomped in puddles and caught their clothes on briars, and hadn't any inclination to pause in reflection and notice how the air was freshly scented. If Anne lost sight of the sisters and their brother running on ahead or, more likely, straying from the planned route and not all in the same direction, she said a quick prayer to keep them safe and made the most of a more satisfying stroll with her thoughts and Mother Nature.

Oh, let me be alone a while, no human form is nigh. And I may sing and muse aloud, no mortal ear is by.

A rarer divergence from Anne's ups and downs in the Hall's east wing was a dinner party at Thorpe Green. Mrs. Robinson was inclined to show off her progeny for other significant folk to see how well they were growing and Anne was expected to keep them on their best behavior. Elizabeth and Mary were fairly cooperative, perhaps because they felt the opportunity to be seen and not heard was better than not being seen at all. Lydia was more inclined to upset her mother, not because she didn't value social status but with her own ideas on how to achieve it. She went along with dancing to show off her figure, and singing if someone else played the pianoforte, but used her charms to choose male victims according to her preference for enjoying the present over considering the future.

Ten-year-old Edmund had the knack of pleasing his mother even as he exasperated her. Mr. Robinson would impatiently summon Anne to do what she was there to do and control the lad's willfulness as no one could.

Anne had been hired like and unlike any of the kitchen, house, stable, or grounds staff. She was expected to accept her lowly place and yet dress and act better than the other servants and not associate with them, which was their ruling as much as the Robinsons'. There wasn't cozy time by the kitchen fire like at Haworth with Tabitha Aykroyd and young Martha Brown, Anne missing their stories, gossip, even Tabby's scolding over the extravagance of lighting another candle.

Anne was a governess. It was her job to watch, follow, teach, and endure, every day at any hour, her life crowded without true company. She was to act like a lady without ever expecting to be treated like one in respect to her class, experiencing snobbery from every direction and disorder in her sense of herself. At least, that was how it was before she began believing there might be a different future for her, one full of tenderness and affection. It was still unclear but not uncorroborated, not since those summer solstice days that encouraged a touch and trust and thoughts of what more a next meeting might offer.

***

On a chilly afternoon in the third week of September, Anne should have been in bed with a compress on her chest and wool wrapped around her neck. Her breathing was difficult and her voice weak, the effects of a cold and asthma attacks brought on after her charges talked her into conducting a lesson outside in unsuitable weather. They had all sat on damp grass, but only she and Mary were caught in a driving downpour, because they had gathered the books and papers the others had abandoned to avoid getting wet.

While the Misses Robinson and their brother did schoolwork Anne had assigned them, she sat at the table intending to write a letter. It was almost two weeks since she had received one: most reproachfully, none from Charlotte or Emily, who seemed lost to her while they were in Brussels. She was less likely to hear from Branwell, but it was unusual for her father and aunt to leave her so bereft of correspondence, theirs usually regular if brief.

"I think I've studied enough today." Edmund sat back, holding onto the edge of the table, the front legs of his chair off the ground.

Anne knew he was goading her with the chance he would fall backwards as he had more than a few times before. "Who will have sympathy if you hurt yourself?"

"You will, Miss."

"Have you conjugated all those verbs?"

"He's done more silly pictures than Latin." Elizabeth huddled with Mary as they both giggled.

It was fortunate the rigors of public school were still a few years off for Edmund. "And what have you two accomplished?" Anne was more frustrated with the girls' resistance to being studious. She offered them a curriculum of the three R's, French conversation, history, and the use of globes, as well as drawing, the rudiments of music, the example of modesty, and, without a hint of criticism of their parents, a moral compass for knowing right from wrong.

"I've decided what color my next ball gown will be." Lydia, looking very well, had separated from her sisters and was reclining on the divan designated for ailing students only. Her shoes were off and there was a book in her lap, in this one way only reminding Anne of Emily. "And the style, too."

Anne's sigh was louder than she intended it to be.

"Oh, but I'm doing my French, Miss Brontë. *Une robe de bleue paon avec une décolleté en dentelle*," Lydia read with exaggerated enunciation from her notebook.

"Peacock blue?" Edmund slapped his Latin book shut. "You hardly need encouragement to strut around more than you already do, Lyd."

"You may one day appreciate a girl's proud posture."

"Never. Girls are annoying creatures. I'll be glad when I'm not surrounded by them."

"Is your brother as impossible to love, Miss Brontë?" Elizabeth almost seriously wondered.

"You may find out."

If Anne guessed Edmund's meaning correctly, it was the first she had heard of the possible outcome of an idea she had presented to his parents on the return from Scarborough. A fit of gasping and coughing prevented her questioning him further.

She rushed out of the room and upstairs to her own, seen by Mrs. Robinson who called her back to give her a letter.

"Is that your brother's hand?"

Anne was forced to look rather than tuck it into her sleeve and imagine who its sender was for a little while longer.

"Well, it's legible enough." The older Lydia Robinson hesitated to leave, her skirts filling the hallway, not seeming as handsome as she did in better light, her bosom out of balance with her small shoulders, her wide eyes colorless in the shadows. As she finally moved, the candlelight above caught the redness of her large nose and full cheeks, and, also, the wetness of her mouth. "When you reply, tell him my husband is willing to interview him."

Waiting for letters wasn't something Anne could become used to. Missing home was a trial, and wondering if she was forgotten caused more than a few confidence crises. She might have been valued by the Robinsons, but never felt approved of, the master dissatisfied with everything, his wife lazy and noncommittal, and the children almost sweetly glad of the return of "Miss Brontë" until after an hour or so they were misbehaving. Anne tried not to complain, not even to her sisters who knew what it was like to be exiled and harassed, as Emily put it or, in Charlotte's terms, to long for a way out of the land of Egypt and house of bondage.

Receiving a letter was a chance to escape immediate circumstances. Anne liked to carry it around, carefully break its seal, slowly meet its words, realize its consolation and companionship, read and consider and read again. She also delayed her response to be sure she measured it and didn't raise suspicion she was unhappy or, on the other hand, like during the last few months, harboring a joy it was difficult not to express.

The letter was from Branwell. He had addressed it without the artistic flourish of his better moods, Anne thinking he might be depressed because she hadn't let him know the status of his possible employment as Edmund's tutor. That could finally be remedied.

First Anne must return to the schoolroom, no matter she wasn't feeling well, Mrs. Robinson having stepped in and then out because the children were such a strain on her nerves.

Books were opened and closed on geography and French idioms, more Latin for Edmund, arithmetic even for the girls, the last hour for drawing or quiet reading without resistance as droopy eyes and even yawns explained. Anne considered opening Branwell's letter there, but with her head hurting, her patience for whatever he had to say seeming endless, and an audience she didn't wish to share it with, she told Miss Lydia to ring for tea and corrected some lessons instead.

***

"Won't you walk in the garden, Miss Brontë?"

"She's unwell, Mary. You know that."

"Yes, Bessie. But Mama only lets us go out before supper with Miss Brontë."

"Good night, dear girls," Anne uttered hoarsely. "I'm sure I'll feel better tomorrow."

Her room was cave-like, at the top of steep spiraling stairs and down a narrow passageway. The morning's strongest sunlight was blocked by farm buildings beyond that side of the house. Sometimes moonlight found its way in. If she opened and leaned out of her little sash window, she could catch its reflection on the crystal-clear pond below and even the sheen of ornamental fish swimming round and round. It had been an overcast day, very still, chilly yet humid. Usually Anne would hope for some clearing. The goal of an evening walk, if only as far as Monk's Lodge, was to see the sunset through the trees. A look to the west was almost a journey home to family and one who might yet be, until just before dark she reluctantly turned back to the great red-brick house that signified a livelihood and loneliness.

That evening's continuing clouds meant the night came early, a candle enough to read a letter by, her throbbing head not patience convincing her whatever Branwell had to tell could keep until morning.

Once her breathing eased she slept soundly, until she started to a screech that might have been an owl or a vixen, an unremembered dream shrouding her ability to distinguish which it belonged to. It was just beginning to get light, although there was an unusual cast to the dawn. She wrapped her bed's top quilt around her and went to the window that glowed strangely. It was said if the morning sun rose with a dazzling ray, by noon all such glittering would fade, overcome by clouds and rain.

Anne propped herself against the window, the peculiar light spraying on the letter in her hands. Its seal was stubborn and its paper tore. She held it together to mend the first few lines. *Impossible, impossible.* Branwell reported little, but enough to change everything. What had been hope at first sight, a stir of her heart, amiable reserve, foolish diffidence, a February keepsake, time standing still and looking forward with a gentle exchange of words and glances in a trusted parting, was, in a moment more than a week after the fact, all that was left of William, her William, never hers except as she imagined, always hers as she would forever know him.

Where are your feet, Anne? She scolded herself as her aunt had done when she was a child. *On the floor, on the floor.*

Then why can't I feel them there?

She went down and after a stunned few minutes got on her knees, waiting for pain to become prayer. If her faith deserted her than so would the sunny smile, the speaking eye, the changing lip, a voice's music, her fondest thoughts and deepest belief—no reminiscence or expectancy, if now of a truly divine reunion, remaining as an antidote to despair. She crumpled and curled her legs into her arms, the shock becoming more intense, not only the news but, also, the dust of the carpet threatening to suffocate her. She muffled her coughing with a handkerchief as she pulled herself onto the bed with one thought, one entreaty left to her, at least the relief of knowing she could still pray.

Oh, dear God, let his memory stay with me and never pass away.

***

No one questioned the redness of Anne's eyes, lack of color in her cheeks, or weakness of her walk. They put it all down to her chest infection. Miss Lydia decided it was worse than any Anne had while working at the Hall, Edmund that Miss Brontë was too sick to teach them. It was the middle of the week and Mrs. Robinson allowed Anne a day or two in her room.

"Should the doctor be sent for?"

"No. Please. I would rather—"

"What about a vaporizing pot, honeyed tea, beef broth, or a mustard compress? Just say what you need and it will be brought up."

"We'll do it." Elizabeth offered Mary's help, too.

"No, no." Their mother folded her arms.

Anne refused special treatment. Servants waiting on her would aggravate their antagonism. Also, she might sink irretrievably with only physical healing to accomplish. She needed the distraction of her duties, of the children who hardly knew her, of her insignificance. Her secret must be put in a safe place, her going on as unremarkable as possible. It was actually better she wasn't at home, her almost sightless father bereft of the best curate he'd ever had, a better son than his actual one. Even Branwell, his script shaky with the passing of a dear friend, couldn't fully realize what cholera and God in his infinite wisdom had taken. Emily, with her armor against shocks, might have been a comfort to Anne as she had been with other difficulties throughout the years, but she was far away. Charlotte, restless, intelligent, contrary, and controlling, could not be told, could never be told what Anne had lost.

CHAPTER FOUR

Haworth, three months later, December 1842

Anne was once again in the company of her father, sisters and brother. This reunion hadn't forgotten the sorrows of the last.

The Waits' Christmas Eve caroling attempted to bring some cheer back into their lives and a community still dealing with privation, chapelry battling, and constant heartbreak. Anne and Emily, thinly coated and, in other respects, not warmly receptive to the season, walked down to Church Street to acknowledge the official singers with mince pies, a few coppers, and a note requesting the money be given to the neediest. They assumed coins found in a drawer in their aunt's room were put aside for that purpose. If not, they were certain she would have approved the use made of them.

There were also the young Vessel Maids singing carols, carrying a decorated box, and knocking doors. A penny was enough to open their Wassail Bob and a look inside at the baby Jesus doll nested in sprigs of evergreen and scented with cinnamon promised good luck. Last year Anne had given two pennies as wishfully as she had given her heart. This year tradition continued in a kind of trance, sweet voices rising and falling as did the box's lid.

Anne wished the girls the joys of the season, which closing a door left outside.

The delight of homecoming, the simple happiness while there, a break from work and isolation for rest and liberty, familiar conversation and easy silence, loving and being loved, none of these usual comforts consoled her now, and she could not yet allow they would again.

"All Emily could talk about was getting home and staying there," Charlotte remarked in her sister's absence at the parlor table still not large enough for the family to sit around.

"Martha will be keeping our Emily company, or the other way 'round," assumed the Reverend Brontë.

"We always give Martha Christmas afternoon and Boxing Day off to be with her family," Anne reminded or, more likely, informed him.

"The least we can do for the Browns."

"How's Tabby?" Charlotte wondered. "Has anyone seen her?"

"Not since Aunt's funeral. Her leg seemed a little better."

"Then we are bad girls, Anne. Ellen and I will pay her a visit tomorrow."'

"Ellen?"

"Nussey, Father. She comes in the morning for a little visit."

"Ah. A sweet and suitable girl."

"Yes, she is. Anyway, I've brought Tabby a little trinket from Brussels and I believe Emily has something for her, too. Of course, she may have already given it to her, slipped out without asking us to go along and not telling where she'd been."

"Well, Charlotte," their father's back straightened, "I hope Emily didn't do so in Brussels."

"If she did disappear, I knew I'd find her in her room writing without much light or consideration for anything else."

As if knowing who was talked about, Keeper, Emily's only companion in the kitchen, barked, or, as Anne surmised, begged his mistress to bend the rule of not giving him food until it was considered scraps. Mastiff, bulldog, terrier, or a bit of all three, the lumbering four-legged creature had been making the most of Emily's sense of guilt for being so long away and her enraged sorrow because of the loss of her merlin hawk until she was nearly tolerant of his offences.

"Emily seems to have been visible to Monsieur Heger. His letter expresses disappointment she won't be going back, just when, at least as he reports, she was losing her awkwardness." Reverend Brontë leaned close to his plate to see what his knife might cut and fork scoop up. "He says so many good things were about to be begin: Emily to receive piano lessons from the best teacher in Belgium and you, Charlotte, to teach French and gain enough confidence for him and Madame Heger to offer you a permanent position at the *Pensionnat*."

"I'm humbled they're considering it."

By the squint of Charlotte's eyes and stiffening of her lips, Anne could tell her oldest sister was more resolute than self-effacing. She not only knew Charlotte's nature but also her secret. Anne didn't need to approve to be sympathetic.

"I thought you hated teaching." Their father took off his spectacles to wipe food splashes. "I suppose when one is obviously appreciated, there may be a conversion." At least he was talking to them again beyond the bare minimum of uttering greetings or letting them know he didn't want to be disturbed in his study. Or at nine o'clock, while winding the long-cased clock at the turn of the stairs, feebly telling them not to stay up late, which they heard because it was his habit to more clearly articulate the same words every night on his way to bed.

Death had intruded on them all, but Branwell and their father had spent the most time with it and were physically and emotionally wearied by its visit not once but twice in a little over two months. Anne and her sisters weren't spared its ruthlessness, although with the loss of her aunt,

Anne found some relief, not from grief but the concealment of it.

"However did we all fit in this room?" Charlotte prompted Anne to find courage, even a little delight, in remembering.

"We pushed up the side table, didn't we?"

"Yes, I believe so. And Branny straddled its pedestal, could hardly eat for its wobbling, and sweated as he was so close to the fire."

Their brother didn't look up, his plate as full as it was half an hour before.

"Aunt hated when we teased him," Charlotte continued to talk about her brother as though he wasn't there, knowing how to both irritate and indulge him. "She doted on him more than she did you, Anne."

"She knew his weaknesses," Reverend Brontë immediately clarified, "but, at the end, his devotion."

Branwell spoke softly with his hand over his mouth.

His father reached across the table to pull it down. "Say again."

"I don't think so. How could she? Her suffering, such pain as I wouldn't wish on my worst enemy."

"She's not suffering now, my boy."

"Just regretting."

Anne, who was sitting next to him, stroked his hand crumbling a piece of bread.

"Oh, I think she's comfortably settled on her heavenly throne thinking she did her best and we're no longer her problem." Charlotte wasn't eating much, either.

"Not how she wasted her life on us?"

"Well, you must let such a question influence your own choices, Son." Reverend Brontë spoke without a hint of guilt in any reference to his wife's sister, who had saved him from foolishly continuing his search for a second wife and his children from being motherless, although not any of them from being sinless.

"Not done yet?" Emily stomped in, her arms folded, her apron askew. "You talk too much. No, Keeper." Her hands were swinging, the dog whining. "Anne, he's already had what he's getting."

Their father was finished eating. He always cleaned his plate, lately never filling it more than was necessary for getting through another day. Even on Christmas, dining with others, a few extra spices flavoring the food and air, and a treat like goose and even port wine sauce, he ate sparingly. He had taken one slice of meat, a small potato, a dab of currant jelly, a smattering of vegetable, a preserved pickle, and only enough bread to satisfy young Martha's hope that she was getting better at making it.

"Time for pudding." Emily began clearing the table. "It's been steaming up the kitchen for hours, like washing day."

"Yes, you do look wilted." Charlotte stood to help her, Anne meaning to do the same. "No, no, delicate one," she was both patronizing and considerate, "you're home to rest and recover."

Anne sat down, feigning a smile.

"Fortunately, I've no reason to care how I look," Emily said without a hint of feeling sorry for herself.

Charlotte and Emily left the parlor as if burdened only by what they carried in their hands, continuing to amuse themselves with affectionate insults. Their father benignly shook his head while his son bowed his even lower. The food Branwell had hardly touched removed, he fiddled with the dingy cuffs on his shirt instead.

Anne couldn't share in her sisters' forgetful, almost lighthearted banter, either, but, unlike her brother, even in happier times, she rarely did. From an early age, under the influence of her aunt and something reflective in her own spirit, she had been called to seriousness as though it was a vocation. The younger Lydia Robinson once said she was too comforted by it. Anne didn't think it mattered what the disrespectful girl thought of her, but since Anne's hopes for romantic affection had died, she couldn't accept being uncomplaining, reliable, in the background, acceptant of what did and didn't happen, devoted to an inner life of strife and tears and religious crisis was all she was made for.

Her sisters returned. Emily led the way with a strong stride, carrying the powdered otherwise dark mound of a pudding on blue and white china. Her arms outstretched, chin up, mouth and back taut, she fulfilled her role as the Major of their unconventional regiment. Charlotte came just behind holding a lit candle, small but bold and hoarsely determined to sing the figgy pudding verse of *We Wish You a Merry Christmas* once through before declaring, "And now we must do without Miss Celia Amelia to set the pudding afire and Auntie to worry his sleeves might catch."

Charlotte continued insensitive, not about to acknowledge her offense, and Emily wasn't about to accuse her. Anne felt her stomach and throat tighten, but managed not to tear up or judge her sisters harshly. Branwell, his eyes downcast, pushed his chair back and left the room. Emily put the pudding down hard at his empty place, creating a burst of confectioners' sugar and brandy fragrance, and removed the sprig of berried holly decorating it as Charlotte brought the candle closer.

"Anne. Go fetch your brother back," their father hardly insisted.

"I think he'll do better left to himself." Anne could only articulate Branwell's need to mourn longer, hoping her father also heard she couldn't lighten her heart, even if he was unaware of what inconsolably did and would, for the remainder of her earthly life, weigh on it.

"So, the prodigal brother returns," Emily announced Branwell leaning on the doorframe, his glasses steamed.

"My son. I am glad."

Charlotte saw her cue to at least brighten their faces. Emily stepped back and the pudding momentarily sizzled and flamed, offering the flavor of good memories, whether or not anyone had a taste for them.

***

Anne couldn't wear her mourning for William. Especially not at home. She had little to add to conversations about him and never initiated any. Branwell and even Charlotte would have ridiculed her for making too much of a few flirtations. Emily would have told her to breathe deeply and return to Gondal where everything was in her control. Her father might have been more inclined to believe the possibility she had, but she didn't want him to know he may have lost more than a fine curate and friend.

Her aunt, who was gone herself before Anne could decide for or against confiding in her, would have been proud of her youngest niece holding back and holding in and offering herself to use rather than gratification. In spite of having often spoken of her own sacrifices, the warm winds, nearness of the sea, and pleasures of society in Penzance that had nurtured her fondness for silk and snuff and ladies card games, Aunt Elizabeth would have been all too ready to believe she had influenced Anne's stoical silence.

Since William's death, not a word of her heartache or shaken faith had passed Anne's lips. No poetry or prose leaked her sadness through her pen. She didn't send letters and didn't receive any, until one dated the 26th of October was put in her hands almost twelve hours after Mrs. Robinson "meant to give it to her immediately." Anne's request to return home to bid farewell to the woman who had offered, albeit with melancholic affect, the only motherly affection she could remember, was further delayed when it was initially refused.

The elder Lydia Robinson didn't show compassion or understanding, instead complaining of a headache and Anne rushing at her and making demands. Fortunately, her husband intervened, believing "Miss Brontë's troubles" warranted her going that afternoon and even the use of their phaeton and driver to take her as far as Keighley.

"Why not to her door then?" Mrs. Robinson resorted to sarcasm.

Within the hour Anne was on her way, enough time to pack, Mr. Robinson to write a note for her brother, Mary and Elizabeth to worry she wouldn't come back, and their older sister to wonder why she would want to. It was too late to be by Aunt Elizabeth's side before her life and, therefore, agony ended. Anne was there sooner than her sisters who would miss the funeral and Anne's first days of passing through the old church door to stand upon cold damp stone and think of more than one lying frozen below.

She managed to slip as inconspicuously away for the same purpose on Boxing Day morning. Emily was busy with her own and Martha's work, Branwell still asleep or brooding in his room, her father shut away to contemplate his next sermon, and Charlotte gone down the village to meet the coach bringing the too pleasant distraction—Emily's words—of Ellen Nussey to them all. On the way back, Charlotte and Ellen planned to call on Tabby who, since becoming lame from a leg ulcer, had been living in Haworth with her sister in a little house constant frugality had allowed her to buy.

St. Michael's and All Angels' slabbed floor was bathed in stingy, moody light falling through its few deep, narrow windows. Anne sat on the end of a hard pew, closing her eyes to bring back the zeal, morality, intellect, mildness, and affability of one of the church's finest shepherds, eventually kneeling to pray in grief and gratefulness, one not bearable without the other.

"Charlotte tells me a memorial will be erected for William." The soft voice of Ellen was unmistakable, even in December the scent of roses about her. Anne would have rather greeted her with dry eyes and a steady hand. Ellen might have had the same regret, sliding her fingers away from Anne's to wipe her own tears and brush back the delicate light-brown curls fallen forward with her head. "It's just the thought," she tried to explain, Anne finding some distraction in remembering a portrait Charlotte had done, capturing her friend's curvaceous mouth, "of such liveliness and kindness gone. Of course, your dear auntie, too. How you'll miss her faithful guidance."

"Yes, but she'll advise me still."

"She wasn't without her contradictions, was she? Those dainty caps and lacey shawls. She even made snuff-taking seem respectable. Although how she would have objected to me visiting in the winter."

"She had her particularities; some she passed onto me."

"Excluding the snuff."

Anne tried to laugh. At least she smiled. "That was her gift to Branwell. Where's Charlotte? She did meet you, didn't she?"

"She did indeed, bundled, so she described, like a Mongolian. A good thing as the coach was late. And look at me dressed for fashion, not sense. I'd forgotten how the cold grips Haworth, especially coming up the hill. Even more so here. I can't stay longer in this gloomy place. And neither should you." As they walked out of the church, Ellen's sigh was loud and long. "Sometimes I wish I hadn't listened to Charlotte. Well, perhaps, she was right about Mr. Vincent. But poor William. What have I missed by continuing heart-whole, as she dubs it?"

Anne couldn't answer, blaming the bitter blast of wind, leaning into it, shielding her eyes that stung from it. Ellen—at least, the pretty, playful, slightly vain and irresistible Ellen who might have stolen Anne's future if heaven hadn't first—probably expected Anne would be more sympathetic than Charlotte.

"On the other hand, as Charlotte also tells me, I'm without romance." Ellen touched Anne's arm and was once again a conscientious, calm, loyal, well-bred Yorkshire lass. "William would have soon realized my dullness."

Anne knew what she meant, for Charlotte had often spoken of her relationship with Ellen as based on her longtime friend's goodness and faithfulness and not for anything profound or poetic stirring in her. Charlotte had Mary Taylor for more intellectual and passionate exchanges.

"I'm better suited to advising Charlotte against any cupid nonsense Brussels has made her vulnerable to."

Anne walked a little slower, hoping Ellen would continue at her normal stride and be the first Charlotte greeted as she opened the door of the parsonage. Instead, Ellen turned back to her, so that Charlotte's attention was on Anne trying to discreetly wipe her eyes.

"Now, now. You contradict my promise Ellen wouldn't find us melancholy or depressed."

"It's the wind. Normally I don't mind—"

"Yes, it's wicked today." Ellen also supported Anne by grabbing her hand. "We weren't prepared for how it would hit us on our walk from the church."

"Get inside at once," Reverend Brontë's voice moved Charlotte aside. "I won't have Miss Nussey returned to her family unwell." He further welcomed Ellen with a ceremonial handshake and then disappeared.

"The kitchen fire is blazing," Emily shouted, so Keeper barked. "Leftovers have made a hearty stew and there's much to catch up on."

"Yet she'll hardly say more to you," Charlotte voiced what Anne was thinking. "Branwell, under threat of the Duke of Zamorna, took your case upstairs."

"She didn't even have to ask." Branwell seemed to have forgotten all his cares, teasing as he knew pleased and embarrassed Ellen. "I see that, despite the weather, your curls are intact."

"That's because, like Anne's, they're natural."

"Except, Charlotte, mine are prone to frizz and tangle."

"There's a trick, Anne," Ellen was finding her stride, "to smoothing them and making them hold."

Branwell was po-faced. "Is it lard? That would do it."

Ellen didn't seem to mind being ridiculed, thinly laughing as visibly annoyed Branwell, challenging his attraction to her.

"Don't put your cloaks away."

"We've had enough of being blown about today, Branny."

"Oh, Charlotte. Does that mean you won't be up for a walking adventure?"

"You know it does. We'll sit in the parlor and talk and, when we've run out of things to say—"

"If that's possible."

"Maybe not, Branny. But, if so, thanks to Father's unfailing gift to us every Christmas, we can always take turns reciting from the *Forget-me-not* annual."

"I'm here for the rest of the week," Ellen conciliated. "There'll be plenty of time for walks in, perhaps, pleasanter weather."

"At the end of December? The north-easterlies won't allow it." Branwell sounded argumentative until he winked and Ellen fluttered her hand over her mouth.

Anne felt embarrassed, or, as she was less able to admit, without her whole heart to appreciate their fleeting flirtation. Rather than warm herself in the kitchen, disturb her hunger with Emily's hearty cooking, or be amused by parlor gossip and poetry reading, Anne excused herself to go up to the room haunted by all those nights she had shared with her aunt. Although overwhelmed by sorrows and anxieties for which she couldn't overtly ask for sympathy or advice, verse might once again soothe her, while prose, some begun, some only thought about, was waiting to help her pass into uncharted territory.

CHAPTER FIVE

Thorpe Green Hall, three months later, March 1843

"There's no doubt you're a Brontë lass, too fond of wild weather than is good for you."

Branwell, unambitious in his leisure hours and warm low-timbered parlor, declined Anne's invitation of a walk. "I don't want to soil my boots. I just wiped my one pair and set them to dry by the fire."

Anne thought he might insist she spend that Saturday afternoon with him in his "old hall" lodgings rather than on her own traipsing around fields and woods. He leaned forward with a melancholic expression to match his Byronic surroundings and no longer tried to hide the hip flask he knew would send her on her way.

"You'd better eat as well."

When Branwell first took up his post as young Edmund Robinson's tutor, he seemed to enjoy the close proximity of his and Anne's employment. If not always willing to brave the elements and explore the countryside with her, he was often amenable to a few hours of shared conversation, reading or writing in the schoolroom. Recognizing Anne's need to get away from the main house, he encouraged her visits to the gabled red brick lodge with underground passages and a supposed romantic history that pleasantly and perilously accommodated him.

After two years of being solitary and far from family most of the time, she wanted to be utterly pleased to see and speak with her brother every day. She also saw the chance to learn more about his final months, days, and, especially, moments with William.

It wasn't enough her father had spoken of the tranquility with which Curate Weightman had, at only twenty-eight years old, closed his eyes on the world, at peace with his mortal end and hopeful for the glory to come. Anne hadn't heard his eulogy of William's bright if brief tread upon the earth in private or even from the pulpit, but read it in its subsequent publication.

Anne longed for an intimacy with William's dying she had been denied in his living. As difficult as it would be, she needed to experience the demise of his flesh before she could fully accept his presence in spirit. Her mourning needed companionship, the kind only Branwell, a dear friend to her dearest, could offer. She already knew her brother had devoted himself to William's care and, in the end, kept vigil by his bedside, just as he had with Aunt Elizabeth. She couldn't ask Branwell anything that might give away, through words or trembling and tears, what she hoped had been born before William's death. She wasn't sure how her brother would react if he knew. Surprise? Ridicule? Pity? Offering not only his opinion, but proof of how mistaken she had been?

What if she had been there without any rivals, not even Branwell, to hold William's frail hand, attempt to keep him warm and get him to swallow a few drops of peppermint oil to quell his vomiting? Not repulsed by the smell even helping Martha change his gown and bed linens frequently didn't alleviate, she would have rubbed hot dry flannel wherever he had pain, and placed vinegar and mustard flour poultices on his stomach to ease his cramps and diarrhea. She would have assured him there was no need for embarrassment or apology, because he wasn't a bother but her first and last love. Nothing and no one would come between her and his fitful sleeping and waking, the grateful reach of his hand, his last smile and attempt at saying what she longed to hear.

No, she was fooling herself. She knew about cholera. William had told her. Actually, he had told Branwell, what he witnessed in his rounds of the parish's victims not fit for female sympathies. Eavesdropping and reading had informed Anne of the disease's mercilessness, her heart even more wasted by William quickly becoming unrecognizable, his skin aging before her eyes, his sunken and shut most of the time, and his mind so altered even when they opened he didn't recognize who was there. His final days must have been consumed by seizures and, mercifully, long periods of unconsciousness, until the cruelty of cholera resumed, his final breaths so labored he wouldn't have been able to speak.

She wanted to believe her father and envision a pain-free William accepting the eternal benefits of a life cheerfully, compassionately, and charitably lived. Only in faith could she not regret her shyness at his bold glances and flushed cheeks and overrule any conflict with him posing as every young lady's desire, convinced he did so for their pleasure not his conceit. Only through faith could she not be angry he sacrificed himself in service to others. Even her father hadn't expected that much from him and Charlotte took back her assertion, "He ought not to have been a parson."

Anne, more convinced than ever of her own exalted purpose beside him, had begun to, slowly, heart-wrenchingly but devotionally, relinquish her loss to heaven's gain.

"Don't forget Father is coming on Monday," was the last thing she said to her brother before setting out towards the long plantation east of the Kirby estate, a destination that would provide sufficient cover as long as it rained in drizzly episodes and not downpours. It was her plan to follow the maze of indistinct trails made by deer, foxes, hedgehogs, and prowling boys all the way down to the river, where she might come across a fallen tree to rest on. With any luck, by the time she made it all the way around the woods to exit where she had entered, quickening her pace and taking a short cut, she would return to the Hall before dark.

Sheltered by high hedges, Anne went north on Thorpe Green Lane, past laborers' cottages and the flat arable fields their inhabitants worked, making a little detour for a handful of primroses. Eventually she left the road completely and, with the on-going permission of the Thompsons, her employers' nearest comparable neighbor, she entered the Kirby Hall grounds through a grand pillared gate. It was a gusty walk across open fields to Lower Farm, over a footbridge spanning a fish pond, and following a bridleway cutting the east corner of the estate. The wind couldn't decide whether it meant to push or obstruct her, the clouds at first interrupting the blue sky here and there, gradually thickening and blackening until she was running towards the plantation in sight and then reach within moments of the rain lashing.

The thickness of that wood, unmanaged for years, made the day darker, drier, and eerily silent as she moved on a mulchy carpet of conifer needles, missing the wind and any birdsong. It felt like she had passed into the wish she made when losing everything to death seemed preferable to finding something left of life.

She never made it to the river that afternoon, didn't go deeper into the plantation but waited at its edge. She could easily get sick again and needed to moderate her love of wild weather, which, even without the influence of Emily and the rugged landscape of the moors, tempted her to forgo good sense. She stepped into the open, a roaring above and around her, whirlwinds of spray making her even damper, thunder crashing once and then again, breaking the clouds apart a little, the rain letting up but not stopping. It could be a long while before it did.

***

It wasn't the first time Reverend Brontë was invited to Thorpe Green. Anne wondered why he accepted now and not before when her loneliness and homesickness didn't have the relief of Branwell being a short walk away. She acknowledged and appreciated her father's undeniable affection, but regretted he was more attentive to his son than daughters. Emily reported that when he traveled with her and Charlotte to Brussels, his sightseeing goals were more urgent than scrutiny of the situation he was leaving them in. She claimed he was easily confident of their good behavior and convinced of their good care once he was assured they wouldn't be required to attend daily Mass.

As Charlotte, who couldn't let Emily be the sole talebearer, added, "Without further ado he was off to invade the fields of Waterloo."

The Robinsons offered her and Branwell the use of their four-wheeled bonneted phaeton to meet their father in York so he wouldn't have to endure more public transport than was necessary. He was in the city to give evidence at the Assizes in a forgery case. For a man over sixty with failing eyesight, who only a year before had traveled by rail to London, bravely born fourteen hours on a small steam ship to Ostend packed with passengers and mail bags, anticipated the rewards of a long, slow ride by stagecoach to Brussels, and a mere week later made his way back home in the same manner and companionless, traveling around Yorkshire was a jaunt, not journey.

Branwell boldly displayed his attitude of deserving the privilege of "living in a palace" and driving himself "in style". He believed he couldn't do wrong in his new position, was a favorite of all the household, and that curling his hair and scenting his handkerchief made him as good as a squire. His tendency to posturing and exaggeration had always worried Anne, more so since her recommendation and expectation had brought him to Thorpe Green. After just a few months, there were already signs of it turning him sharply away from finally leading a sober and productive life.

He admitted it. "Well, our mistress might admire you, Anne, but she is too damnably fond of me."

Anne wouldn't say *how do you know*? She could only hope Mrs. Robinson wasn't so foolish or bold. It wasn't correct for a woman to presume a man's interest and certainly not to speak of it before he did, absolutely not if it was improper. For a man, even one as languid as her brother, it was expected he initiate or ignore, encourage or cast off, make right or wrong; in short, be in control of a woman's attention.

Within her brother's bravado Anne heard vulnerability. Despite the benefits of his sex, she was afraid Mrs. Robinson's physical attributes, place in society, and flair for having her way were going to get the better of him. On her way back from her Saturday evening soaking, Anne's intention to warm and dry herself at Branwell's hearth required immediate revision when she discreetly witnessed Mrs. Robinson, with young Edmund in tow, at the door of Monk's Lodge.

The sight made Anne think of the evenings in the parlor when she was called on to play the piano and sing with Mary, and Branwell to recite, even some of his own poems. Mrs. Robinson slightly applauding his efforts didn't pose a problem, but her inviting him to sit on the settee beside her so she could leaf through his poetry book or journal did. Even when he was seated away from her, all engaged in silent reading and needlework, the raising of her eyes to Branwell's restless concentration indicated, to Anne, and, as was becoming obvious, to Branwell, the development she had in mind.

Anne was astounded that any, let alone two, of her siblings would consider an amorous involvement with a married individual. She already knew of Charlotte's weakening and been warned by Emily that any sensible advice wouldn't be welcomed. Branwell was even more susceptible to being misled, especially emotionally, and less inclined to accept guidance from his youngest sister, who was "naught" but another sibling to him.

***

Branwell drove at an uneven pace southeast from Thorpe Underwood through Green Hammerton on the bumpy Boroughbridge-York Road. Anne managed to replace her frowning with small smiles. She was on her way to a favorite destination, the day cooperative after the rain and wind of the two before, and had cast off her envy of her father's stay in York because it had made a visit there possible for her, too. The Minster's Gothic height and medieval pinnacles could be seen as they crossed the River Ouse into the city's lively center, but its ethereal light, echoing spaciousness, antiquity and restoration, artworks of man reflecting God everywhere one looked, and serenity despite the streams of visitors and surges of music were only for remembering this time.

Their father, waiting in front of The George Hotel on Coney Street, the very place Anne had stayed with the Robinsons, stepped out and raised his hand before they expected him to see them. Branwell complimented himself on his estimation of how long the journey would take, if only because they had arrived in between the times public coaching dropped off and picked up travelers, the clock anchored to St. Martin's church a few buildings up from The George striking eleven-thirty.

Almost the moment Branwell jumped down, Reverend Brontë gave him a small bag to hold and relegated him to the back seat on the phaeton. Their father stroked the nose of its chestnut horse, offering her something pulled out of his pocket before he stepped up to sit next to Anne and take the reins. He hardly reacted to his daughter timidly kissing his cheek.

Branwell had yet to obey his father's instructions. "I thought we might give the mare a rest and have something to eat before we go back."

"And drink?"

"I hear Little John's in Castlegate is welcoming and only a few blocks away."

"And what should your sister do while you find out and I accompany you to make sure it isn't too hospitable?"

"A bit of shopping? You'd like that wouldn't you, Annie?"

"Not—"

"By herself," her father finished her objection more adamantly than she would have.

Sensing Branwell's obstinacy, which was bound to irritate her father even to the point of setting the tone for his entire visit, she tried to appeal to her brother in another way. "The Robinsons are expecting us for dinner."

Anne thought she heard her father grunt.

Branwell obviously had no doubt he did. "I was thinking of you, Father, knowing you don't like eating with others, especially strangers."

"Difficult to avoid in a public house. Surely, your fine employees don't eat so early, Anne."

"Miss Marshall, Mrs. Robinson's maid, heard her tell cook they would be dining Sunday hours and fare as she suspected 'Reverend Brontë would have missed his roast beef and pudding while being away from home.'"

Branwell wouldn't give up his plan. "Little John's might offer the snug where even I wouldn't interrupt your thoughts and Annie could be discreet, as well as the excuse of us having already eaten."

Anne thought how her father and brother might have a meal and drink nearer the Minster, surely no harm in her walking around and sitting unaccompanied within the cathedral's sacred embrace. However, she knew what the prudent argument to make was. "We must not frustrate the Robinsons' generosity, Father."

"Of course not, my dear. If we set out now, Branwell, you'll eat—and drink—soon enough. When I venture from home I cannot always avoid dining sociably."

Within ten minutes they had left York for purer air and sharper sunlight. Once across the Ouse, the stop and go of the crowded city turned into a continuity of movement and pleasant views ahead as the road tunneled through blossoming hedges and to the left or right where fields were overturned for planting and naturally greening meadows recalled spring in wispy daisies and two- or three-week-old lambs. Trees, singular and in clusters, seemed to open their leaves before Anne's eyes that moistened as she reflected on what began so bright and hopeful but was bound to wither. Strangely, she felt grateful just because life's joys were fleeting; after all and often noted too late, meant to be treasured all the more as they might only last a few years, months, days, or moments, or merely the eight miles back to Thorpe Green.

Posed in the ivied shade of their columned porch, Mrs. Robinson, the girls, and even young Edmund were dressed in their Sunday best to welcome the man who had given them the use of two Brontës. Mrs. Robinson couldn't sustain a smile and didn't let her hand linger in his, but, if his stuttered greeting was anything to go by, charmed him all the same.

CHAPTER SIX

Haworth, three months later, June 1843

Emily held Keeper back as he growled at the curly-coated black and tan dog standing his ground and expressing a high-pitched opinion.

Anne lifted the squirming King Charles spaniel away from the meeting she had worried would be confrontational. "More Flossy's fault than Keeper's," she acknowledged.

Flossy was a small dog with a large sense of himself, as cavalier in character as breed. Relishing a soft lap and stroke by a warm fire, he also went wild in the fresh air, digging holes to set the Thorpe Green gardeners cursing. Other times he flew across muddy fields and disappeared into thicketed distances, enticing young Edmund to escape with him. The greatest threat to Flossy's well-being was he wouldn't acknowledge his youth and size in the company of larger, more seasoned four-legged creatures. If he didn't actually attack them, he barked in a shameless tone like he had with Keeper, precariously proclaiming his equal worth.

The Robinsons must have thought Flossy was the perfect dog for their timid, sorrowful governess, and so he was. Just as Anne loved her sisters and brother because they challenged and complemented her, she excused and embraced Flossy. She suspected the idea of giving her a dog was Mary's, with Elizabeth helping to find one. Lydia was too distracted by coming out balls and the gowns and manipulative ways they required to think of giving Anne anything other than reason to question the young woman's judgment.

Flossy came into Anne's life on a Sunday, one of many she walked back from church, Branwell not nearly so energetic and, in any case, unable to resist an invitation by Dr. Crosby from Great Ouseburn to join him for pheasant shooting. Mrs. Robinson wasn't pleased, either, not because she had an aversion to men hunting anything, but due to Branwell missing dinner and the chance to discuss literature and art with her afterwards. Mr. Robinson must have been relieved.

Anne's anxieties usually cleared away, at least temporarily, while she was on her own out of doors. June continued pleasant, the sun intensifying so scattered clouds were welcome, along with trees touching their fresh canopies across the road from Great Ouseburn to Thorpe Underwood. She frequently stopped to study and sketch whatever flora caught her eye. Hawthorn blossoms clustered out of bramble hedges and chickweed didn't quite succeed in creeping unnoticed through roadside grass. Dandelions invaded the road, some already bursting into seed. Anne enjoyed their bravado, quickly drawing a couple of them head to head, but not their simple, lobed leaves before she was distracted by bees finding sustenance in clover flowers. Kneeling down before their sacred endeavor, she was and wasn't a careful witness, stung, not by them, their busyness uninterrupted, but by burn weeds.

All the way back to Thorpe Green, her legs, arms, and hands tingled from their nettled encounter. Elizabeth and Mary met her with irritating giggles. Lydia wondered why she looked such a mess. Young Edmund said she was in for a surprise, all three of his sisters immediately shouting at him. It was only when Anne stepped into her room she knew what Edmund had almost given away of someone else's generosity. A little dog was on her bed, its long, feathery ears chestnut-colored like the cushions under its persuasive eyes, its creamy black-tipped nose resting on its front paws placed together. She heard Mary say they had already named him, thinking he was a female. Flossy gave a yelp before stretching out his well-shaped body and lifting his tail-wagging rump onto the pillows, utterly aware of posing for an irresistible first impression.

***

What better way to enjoy time with Emily again than by resuming their habit of wandering west to meet only earth and sky. Their dogs, like themselves, with contrasting physiques and personalities, were intrinsically similar, especially in their need to frequently escape the stuffiness and limited amusement of being indoors.

"Flossy, come back," Anne tried to command the impulsive spaniel off once more to chase sheep.

Emily had no trouble getting Keeper to lie down with a firm annunciation of his name while she pointed to the ground, although his whimpering implied he was still thinking about following Flossy's example.

"Flossy. Bad boy, bad boy."

"If you control your little Robinsons like you do that sassy mutt, I fear they won't live long."

As if it heard Emily's prediction, a large ewe turned on Flossy, which brought the dog running back up the steep slope to his forgiving mistress.

On second thought, Anne tried to be tougher with a disciplinary tap on Flossy's nose, then embraced him again. "Good boy."

"Methinks he's exactly what you always wanted … to be." Emily was walking again, her direction declaring her destination. Their ascent to Top Withens would be delayed an hour or more, if Emily's mood was more for reclining and swirling her hand in the water to stir up tadpoles.

When Ellen Nussey was with them, from crossing the slabbed bridge over Sladen Beck to climbing a rugged bank, navigating greasy stones and not minding a little dampening, there was always an echo of "watch your step". With just Anne and the dogs following her lead, Emily didn't have anything to say until they were at the best seat in view of the waterfall.

"No, you take it, Annie. I relinquish my throne to you."

"Any of the other stones would do for me."

"I insist on taking care of you."

Anne didn't mind Emily acting more like an older brother than Branwell ever did, or even a gallant lover, reminiscent of childish acting-out. In truth, she depended on it. In that small oasis of time, standing still where they were hidden from the world, their faithful companions conspiring to find something to occupy themselves, there was so much to enjoy and be grateful for. The sky was open in sight of heaven, high ground around and beyond them, the sun warming and a breeze cooling, the sound of water calming, and faintly fragrant moss glistening on the rocks with tiny white stars appearing between some of them.

Yet, more as if she was on a stormy ocean than in a quiet cove, panic overwhelmed Anne until she could hardly breathe.

Emily lightly rubbed Anne's back and twisted up a strand of her hair loosened from its simple arrangement.

Anne cleared her throat, choking, Flossy pawing at her knees, Keeper barking.

"Go ahead and spit." Emily helped her sister lean over to do so. "Other than me, there's only the dogs, flies, tadpoles, and, perhaps, God to witness it."

Anne laughed and spoke hoarsely, "What would I do without you?"

"Better than I have done without you."

Anne supposed Emily was referring to their Gondal writings, but also wondered whether she was admitting a reliance on something besides her own fortitude and segregation. That was a rare occurrence. It might be Anne had learned true stoicism from Emily, not Aunt Elizabeth. Even when Emily was released from her teaching post at Roe Head because there were fears she would go the tragic way of their sisters Maria and Elizabeth, or after suffering a whole semester teaching at Law Hill, once more to the point of being ill, Emily was only in need of coming back to herself to be well again.

Her return from Brussels had been less dramatic but more conclusive. All the knowledge Emily needed to gain or impart could be found at home.

It was never easy to tell what was stirring in Emily's heart. That afternoon her touch and words felt like pleading, as much as she could ever be suppliant. It might change Anne's view of her nearest and dearest sibling. Even walking physically tall and strong across the moors, Emily seemed smaller, as if her influence was shrinking.

"You didn't think I meant that, did you?" Without waiting for an answer, Emily made the unwieldly climb further up the waterfall, exhibiting surefootedness in a natural environment she could never have in a societal one.

Yet there was a visible change in her confidence as she stopped and stood, waving from a pedestal she appeared unusually unsteady on.

***

"Can't you leave that a while, Annie?"

Anne didn't question why Emily was still so absorbed in childish chronicling, currently mostly poetry, her handwriting not grown larger with the aging of her eyes.

Anne was on the second page of filling the music manuscript book she had only counted on costing her three shillings and six pence, not the favorable opinion of her favorite sister. Her last trip to York, longer than when she and Branwell had met their father there, this time sanctioned for shopping, allowed Anne almost two hours away from the Misses Robinson. While the girls spent their time and money on dresses, hats, and confections, Anne browsed a bookstore newly opened, considering any expenditure carefully. She finally settled on two purchases: a German dictionary and a fabric-bound book for music copying to also aid in her teaching, the latter more of a justification than reason for buying it. Anne wanted to make the music she loved compactly portable, even without access to a pianoforte, available for performances in her head — preferably so, for then her fingers were agile and her voice wasn't weak.

"I must have your opinion." Emily abruptly moved Tiger from her lap, swung her feet off the sofa and slipped them into her shoes before she began to recite, "'In the dungeon-crypts idly did I stray, reckless of the lives wasting there away; Draw the ponderous bars! open, Warder stern!'" She stood and stamped. "'He dared not say me nay—the hinges harshly turn.'"

Emily continued to read, Anne giving up on her own work while her sister thumped around the dining table. Emily stopped to perch her notebook on Anne's back and murmured in her sister's ear, "'The captive raised her face; it was as soft and mild as a sculptured marble saint, or slumbering unwean'd child; it was so soft and mild, it was so sweet and fair, pain could not trace a line, nor grief a shadow there!'"

Anne shook Emily off. She immediately regretted doing so and turned as if to explain, but couldn't.

Emily retreated to the sofa. She probably thought Anne's reaction was another refusal to engage in the melodramatic make-believe that had once unfalteringly formed their little society with its pact of keeping secrets from their father and aunt, Charlotte and Branwell, everyone except each other.

Anne glanced down at the hymn she was copying, not one Mary would wish to sing. The music wasn't Anne's, but the words were, written when she thought she knew what grief was, and did, but not as it would have her suffer in isolation and without admission. Was that moment any different than all the others for the last eight months? Would poetry allow regret to whisper and yet be heard? Anne felt it was time to literally reveal the turn her muse—her life—had taken, at least as an explanation for her lack of interest in Gondal. She remained seated, leaning on her elbows, and didn't once look at Emily as she began in a soft and impassive voice, "'I have gone backward in the work, the labor has not sped; drowsy and dark my spirit lies, heavy and dull as lead.'"

She heard little grunts, more animal than human, expecting to see the dogs in the room. She wished they were, so Emily would be distracted by her own temper and Anne would be relieved of reciting more by needing to defend a frightened Flossy hopping onto her lap.

In Anne's long pause there was the rhythm of the mantel clock and a little whirl of wind through the half open window in front of which the canary, Dick, hopped and jangled the bell in his cage.

"Go on."

Anne heard a suggestion rather than an order and couldn't refuse the anticipation in Emily's eyes. "'How can I rouse my sinking soul from such a lethargy? How can I break those iron chains and set my spirit free?'"

"I've grown too serious." Anne closed her book.

"Well, I have my moments. But won't entirely abandon my little rascals as long as they delight me."

"If we were together more often and for longer," Anne was, in that moment, convinced that was what she wished could happen, "I might also be inclined to write to escape my pains rather than expose them."

"Don't go back to Thorpe Green. It won't be long before Charlotte returns and we'll set up our school." Emily's request was lost to the unmistakable rumble of Branwell coming downstairs. "Speaking of rascals, Branwell has been whistling a lot lately."

"A happy noise, isn't it?"

"A suspect one."

Their brother, shoeless, his shirt hung over his breeches, his hair uncombed and beard untrimmed, his spectacles in his hand, wandered into the parlor without a thought let alone care that he was interrupting anything. "Is it only a few days we've been home?"

"Yes. And you've slept away most of them," Emily quipped. "Except when you're out far too late." Then she was even more accusing. "You seem eager to return to your labors."

"You should be glad I've finally found employment I'm content with that is content with me."

"You've managed to get young Edmund interested in his studies."

"Well, Annie, what lad wouldn't rather do something else? Ignore that and you'll have rebellion. Recognize his distractions, make them part of his lessons, and you might teach him something. Saying that, he is a spoiled little bugger." Branwell looked around. "Any newspapers? Ah, the *Leeds Intelligencer*. Two weeks old."

"Father probably has the most current in his study."

Branwell whistled again, this time for the dogs, enticing his sisters with the canines' excitement of an early evening walk and an observation that reminded Anne of how soon she would be among greener pastures, sheltering spinneys, and gentler paths. She felt the unfairness of her own character that put obligation over staying near the stony hills where trees were stunted and few and far between, the heath was unprotected, uninterrupted, and undesigned—except by God—as far as the eye could see, and the way over tufted grass and stony hills caused her heart to beat faster and, paradoxically, her life to seem less harsh.

Emily might have been reading her thoughts. "Come on, the wind might never again blow as it does for us now."

On that warm, wild summer's evening it played with them roughly to their liking with the intention of resurrecting the children they once were and, for a few hours at least, would always be. Branwell battled the swirling gusts with his blackthorn stick, Keeper growling and snapping at and even swallowing the blasts that threatened to blow Flossy away. Anne saved the cocky spaniel, but not her skirt and petticoat from lifting, nor the destruction of her hairstyle, which set Emily heartily laughing as she walked even faster. She exemplified what she would call a withering thing, long-limbed, remote and unclaimed, half savage, a law unto herself, wandering far without leaving home, the only hero and heroine she ever needed, like every tree at that stark height, holding her own but vulnerable all the same.

They all were.

Branwell used his stick to flush something imaginary out of the bracken and then lifted it with nothing to aim at.

"Give me that." Emily wrestled it away from him. "You know there are curlews, merlins, and peregrines still nesting."

"Ah, Em." He rubbed his arm. "Where do you get your strength?"

"Out of necessity."

"I love these long days," Anne said as they made it to Top Withens, Flossy seeming to relish being carried all the way to its barren height and encompassing views.

"I don't." The reason for Emily's answer was known only to herself, her eyes darkening gray—indoors they deepened blue—her cheeks wind-burned, her hair tangled to the point of being unbrushable. Anne was afraid she might take scissors to it.

"Shall we head back through Stanbury?"

"Shall we lose you at the Old Silent?" Emily said what Anne suspected in Branwell's plan.

He reached out for his stick, but Emily wouldn't give it to him. It had become her prop as she probably imagined she wore trousers and heavy boots, had somehow turned into Augusta, her Gondal mountaineer, with a robust stride only Keeper could keep up with, although Flossy, with his feet on the ground again, tried to. Anne didn't, trailing her brother until she realized Emily and the dogs had left Scar Top Road to climb a dirt lane through rough grazing grounds that were part of the Ponden House estate.

With a happy wave, Branwell continued towards Stanbury.

"It's too late to call," Anne advised without meaning to dissuade her sister from what she had in mind, even if it was to revive the hospitality of their neighbors. Before their father had fallen out and even refused to bury one of their own, the Heatons had welcomed his wandering children on aimlessly sunny days and sheltered them on suddenly rainy ones—even once saving them from a storm of biblical proportions. The Heatons had offered them sweet tea and prettier cakes than they were used to, and, best of all, the perusal of the finest library in West Yorkshire. "Do we know they have forgiven us? Do you think we dare, Em, without invitation?"

Anne wanted to believe it was all right, for no other reason than to have another look at the Shakespeare first folio and what she remembered as splendid editions of *Aesop's Fables*, *The Arabian Nights*, and *Bewick's British Birds*.

Emily was bending low with a grip on Keeper's collar as they crept around the manorial farmhouse to its front entrance. "I hear music. I think they're having a party."

"Oh, Em, we mustn't call then."

"We can eavesdrop."

Ordering Keeper and Flossy to sit, Emily slowly lifted the latch on a gate into a walled garden of gnarled trees and light-starved flower beds just outside the parlor window. Flossy was the first in, Anne not catching him before he began digging around some scrawny geraniums.

Emily was right, at least about what they could do even if they shouldn't. The parlor shades were up, the curtains half-open, and the room was lit with more candles than Tabby allowed in the entire parsonage for a month. A ledge to cling to also made it easy to see the Heatons had visitors who demonstrated the hindrance fine clothes and dull spirits were to enjoyment. Someone was playing the pianoforte; only dancing children seeming to be listening.

"I remember when you performed much better on that lovely instrument," Anne whispered to distract herself from feeling criminal.

Emily groaned when Keeper barked so Flossy did, and insisted they all run from the consequences of being seen where they may or may not have been welcomed.

PART TWO

I allow she has small claims to perfection; but then, I maintain that, if she were more perfect, she would be less interesting.

~ Anne Brontë, *The Tenant of Wildfell Hall*

CHAPTER SEVEN

Scarborough, fourteen months later, August 1844

Anne had recently read a review in the local gazette describing Henry Roxby Beverley as a sound, low-comedic, unremarkable actor who exploited his family name, especially as it was distinguished by his brother William's reputation as a fine scenery painter. There was a caricature of "Hell-bent Harry" with a caption that claimed his main talent was winking and smiling at young ladies. Although middle aged, he was eye-catching and robust, his red face needing little greasepaint to play the drunkard Newman Noggs in *Nicholas Nickleby*, a character he knew inside and out from a past production, which was part of an adored feast of Charles Dickens at London's Adelphi Theatre. It had been an afternoon's diversion shortly after Anne arrived in Scarborough in early July with her brother and the Robinsons, and a few times after that, repeated viewings no less enjoyable. One or two matinees each week were set aside for amusement at the Theatre Royal, comprising summer pantomime and other light-hearted offerings, but excluding *Tom and Jerry*, the flash favorite among those like Branwell and a few lads he had met from carousing around town.

On the previous Thursday evening, August made a thunderous beginning, the rain holding off just long enough for the five-hundred-yard dash from Wood's Lodgings to St. Thomas Street. Anne, Branwell, and all the Robinsons except Edmund Senior attended a lavish, if lackluster, performance of *King Richard II* with Harry in the role of the fortunate Duke of Aumerle.

"There he is," Lydia blurted the first time he walked on stage, provoking an inharmonious chorus of "hush", her sisters to lean away from her, and her brother to hiss until Branwell took control of him. Anne assumed it was her brother, the heavily-fragranced Mrs. Robinson thanking him for something.

The following Saturday, Mr. Robinson grudgingly went to the theater with everyone else. A breeze eased the humidity, with no thunder and rain to overthrow the resonant sounds and salty smell of the sea, and no moon to outshine the stars. Anne's long-sleeved, meekly-laced gray silk, her aunt's fringed shawl, and a simple silver comb to join her hair's plaited coils was the best she could do for what the theater billed a fashionable evening by invitation only. More shimmering fabric than she had ever seen in one place swayed and swished in its lobby. Flimsy stoles and capelets slid off bare shoulders and arms, jewelry boasting but also trembling when ringlets did, smiles born of confidence and grimaces of comparison or perhaps just the pain of so many tiny waists. Most of the men wore their affluence or claim to it easily and elegantly in gray or brown trousers, dark green or burgundy jackets, with glimpses of brightly patterned waistcoats. Their hair was slicked back and sidebars and whiskers closely trimmed, which made them, in truth and pretense, respectable. A few were boisterously foppish in their mannerisms and clothing. Anne gave them the benefit of the doubt, thinking they were theatrical in profession as well as appearance.

Henry Roxby, for a reason becoming more and more evident, pushed through the crowd to specifically welcome them. Despite his occupation, graying temples, beard, and eyebrows, and reported reputation, Anne thought him an underwhelming fellow.

Branwell was sullenly histrionic. To Anne, he was a quivering fledgling bird: humped over, swaying, biting his lips, adjusting his glasses or picking at his chin when he wasn't rubbing his hands. To his own satisfaction, he looked every bit the doomed artistic type. Not for the first time, he struggled to contain his anger when Mr. Robinson was less than civil to his wife, Anne hooking her brother's arm and holding him back from behaving as wasn't his place to.

The show that evening was a sophisticated revue rather than serious theater. Robert Roxby, another of Harry's brothers and manager of Manchester's Theatre Royal, was the comedic attraction along with Charles James Matthew in excerpts from plays they had both done and skits it was announced had never been performed before. Anne found Robert a little rigid and his voice weak, but his physical antics caused her to smile and even laugh outright, so she was glad the majority of the audience's amusement was louder. Mr. Matthew's style was more to her liking, subtle and at times even sublime, exhibiting an understanding of the wisdom humor could reveal and the disquiet it could ease. There was music, too, the most delightful performed by Mr. Matthew's lovely wife Lucy Elizabeth Vestris, or Madame Vestris as she was promoted. She sang arias from last year and centuries ago, bewitching the stage with her physical beauty, rich contralto voice, and tiny-footed dance steps. In one number, she was surrounded by her own pet spaniels that, even impeccably obedient, were suggestive of Flossy, who had been left at Thorpe Green. Anne was reminded of how much she missed him.

As the curtain fell for intermission, it was announced there were liquid refreshments in the lobby. Mrs. Robinson preferred to remain seated, Lydia escaping before her mother or father could order her back without making a scene. Anne would have been content to stay in the auditorium and talk to Mary and Elizabeth about the performances so far, but, with Branwell, was enlisted to follow their sister.

The boy Edmund decided he would go along before his father realized he had lost control of his son as well as eldest daughter.

Branwell told the lad to accompany Anne, who guessed Lydia had gone backstage, a now costumed and heavily made-up Harry holding the impressionable girl's hand until he realized Anne watching. Before he could do more than greet her and stop Edmund exploring a world that wasn't meant for him or his sister, Anne experienced a little giddiness of her own, a reaction not as foreign to her as some might assume. She couldn't help being overawed by Madame Vestris and her perfectly groomed and behaved dogs filling the dingy yellow corridor off the dressing rooms.

Madame was small in stature, but undeniably present and a privilege to meet, although she would never know Anne's name. "Such philandering didn't go on at the Olympic or Covent Garden," Madame proclaimed in a speaking voice as resonant as her singing. "Charles and I expected propriety in every corner of those establishments. No loitering, no hangers-on, no improper flirtations, only a few friends invited backstage."

"Miss Robinson, and, therefore, her family … and good acquaintances," Harry finally acknowledged Anne, "are my friends."

Anne saw Madame Vestris as upstanding but too scrupulous to say everything she was thinking. "Perhaps, after the show, as long as the girl has a chaperone. Then you should entertain them in the Green Room, which is barely decent enough."

"Yes, yes, dear Lucy. There's always need for improvement. We have to watch the purse, you know. Don't want to end up bankrupt. Or in debtor's prison."

"Harry," Lydia whined and pulled on his arm as if she had a stake in any disagreement he caused with Madame Vestris. Like Anne, she probably didn't know what he was alluding to. There was little doubt Madame grabbing her chiffon-flounced skirt and holding the rose corsage on her chest to turn and depart with her dogs at her heels was not merely in response to the call boy running and shouting up and down the hallway.

Branwell's place in their section of the house seating was empty as the orchestra began playing.

Unlike her husband, Mrs. Robinson couldn't ignore his absence, leaning and reaching out across Elizabeth's and Mary's laps to tap Anne's knee. "I thought he was with you."

Genesis 4.9 might have influenced Anne's reply, but like Madame Vestris she wouldn't reveal all that came to mind. "He needed some air."

"He drinks too much." Mrs. Robinson sat up again, clapping with the rest of the audience as the curtain rose.

The first picture-framed segment had Harry and Robert Roxby along with Charles James Matthew involved in an amusing if slightly unsavory skit full of coincidences, mistiming, and mistaken identities. Half-way through Branwell finally returned to take his seat, intoxicated enough to fall over Mr. Robinson's knees so his hands landed on Mrs. Robinson's, and he couldn't resist winking at her, young Edmund, and the girls before he sat and grinned at Anne as though aware of what her thoughts accused.

***

"But, Papa, Harry invited us backstage."

"From what I hear, Lydia, you invited yourself."

"Oh, Mother. Not to the Green Room." Lydia poked her brother. "You're such a damnable tattletale."

"Such language, young lady." Mrs. Robinson glowered at her eldest daughter and then Anne.

"Harry, is it?" Mr. Robinson was behind in the conversation and their leaving the auditorium, struggling to straighten his back after sitting too long. "That's enough for me to know it's time we called it a night."

Lydia was crying one minute and smiling the next, slipping through one of the now empty rows of seats to unashamedly move towards Harry stepping down from the stage. He said something to her that prompted the mesmerized girl to respond loud enough for anyone to hear, "Yes, yes, no one will stop me."

"Well, I suppose." Her mother conceded her interest as her eldest daughter explained it was customary—imperative—to attend the after-show party in the Long Room. "After all, we won't be backstage, but quite respectable among those like ourselves," she informed her husband, and then dismissed him. "Take Edmund home. The girls need to socialize more and Master Brontë will insure we're not unaccompanied walking back after dark."

Mr. Robinson did as he was told, venting his own protest by dealing with Edmund's, lecturing his son's grumbling while pulling him into the lobby and out of the theater.

Anne wished she could view Branwell's increasingly untenable situation as primarily Mrs. Robinson's fault. Up until that summer, she had hoped her brother would act out of caution rather than vanity and tactfully deflect Mrs. Robinson's advances. Instead, by allowing, even encouraging, her pitiless whims, he was threatening to jeopardize his and Anne's positions. Anne was more concerned he was setting himself up for disappointment worse than he ever had to cope with before. She wasn't so dedicated to duty, without other purpose, or under the illusion of being irreplaceable, that reaching the end of her life with the Robinsons would cause her hardship. Branwell also had the refuge of home for career disasters, but nowhere but drink and opium for those of the heart. He didn't have the core strength of his sisters and father, and wasn't well disposed to thinking any or all of them might ever direct him better than he could himself. Without a male friend like William Weightman, who had affectionately addressed but never enabled his weaknesses, achieved his trust, and might have proven an example he could eventually follow, poor Branwell was at the mercy of his own more often than not foolish counsel.

All the same, Anne couldn't excuse Mrs. Robinson. It would have been imprudent but not unforgiveable if, instead of the mother, it had been daughter Lydia lifting her bosom and her fan while tilting her head to say something close to Branwell's ear.

The younger Lydia's actions were otherwise irresponsible, causing tongues to wag about her friendship with Henry Roxby. Yet her unselfconscious flirting with a man old enough to be her father—his profession and lack of pedigree being what really disqualified him as a matrimonial prospect—didn't offer a scandal like her very married mother boldly dancing, sipping cocktails, laughing and whispering with her son's twenty-seven-year-old tutor.

It seemed later than half-past nine when they finally left the theater, Anne huddling with Mary and Elizabeth, the three of them yawning and dragging their feet. It was fortunate Branwell wasn't their only male escort, for he lagged far behind with Mrs. Robinson. Henry Roxby was a few steps ahead of them and behaving more like a protector, although he acted out of line in courting Lydia, holding her close.

He proved almost honorable in his intentions as he looked back, asking, "Everyone safe and sound?"

Anne appreciated his attention but didn't really believe any harm would come to her in Scarborough. It was one of the few places where she never doubted her well-being, no matter what disturbed her elsewhere. So far in her life, there were two locations away from home that saved her from doubt and loneliness and even despair: York Minster and Scarborough. The great cathedral reminded her of the eternity of her soul, showering her with God's love in rainbows of light through arching glass. Stretches of sand and the sparkling, lapping motion of the sea invited early morning escapes from practicality and responsibility and encouraged wandering where no one would ever look for her. She equally loved the sea at night, although she never found the nerve to walk on the beach after dark.

At night, the sea smelled saltier. Without gulls, bathers, children on the sands, and the grown-up frolicking that went on all around the town, it sounded sinfully irresistible, hypnotically rushing in and out as though it meant to steal and cast her heart piece by piece into its dark depths. As close as it was, just below and reflected east and south in a frothy moon, it was hard to hear as they walked along, Harry and Lydia chattering, and Mrs. Robinson and Branwell also distracting because of where their behavior was going.

Once Anne was in her bedroom with its seaward outlook, she was reckless to the extent of opening the window, not only to hear the sea, but to feed her imagination with the seduction of all the places she would never go, all the chances she would never take, and all the hopes she would never admit, except in her writing.

Anne left herself vulnerable to the sea's sounds and fresh air all night, the latter as might have been prescribed by the eminent Dr. Arnott to keep enough oxygen in the room. She woke just after dawn with a cough that threatened her plans to take the girls to the noontime Sunday concert at the Spa. It might be wiser for her to go than not to, considering the acclaimed healing power in a slow drink of its water. At breakfast, she initially treated her ailment with vinegar and treacle, resisting Branwell's whispered suggestion of adding a few drops of laudanum to the tincture. Wrapping a shawl high on her neck helped, as did the day's warm sunshine. Nothing was more calming to her lungs than sitting among other reverent music lovers—which Elizabeth and Lydia were not—in the Spa's turreted Saloon, melting into a Mozart symphony, an air by Weber, and a Rossini overture. At least, as the music swelled and soothed and satisfied, she was unaware of any physical discomfort from the afternoon's rising temperature, let alone her earlier asthmatic episode.

The older girls did enjoy dancing to some quadrilles: flutes, coronets, fiddles, and rather heathen-looking drums meeting the challenge of rousing the up-until-then sedate crowd. Mary refused to make such a spectacle of herself, even though Anne urged her to join her sisters and another young lady to make up the number required. Perhaps the girl knew what would happen next, Henry Roxby seeming to step out of an extravagant flower display, his smile manipulative as he extended his hand to Lydia. Anne also saw his intention to court any member or, with a nod in Anne's direction, advising acquaintance of the Robinson family. Anne smiled, not so much in response, but because he was mistaken in regard to her influence.

After twenty minutes, the dancing concluded.

"We'll be expected to return soon," she submitted, frowning at Lydia's frowning and how she tried to lean on Harry who, in conscience or expediency, held her at arm's length. "Your mother will miss us if we're not back by three."

"Not if your brother is keeping her company."

If ever Anne was tempted to lose her patience, even her temper, with the eldest Miss Robinson, this was the moment. Harry abruptly excused himself in response to a group of concert goers who had recognized him. Lydia's sinking posture, reddening eyes, trembling mouth, and a hand rising to where she felt pain in her corporal and emotional heart, reminded Anne how crushing, how hard to breathe, how impossible to be rational, how utterly miserable it was to be harshly jolted out of the beginnings of love.

Lydia allowed Anne to stroke the back of her shoulders and lead her away from the sight of Harry easily forgetting her. Anne put a finger to her lips when Elizabeth commented on his fickleness and wasn't surprised by Mary exchanging her cleanly folded handkerchief with Lydia's dampened crumpled one. Their walk across the bridge was under clouds that hindered the sun and any conversation. The sisters got ahead of Anne because she chose to take smaller steps and make more than one stop to look out to sea. She felt a rush of gratefulness for having had the chance to feel close to it, remembering the brief possibilities of running a school with her sisters and even honeymooning there, knowing that as it once more swept her away the time was fast approaching for her to endure missing it like that other love of her life fate had deemed she live without.

CHAPTER EIGHT

Thorpe Green, two months later, October 1844

Anne remembered she owed a letter, not to Emily, Charlotte, or her father, but to an unexpected friend. Its composition interrupted her gathering of thoughts, characters, and storylines for a project germinating since her Blake Hall days and finally growing into prose much different from, yet indebted to, what she had written for the Glasstown Confederacy and Gondal Chronicles. As far as Anne knew, Emily wasn't aware that anything but music copying, Bible studies, and the odd poetizing about nature and God's mercy distracted her youngest sibling's limited leisure time away from the exploits of the Republicans, Royalists, and Unique Society. Changing interests could be left out of letters but not returns to Haworth. Emily wouldn't accept Anne was no longer eager to play along with those little rascals and escape to the islands. Anne endeavored to pretend a little, out of love and her sense of conciliation, but even if she found some pleasure in them, what was their relevance beyond making Emily happy?

If Anne had gained anything from living among those richer and poorer than herself, it was a confirmation of what she already knew: resistance weakened in the absence of conscience, conscience disappeared in the emphasis on desire, and restraint was overtaken by greed without a care for what might be stolen. To reside within the dissolution of principles and proper behavior without being party to it meant that constant vigilance was required, which left little time or inclination for make-believe. Emily might argue imaginative escapes were a good defense. One day, Anne might return to being as Emily wished her to be, in part if not entirely. For now, Anne needed to concentrate on the practicalities of duty and endurance, and the long-term benefits of maintaining her integrity. Her faith and blessed insignificance helped her to step carefully around the snares and pitfalls of others' unchecked impulses, and remain on higher ground. Somehow she held her own against the testing winds blowing up from the valleys, with a hand outstretched to her own dear brother who was slipping into one of the deepest and darkest.

With Flossy warming her lap, Anne was writing to a woman as old as her sister Maria would have been. The letter couldn't be long as she intended to fold in a copy of *The Misses Brontë's Establishment* flyer Charlotte had sent her. She had to consider the weight for postage. The few times she and Lilian had met, their conversations punctuated by the rush of seagulls and surf, they discovered much in common even as they hardly knew one another. Although Lily was a widow and Anne had barely dared to think of matrimony, they shared the understanding of how love didn't need earthly presence let alone ceremony, children, or years of companionship to be sustained. Within moments of their first accidental meeting on Scarborough's most remote shore, Anne's "dreamy look" was easily read by Lily, who had risen over the dunes with shoes in hand and already graying hair loosened from its plain styling. Her own happiness was revealed in her flushed smile as she mentioned she had recently married.

"Who'd thought, long past the bit o' prettiness I had. If it culd be fer me, then it will fer thee."

She pointed out to sea, loving it more than Anne did, her man and her heart at its mercy. A year later, almost to the day and in the same spot, her tears were shared, although Anne's grief seemed so much smaller when she heard "a babe gone, and a chance of more stolen by the sea". Lily didn't agree that Anne had less to mourn for, drying her own eyes and, with a finger like a cat's tongue, Anne's. They walked up and down the beach, talked and as effortlessly didn't, hands clasped before parting, both looking back at the exact same moment with a questioning wave.

Between then and Anne's next summer holiday, Lily went to live down the coast in Bridlington, a day trip away. Through correspondence she and Anne arranged an assignation in Scarborough for one afternoon. Anne, who was late because Mary wanted to come along and couldn't be convinced not to, found Lily wading out further into the surf than was safe but Lily came back to life when summoned by Anne's friendship. Their privacy invaded by Mary's curiosity, they couldn't speak as they needed to, even a mention of the school Anne and her sisters were hoping to run proving unwise for Mary to overhear.

"Miss Brontë is going to leave us soon," the girl blurted to Lydia and Elizabeth with such sincere anguish Anne forgave her at once.

There was something serious to forgive Mary for, the naïve girl's heartfelt expression offering her often conniving sisters an opportunity to demonstrate how they were inclined to enjoy a bit of news for more than just hearing it.

Anne couldn't help considering the eventual, even imminent, end of her employment at Thorpe Green, but was careful not to broadcast any self-initiated plan for leaving. She reminded herself again and again it should be Mr. and Mrs. Robinson's decision, not hers, and without any blemish on her years of service to them. The best scenario was that long before the Misses Brontë's school had a chance—a remote chance—of being realized, her position would come to its natural conclusion. The worse outcome was becoming more possible, but Anne did not, would not, believe it was inevitable.

While writing to her, Anne thought of something Lily had said: a word, more than a word, a philosophy, simple but profound, out of the mouth of someone who spoke simply and succinctly, not unlike Tabby, or, in the old days, Nancy and Sarah Garrs, who sometimes shared wisdom with just a comment on the weather.

"Fluctuations."

At the time, it was an apt description of who and where Anne and Lily were with the warmth of the sun on their backs contradicted by the wind shifting, so it felt colder as they faced the sea deepening because the sky was darkening long before night.

Now it was a title for a poem Anne decided to fill most of her letter to Lily with.

Anne stroked Flossy's ears as she began to quietly read out loud, "'Fluctuations. What though the Sun had left my sky —'" Her doe-eyed companion looked up, understanding nothing and everything, wagging his tail and letting it drop limply, whining because he didn't like it when his mistress was upset. "Shh, shh. It's all right, sweet pup. 'To save me from despair the blessed Moon arose on high, and shone serenely there.'"

It was all right. It would be all right. Perhaps not every moment, not when she thought of who she must wait until she died to see again, or how there was less heartache but more frustration in believing she would never feel fully useful in society or even at home unless she accomplished something meaningful. Still, it could be worse if she was without the resolve to make her life fruitful, pursue a well-cultivated mind and well-disposed heart, have the strength to help others be strong, or, especially, the faith to endure and rise above endurance.

"'I thought such wan and lifeless beams could ne'er my heart repay, for the bright sun's most transient gleams that cheered me through the day. But as above that mist's control she rose and brighter shone —'" Flossy looked up at her again. "'I felt a light upon my soul!'"

Anne knew life couldn't fail her as long as she acknowledged the blessings of animals and nature, music and prayer. She also valued family and friendship, which, of course, could be one and the same. At times, it was stifling back at the parsonage, as though all the windows and doors that held her to being the smallest, quietest, last and least likely to surprise were kept locked by those who loved her for their own conclusions. Anne could never think of home as a prison, but once she flew the nest and realized she had the wherewithal to, if not quite soar, make survivable landings, she knew it was restrictive. She had always suspected being overly protected was as dangerous as being unguarded, like enjoying the rose without noticing its thorns. It wasn't as though her family was unaware of the world and its ways. Daily and weekly doses of newspapers and magazines initiated lively discussions, mostly between Branwell and Charlotte, with Emily grunting, about religion and revolution and parliamentary reform, potato famine and, closer to home, the plight of the wool laborers and sick in their father's parish.

Anne was afraid responding to political, social, and moral issues through the amusement of fantasy was more about outwitting these realities than addressing them. She even felt some shame at having gone along with the juvenilia that made believe the world was at her fingertips, its maneuverings entertaining, romantic, and escapist, although she could almost forgive the child she was then. Halfway through her twenties, having lived most of the last four years away from her family, she was finally fully-fledged, the nature she was born with at last standing up for itself, wanting its voice to be heard, with the courage to admit she was meant to wear truths not masks.

In or away from Haworth, the best companionship was often with herself alone: the best being the reflection that wouldn't falsely flatter for the sake of avoiding hard feelings, wasn't eager to congratulate in order to keep her friendship, and didn't encourage self-pity because it was wanted in return. Anne had long since decided to be honest with herself even when it meant facing a harsh reality, like the prospect of never marrying and having children. Whatever God's will, she hoped a few of the schemes in her head, humble and limited as they were, might come to something. She could hear Emily guffawing. *Why shouldn't they? You worry too much.* Yes, she did, a correction that was one of the most difficult to make if she thought she must choose between passion and dispassion. *Of course, not. You only need to choose to breathe or die.*

Why should Anne be guided by Emily, differences in temperament, experiences, and responsibilities challenging their cohesion? How could she not? Even when her closest sister was miles away she was present in spirit. The phantom bliss, as Emily called her imagination, had once cast a spell on Anne, but the clingy little sister had become self-reliant and more rooted in reality. If Anne was truthful, she did envy Emily settled at Haworth, never having to apologize for withdrawing from the world and into her writing.

Emily's life was delicious without divisions, like a stew with just the right flavorings blended, all its ingredients slowly simmered.

Anne wasn't yet so comfortably put together. Despondency, too often a visitor wherever she was, set her at odds with her highest intention of actively doing some good in the world. Instead, because of the increasingly objectionable situation she was in, she was afraid she might step back from progress for the safety of home. Unlike Emily, she couldn't be conscionably content there. Emily was because she always knew how she could be, a creature of returning not seeking. Anne didn't expect to ever make peace with her conscience, to stop strengthening her nerve or moderating her sensitivity. Much of the time she hid the ambitious side of her nature, but in neglect it seemed to grow larger and harder to control, a dangerous thing if ever it had more sway over her than responsibility and faith.

As Emily pointed out, she was far too dramatic. Fortunately, Flossy, such a languid dog when it was just the two of them cocooned in her room at Thorpe Green, was a reminder that sometimes retreat was necessary and not irreparable. The precious spaniel proved life needn't be all one thing or the other, curling up his legs on the sofa or bed to catch a nap and once out-of-doors stretching to chase after a rabbit, just alternating parts of the whole of who he was.

"Oh, Flossy. You're snoring again."

The object of Anne's amusement opened an eye and lifted a paw to cover his nose.

The candle Anne was writing by had almost burnt down. She wanted to finish the letter to Lily and get up early to post it in Thorpe Underwood village before Mary knew she was gone. She had heard Mrs. Robinson mention that she, the girls, and young Edmund were going to Great Ouseburn and the Greenhows for lunch and riding. Anne half expected to be asked along as there had been talk of her teaching their young children. The invitation never came and it seemed tomorrow, a schooling day, might be a full one off for Anne, another hint her employment with the Robinsons was nearing its end.

The nine verses of *Fluctuations* took up most of the inside of the letter to be folded, sealed, and stamped without an envelope. She scratched the remainder of it vertically across what was already written, like Charlotte, never one to be brief, often did. Anne smiled to think of her oldest living sister and her well-meaning verging on oppression. Lily had reminded Anne how private even casual acquaintances, those who didn't know anyone she did and were unrelated to her past or future, were akin to that other side of solitude, not censorious but releasing. They were like shooting stars and meteors appearing and disappearing, brightening and lightening moments otherwise rendered bleak and burdened by inescapable bonds and unbearable losses.

On impulse Anne reached for her *Book of Common Prayer*, opening it to the blank back of its inside cover and wrote "sick of mankind and its disgusting ways", causing injury to her prayer book and merciful nature.

The letter, finished, was lighter than her mood and heavier than a penny stamp might handle. She didn't doubt her decision to put the brochure in it, but had second thoughts about including the poem, remembering Lily had shown an interest in the school plan, but not knowing if she appreciated poetry.

***

"I thought you would have gone to the Greenhows," Branwell called to her.

He caught Anne turning away from Monk's Lodge, changing her mind about calling on him. "No. It never came up."

"Did the beast stay behind?"

"Flossy? I didn't want to deal with him running off, constantly tugging if I kept him on a lead, or having to clean him of mud and, worse, burrs."

"I didn't mean Flossy."

"Then I don't know whom you're referring to."

"Yes, you do. You don't like the lord of this manor any more than I do."

"You mustn't be uncharitable, Branny. Mr. Robinson hasn't been well."

Branwell laughed. "Glad to hear it. Will you come in for tea?" He stepped out of the doorway to give her access to it. "Of course, you'll have to do the honors."

Anne felt her moralizing rising to the surface while the summer-like mildness and autumn colors begged her to see the calmer, brighter side of the day. "Why don't you come for a walk? If just around the grounds."

She wasn't prepared for his agreement, but wasn't displeased by it, either.

"I don't even need a coat."

"I'm too warm in this lightweight one. It's like early September." Anne involuntarily regressed, small and vulnerable walking beside him, waiting for him to take her hand as he had when she was the youngest of six. Of course, he didn't.

"Look at all of this—the rolled lawns, trim borders, flourishing trees, picturesque approach to a mansion high and all its comforts inside—that might be mine"

Another kind of hold on Anne allowed her brother to lead her through his misguided expectations: the hope she might yet prevent his thorough downfall.

"It's not home for us, Branny. It never can be."

"So what ails the mister now? Perhaps the complimentary letter I received from Macaulay has sickened him again."

"Anne Marshall said he blames it on last Sunday's dinner."

Branwell clapped his hands. "'Twasn't me. Although I have good reason."

Anne trembled in silence, because of what she should say.

"Miss Marshall is an annoying fly buzzing around my dear Lydia."

"She's doing her job."

"And some. She sees enough to hang me."

Anne could no longer refrain from preaching, stopping and forcing herself to grab his arm to prevent him from moving on. "Only because you provide the rope."

Branwell patted her hand before he pushed it away. "You can do better than such a cliché, my little nothing. Don't pout. You know I only chide you with affection."

Anne tried to ignore his condescendence. "I know Miss Marshall. She's discreet and loyal to her mistress."

"A mistress so deserving of loyalty as well as more return in kind of her unselfish sincerity, sweet temper, and unwearied care for others."

Was Anne really almost to the point of giving her brother up to his emotional weakness and ultimate moral decline? "I'll leave you here. I'm feeling tired. Also, I'd be wise to prepare a German lesson for Misses Mary and Elizabeth in case I'm expected to teach them later, as you might be with Edmund. I don't like to go in through the front door."

"Well, you should like it. You will like it when—" Branwell sounded determined until he saw Anne was more so, standing straighter and folding her arms. He raised his voice to ignore her resistance and further his delusion, "—when I'm the master here."

CHAPTER NINE

Haworth, three months later, January 1845

"As I told Ellen, we're not about to break our hearts over it."

"Well, Charlotte, I'd say Emily is bursting with joy."

"And wanting to mention she told us so, Branny."

"You've done it for me."

"With or without your gratitude, Em? Anne's quiet. All this holiday." Charlotte didn't linger on that thought. "Why is the post late?"

"It's not. You're waiting for it." Emily tugged the thread she was darning with through her front teeth to cut it before Anne could pass her the scissors.

Branwell noticed and remembered. "Aunt would have needed her smelling salts."

"Also if she saw me do this." Emily held up his drawers, trying to hide her grin in a grimace as he snapped them away from her. "She would have approved of my stitching."

"All the same, they're pathetic for a man with my prospects."

"Or exactly right."

Charlotte clapped her hands to bring them back to what she wanted to talk about. "Ellen has believed in our plan as much if not more than we have and troubled herself too much over it. I told her not to. Even if she persuaded any mother to consider bringing her child here, the aspect of the place would instantly frighten them away. I hope you're taking it all right, Anne."

Anne had already experienced disappointment to do with the school scheme, her idea of having it at Scarborough never considered by her sisters, which didn't prevent it happening there in more imaginative circumstances. She deflected Charlotte's obligatory concern. "I was thinking about Aunt, whether she would feel we're giving up before we've really tried."

"Well, she wasted her money on my Brussels fiasco." Emily's voice was hoarse as if upset. Nothing else about her appeared disturbed, not her expression or posture or her making precise stitches in a pillowcase's torn seam.

"We still have most of our inheritance and it's building thanks to Em."

Emily nodded. "Well-invested in railway shares."

"At last." Reacting to the front door bell, Charlotte abandoned her pacing in front of the over-heated range.

"Speak of the unachievable," Emily muttered.

"A stoic like you cannot know," Branwell scolded vaguely.

"What do you think, Annie?"

Anne was offered an alibi for not answering, Charlotte returning just as Martha came out of the back scullery with the bucket of potatoes for peeling Tabby had promised—threatened them with, especially to boil to glue, as Emily noted—before she left for an overdue visit with her sister.

Martha noticed, as they all did, Charlotte separating one letter from numerous others she pushed into her apron pocket.

"Oh, is it?" Martha blurted.

"Is it what?" Charlotte's hostility thrust out like a blow.

Anne was glad Martha also chose to respond with silence.

"Help me here." Emily came to the rescue of the gentle, hard-working seventeen-year-old and the bread in the oven. "Don't want them too well-done like Miss Martha … Brown."

"That's pretty lame." Charlotte acted as if no one suspected the cause of her bad temper and recent bilious attacks. In living for the post, she revealed the breaking of her own code and heart."It's from Mary. Mary Taylor," she finally answered the inquiry no one was brave enough to ask.

"Is she still intent on emigrating?" Branwell was already sitting at the table wielding a knife as Martha put a steaming loaf there. After her run-in with Charlotte she wasn't about to thwart his intention and stepped out of the way so Emily could boss him.

"You'll make mush of it. Let it cool. I'll tell you when." Emily put down a second loaf as Martha brought over a third.

Branwell surrendered the knife without relinquishing his focus on the object of his desire. "Get the butter and jam, Martha."

"And what can you do for yourself? Except what you shouldn't?"

"Go easy on me, Em."

Charlotte curled around her letter.

"Only a few weeks back, when she was here, Mary was intent on joining her brother in New Zealand." Branwell tried again to get her attention.

"What?" Charlotte looked up, her eyes vacant yet wet. "Yes, she will leave our hemisphere soon, like a great planet falling out of the sky."

"It seems such an unnatural choice … for a woman." Branwell leaned over the bread to at least enjoy its aroma.

"Not for clear-headed, independent Mary. Long ago she made up her mind to not be one of those women considered redundant because they don't marry, but to have opinions and purpose and employment other than as a housekeeper or bonnet-maker or even a governess or teacher.

She sees no chance of having a meaningful life in England."

"She's gutsy," Anne said softly, "and, perhaps, will prove wiser for being braver than the rest of us."

"You've shown courage through years with the Robinsons." Emily dropped her head to look sideways at her younger sister. "Now you need to use your wisdom and stay home."

"I fancied Mary Taylor once." Branwell finally sat back from ogling the bread, looking as satisfied as if he'd had all he wanted. "Or thought I did until I realized how ashamed she was with even the inkling of being pursued. That's where you two agree, isn't it, Charlotte? That *une grande passion est une grande folie*? Or, at least, you used to."

Emily jumped up. "What are you waiting for, Branny? Cut us all a slice. Martha, where's the butter and jam?"

"Not for me." Charlotte folded Mary's letter. "I'd better take the rest of the post to Father. He might want me to read it to him. Not that my sight is much better."

"Perhaps, you just need new spectacles."

"I probably do, Anne."

"When the weather breaks, you might walk to Keighley for an examination. I'd go with you, if I was here. Emily might—"

"If only it was so simple to correct my wretched nearsightedness." Abruptly, roughly, Charlotte took off and lifted her spectacles as if she was about to throw them.

***

It was years since Anne was home on her birthday. Emily baked an oatmeal and treacle cake a couple of days ahead of the teatime designated for its consumption to soften it in a tin.

"I'll allow no one to refuse a piece of Annie's parkin." Emily, unusually, looked very pleased with herself. "I mean to give my bet'r sen some happy thoughts." She even sang some lines from an old ballad supposedly from the time of Robin Hood. "'Now the guests well satisfied, the fragments were laid on one side when Arthur, to make hearts merry, brought ales and parkins and perry.'"

"'When Timothy Twig stept in, with his pipe and a pipkin of gin,'" Branwell followed on singing.

"Always the spoiler." Emily didn't look at him.

"Well, part of a song doesn't tell the whole story."

Anne briefly escaped their argument to take a piece of cake out to Tabby in the back kitchen. Easily wearied and hard-of-hearing, the old servant was trying to nap in a straight-backed chair positioned in the draught from the back door.

"Where's your shawl?" Almost as soon as she wondered, Anne found it draped over the handle of a broom leaning against a wall.

"Eh? What yer fuss?"

Anne gently laid the loosely-knit shawl around Tabby's shoulders and gave her the plate of cake.

"Dear angel-lass."

Later, as the sisters spent a final parlor-cozy evening before Anne returned to Thorpe Green, Branwell off to take advantage of his last chance for a while to "stept in" at the Black Bull, even Charlotte admitted the liability he presented to their progress.

"The way it's going with him, it's better our school scheme comes to nothing. No doubt he'll soon be home again, unemployable, even less able to provide decent company. Certainly not an example of manhood young girls should witness."

Anne never told Charlotte as much as she did Emily, but there was no way to prevent the disturbance of her and Branwell returning home for the holidays together but estranged. As soon as they arrived, Anne fled the hours of traveling with him as though nothing ever disgusted her more. Over the weeks, Branwell tried to converse with her beyond yes and no and maybe. Normally, her forbearing nature wouldn't allow her to slight anyone, but with agitated busyness she dismissed him—to comb Flossy or clean Dick's cage or help in the kitchen, which she rarely did, or beg Charlotte to let her read to their father who didn't know of his son's latest sin but might notice his guilt, so Branwell kept out of his way.

For a while Anne was as cowardly avoiding her brother, even if it meant staying in her room when he was in the house.

She wasn't proud of her behavior. Gradually she felt more ashamed of her own choices and failings than Branwell's, blaming her intransigence and righteousness for her failure to persuade him to stand stronger against temptation. Love was what she was made for, understanding, forgiveness and faith at the heart of her, good memories soothing the bad. Flashes of the gentle brother with his little sister on his knee, proving his talent for telling stories too entertaining to question and drawing pretty pictures he inscribed *for Anne*, tempted her to once more hope he might yet chose rationale and, especially, what was right, over ruin.

"Let's expect he'll be better and do better." It was as if Emily had read Anne's thoughts. "Speak no more of it tonight. Are you still working on the same poem, Annie?"

"Still wrangling with it. You know how it is, thinking it might be better with a different word or different order of words, more metaphors or less. That it might benefit from leaving some sentiments out altogether."

"I hope it isn't gloomy." Charlotte was sitting across the parlor table from Anne, the paper she was fingering easily in view as the beginnings of a letter in French.

Emily's lounging took on the look of someone double-jointed with her right leg slid off the sofa and her left one lifted and bent, its stockinged foot pressed against the back of the couch. She made a feeble effort of controlling her skirt for modesty's sake. "It's rather pleading."

"Entreating," Anne corrected as she knew Emily would appreciate.

Emily winked. "If you say so."

"Let's hear it entreat then," Charlotte challenged.

Anne didn't want to read the poem out loud and spoil the evening with dread of what she was going back to the next day. For a moment, she considered sharing a little of *Passages* instead, an excerpt that was well-worked and entertaining. Sensing her sister's impatience, she stood with one of her journals, opening it to its middle and flipping a few pages further. With a slow, almost tiptoeing stride, she recited as she moved around the table, because of the limited space brushing Charlotte's back with each passing by.

"'God. If this indeed be all that Life can show to me; if on my aching brow may fall no freshening dew from Thee; if no brighter light than this the lamp of hope may glow, and I may only dream of bliss and wake to weary woe—'"

Emily sighed as dramatically as she never naturally did.

"You always cheer us so."

"I'm sorry, Charlotte. I won't continue." Anne had reached her chair after a second circling.

"No, go on. The writing itself is lovely."

"'If friendship's solace must decay, when other joys are gone, and love must keep so far away—'"

"Enough." Charlotte groaned.

"Not for me." Emily threw her head back and closed her eyes.

Anne continued, realizing the poem was quite good and nearly as she intended. However, she hesitated when she reached the fourth verse, mustering up the courage to take a risk.

"Vice and sin?" Emily echoed. "Nothing to do with anyone we know, of course."

"That's it for now. I have yet to perfect the rest of it."

As Anne sat down and closed her journal, Emily offered no resistance, just a suggestion. "You might lift your spirits to Gondal as I do."

"We should leave the past," Charlotte seemed to wake from her wallowing, "and expand our literary ambitions. Branwell says what publishers want these days are novels—portly novels gushing with drama—because readers do. I believe he's writing one."

"Or living one."

Anne glanced at Emily to make sure she knew not to go beyond what she had implied if Charlotte was curious to know more. Fortunately, their older sister was leaning over her half-written letter again, crossing out more words than she was adding.

Charlotte realized they were watching her and put down her pen. "Today Father had another application for replacing Mr. Smith. He said it looked to be one he should seriously consider."

Anne was seized by heartache as she hadn't been for a long time. Of course, William had to be replaced, except he couldn't be, as Mr. Smith had proven.

"You never met Mr. Smith did you, Ann?" Charlotte slipped the unfinished letter into her desk.

"I did. When Branwell and I were home last June and he'd only just taken up his post as … Father's … curate." Anne cleared her throat, so as not to allow distress to influence her speaking again. "He accompanied us on a walk when Ellen was visiting."

It was as if Charlotte heard what Anne didn't say. "Yet another fickle fellow. He didn't mention Ellen once after she went home. Until Father put it to him she was a nice girl and he agreed while supposing she didn't have any money."

Emily's listening was almost always distracted, this time by her writing in a handmade journal a little larger than any they had made as children. It peeked out from under her leaning on an elbow. Somehow she never missed much. "I didn't think Ellen was impressed by him."

"Our father thought so. I never saw him so uneasy about such a thing before. Usually his opinion of such matters is sarcastic, not fearful."

Fearful. Charlotte had no idea how that word took hold of her youngest sister, so much so Anne felt a cramp in her stomach and coldness up her spine. Fearful. Yes, that was it. That was exactly what Anne was as the relief of being home—of Branwell being away from Thorpe Green—ran out with the days until they would walk to Keighley, catch an omnibus to Bradford and Leeds and the train to York. The Robinsons' driver William Allison would meet them and take them the remainder of the way back to secrets in danger of becoming known, young Edmund snickering and even threatening to use what he saw and didn't see to some frivolous advantage. Anne fought the impulse to quit her employment of almost five years without giving notice, to ignore her own sense of duty and decorum, to set an example of cowardice to her girls, even to leave Flossy with the Robinsons, as she had for the Christmas holidays, permanently.

Anne welled up at the thought of the puckish little dog jumping out of Mary's arms into hers, licking her face and wiggling to get away, so someone would call and run after him. No, she must do the right thing, by Flossy and herself and the young women she cared about, and believe she might yet influence Branwell. She must return to Thorpe Green, at least once more, to hope for the best and plan for the worse.

"What are you writing, Em?"

"Some of my little rascals have escaped the palaces of instruction to join the Royalists."

"You waste your talent," Charlotte charged.

All three sisters heard the slow methodical steps in the hallway and up the staircase until they stopped on the first landing.

Anne felt her liberty slipping away. "Is it nine already?"

"Of course, Father," Emily answered his call for them not to stay up too late.

"How easily you lie to him," Charlotte was accusing again, this time without a hint of criticism.

"He knows the truth. He sees it in my bleary eyes in the mornings, but appreciates I do the things that need to be done around here no matter. And so he does his duty, too."

"I could never function with so little sleep." Charlotte opened the parlor door a crack. "Goodnight, Father. What? Oh … yes. He just came in … ah … you were still in your study, so you didn't hear him." She turned to see her sisters as conspirators.

They all listened to the whiny opening of the long-case clock's face.

Once he had gone upstairs, Charlotte resumed the banter between her and Emily. "You're like a mole in your tiny room, burrowing an inspired way through the night."

"More like a cat, catching a few quick mice and naps in between."

"As clever and self-contained as a cat, I'll give you that." Just as Charlotte seemed about to smile, a rare occurrence since her Brussels life, she scowled instead and urgently took her box from the table. "I feel so tired. Of everything. I think I'll obey Father for once," she only partially explained.

Anne was prompted to follow her lead. "I hope Branwell does come in soon. We have to set out by eight."

"And Father mustn't hear him," Charlotte reminded.

"I'll stay downstairs and stop him making noise," Emily offered. "After all, it's not my bleariness that will give away your white lie, dear Lotte."

Charlotte looked surprised and then gave in to smiling, just a little. Anne was less hesitant to being drawn into Emily's simply lived yet creatively complex orbit, but then Anne had grown up in it, been sustained by it, and found true friendship in it. She knew, welcoming the hope in that knowledge, that even as Emily seemed unsentimental, letting them go to their beds and disappointments and fears and useless efforts to change what couldn't be changed, she was keeping a place for them by the fire of her imagination and fidelity.

CHAPTER TEN

Thorpe Green, three months later, April 1845

The fields were still too wet for Anne to take a shortcut to the Greenhows and Great Ouseburn. If she had been walking at leisure, for sketching or physical exercise or clearing her thoughts, it wouldn't have mattered if mud splattered her boots and skirts, as it wouldn't when she returned to Thorpe Green by cutting across the Kirby Hall estate. She would use the back door, remove her boots and steal up to her room to make herself presentable again. If she didn't get away with such "wildness when wandering in nature," the Robinsons would only be playfully dismayed with what they had come to expect and, perhaps, even enjoyed about her.

That day she had to prove herself to new employers, which meant presenting an impeccable and undistracted demeanor even before she demonstrated her ability to manage and teach as well as commend herself to their children.

It was left to Mrs. Robinson to inform her that, because Mary, at almost seventeen and except for a music lesson now and then, didn't need more schooling, some of the expense of Anne's wages could be recouped by her instructing the Greenhow daughters three times a week. Despite Anne's displeasure with the circumstances that brought her to them and the anxiety she felt when faced with teaching young children again, she also realized the relief of being away from Thorpe Green.

What was more surprising was the warming of her heart to the dreamy personalities and optimistic possibilities of girls before the future was imposed on them.

Eliza was twelve and already knowing better than anyone, Eleanor nine and thinking she couldn't grow up fast enough. Sophia, seven, and Charlotte, five, were cuddlers, the older pushy and the younger pouty to lean into Anne's arms, sit on her lap and feel her slow caress of their hair. Before she knew it, Anne was equally in need of their affection, of her hand expectantly pressed and her arms opening to their small sweet-smelling forms. It was good to have another chance to influence children, to see their earnest looks as she taught them something new. Her experience with them was especially satisfying when she could open a window to the freshness of a breeze carrying the scents of spring and promise of rain, the children eager to identify trees by their shapes and birds by their songs, interested in understanding the formation of clouds, and willing to engage their blossoming souls in nature's wonders. There were other lessons found in books, on chalkboards and globes, in recitations and writing, addition and subtraction, music and sewing, even those reflective of Anne's belief in free will and expression if tempered with respect for the free will and expression of others. Although she felt exploited by the Robinsons, she made the best of her time with the Greenhows or, at least, made little of the worst of it, taking charge of these innocents with a devoted educator's and mother's care.

The first weeks might be considered successful, her objections and doubts nearly overcome, her teaching style approved and showing results, her affections given and won even by Mr. and Mrs. Greenhow, who wished they could keep her all to themselves. Then, with less than a day's notice, Branwell was also on the road to Great Ouseburn to tutor the Greenhows' only son and eldest child, young Edmund Robinson's best friend, William.

Anne was apprehensive, wondering if she had been sent to the Greenhows because Mr. Robinson was looking for a tactful way to get rid of her brother, at the very least for Branwell to be at Thorpe Green less. If so, did that mean Branwell had gone too far in his admiration of Mrs. Robinson? Had something finally been said, seen, written, somehow admitted? She knew so little of what her brother had been up to, but didn't have to guess how much hung in the balance, employment the least of what was at stake. She knew Branwell too well to believe he could walk away from disaster without his emotions hanging on to the mess made.

"I'd heard something was happening to this road," he said, looking intimidated by two wide-shouldered, thick-armed men chopping at and grubbing up the hedging on the east side of Thorpe Green Lane. A third worker, much less muscular, gray hair matted with sweat also dampening the front of his shirt, was collecting brash to dispose of in a bonfire spitting and collapsing in an adjacent field. Branwell's apprehension didn't stop him inquiring, "It looks so bleak. Will you be replacing the quickthorn?"

"Aye. W'th'same, 'cept'n straight lines." One of the grubbers nodded towards Anne. A few days earlier she had begged some hawthorn branches, blooming early due to an unobstructed view of the morning sun, before they were discarded.

The Greenhow girls had enjoyed that day's lesson about the parts and function of flowers, not so much the tiny ants that jumped onto their arms and even into their hair. Except for little Charlotte, who, unlike Anne's sister of the same name but with a pluck often shown by another, pretended she was the bravest.

Perhaps, like Emily, she really was.

Anne already realized William Greenhow was shrewder than the younger Edmund Robinson, having seen him treat his sisters unkindly without them noticing, although Eliza, embarking on adolescence, was, as might be expected, sometimes sensitive to his tactics. Branwell dismissed Anne's gentle warning about William trying to manipulate and mislead him, countering he could handle any boy having been one himself. She could only despair of her brother put off guard by the fourteen-year-old's willingness to study and be corrected and even contained by whatever lesson was put before him. "He never whines about being bored or weary or hungry, and never looks out the window," Branwell reported, as if unaware of William watching and waiting for any opportunity to learn something more intimate about Mr. Branwell Brontë than his obsessive love for the classics.

Branwell's new student was expected to grow up to be a solicitor or barrister. He had the makings of a politician or spy, even reminding Anne of the two-faced King Brenzaida of early Gondal, after all a saga not left behind but maturing as she was coerced into facing a less idealized view of life. Would Emily be pleased or disappointed her little sister was sinking into pessimism? Her sights were lowering enough to see scheming, her nobler thoughts bowing to suspicion, her better angels cowering from confronting the devil's influence so close to her until the light of redemption was put out by the worst of human nature.

She hoped Emily would not judge but soothe and buoy her back to her best and most fortified self as, perhaps, only Anne knew Emily had the capacity to.

***

Anne did consider her perception of William Greenhow might be more a symptom of her own hysteria than his conduct. Still, she was unable to dispel the thought her brother was threatened by this clever and disarming boy, who, through his friendship with young Edmund, had been willingly enlisted into the conspiracy to tell about Mr. Brontë.

Even before she and Branwell had gone home for the Christmas holiday, the Robinson girls and their brother were hinting at the matter, which caused Mary and Elizabeth visible distress and seemed a source of amusement and means of retribution for Lydia and Edmund. It was still all supposition then. On their return, there were a few weeks when Mr. Robinson's failing health monopolized his wife's time. Eventually, she grew needy for attention herself and resumed her enticement of Branwell's sympathy, which in turn rekindled the madness that caused him to abandon any sense, especially of morality.

Once during a music lesson Mary began crying, reminding Anne of a baby bird fallen out of the nest in a rainstorm, trembling, weakly flapping and curling into fatalistic submission. Flossy's licks consoled her a little. Anne's embrace and careful questioning only persuaded Mary to admit she was upset because her father was ill. When Elizabeth, still in her riding habit, brought in mud and further agitation to lean over the piano's shawl covered lid and not only insult her sister's singing but also announce she could no longer enjoy riding because the stable lads had taunted her with gossip about the goings on, Mary couldn't pretend any longer.

"How could they know? What do they know? It's horrible. We are ruined," Mary blubbered and banged the piano keys, something her mother forbade. Still they were taken by surprise as Mrs. Robinson rushed into the parlor, the bottom of her skirt and petticoats crushed by the doorway, springing out as she pushed through it.

She reprimanded Anne for allowing Mary to commit such a sin.

"The irony," observed Lydia, who was sitting on a window seat, a cluster of primroses wilting in her lap.

Anne wanted to tell her a second time to put them in water.

"What was that?" Mrs. Robinson didn't wait for an answer, quickly glancing at Branwell coming into the room. "Now you must play properly, Mary. And sing. Perhaps, Miss Brontë will, too."

"'Music, when soft voices die, vibrates in the memory.'"

"Shelly, Mr. Brontë?" Mrs. Robinson made an exhibition of deciding where to sit, biting her lip, fingering the tape-lace of her collar, turning this way and that, the side sweeps of her hair swaying, the late afternoon light burnishing the topaz of her perfectly fitted dress. "I always consider the music resonates better over here," she explained as she didn't need to when she chose the Chinese-silk poppy-red loveseat, shoving Flossy off, spreading and slowly stroking some of her skirt over its entire seat.

"I thought you said Papa was better." Miss Lydia hit the heel of her right shoe against the baseboard beneath the window seat, primroses falling to the carpet.

Anne stepped away from the piano to rescue them.

"Oh, no. Hours since I picked them, so they're past their best. The maids will clean them up in the morning."

Anne bent over to gather the scattered flowers anyway.

"Well, you might press them, Miss Brontë. I forgot you and Mary like to do so."

On rising, Anne saw her brother hesitating to sit next to Mrs. Robinson as he also may have thought she was slyly inviting him to. One minute Anne was proud of his resistance and the next horrified by him settling on the rosewood framed armchair he knew was Mr. Robinson's favorite.

"Did you hear me, Mother?"

"Louder than my own thoughts, Lydia."

"Well. Isn't Papa much better?"

"Not today."

"I hope you're not poisoning him." No one else but young Edmund, who completed the spontaneous gathering of the Robinson offspring, could express such a possibility and sound playful, even creative. He reminded Anne of Branwell when he was an imaginative, mischievous boy intending only to entertain himself and his sisters.

Mrs. Robinson invited her son to sit where Branwell hadn't, throwing her arms around Edmund, smoothing his hair, and kissing each of his reddening cheeks.

For some reason, perhaps because Edmund screwed his eyes as he looked at Branwell so relaxed in his father's place, Anne felt there was little playfulness left in the lad.

"So, what will you perform, my dears? Nothing too pious."

Edmund squirmed to be released from his mother's calculations.

"Miss Mary has been practicing an air of Thomas Moore's."

"Augh! My sister is going to sing." Edmund finally broke free and ran out of the room.

"No, Flossy." Anne was surprised the little dog stopped and sat rather than continuing to chase after him. "Come here."

"Should I follow Edmund?" Branwell finally spoke.

Mrs. Robinson seemed affronted by his voice and without looking at him waved her hand dismissively. "Do as you like."

Branwell didn't move, as Anne saw it, paralyzed rather than choosing not to.

"I hope the piece isn't melancholy."

"No, ma'am. Well, only lightly so. It suits your Mary's voice, as so many of Moore's songs do."

"The Irish melodies can be quite lovely."

"Actually, it's set to a French air, from his later collection."

"Even better. More to her station than anything Irish. What are you whispering about, Elizabeth, Lydia? Be quiet or leave."

Anne, standing beside Mary sitting on the edge of the piano stool, touched the girl's shoulder with her left hand and lifted her right to the top of the music so she would be ready to turn the page. She counted one, two, three and Mary began playing. A short introduction and Mary was singing, at first too softly, but soon as confidently as Anne could never do. "'Come, chase that starting tear away, ere mine to meet it springs; to-night, at least, to-night be gay, whate'er to-morrow brings. Like sunset gleams, that linger late when all is darkening fast, are hours like these we snatch from Fate—the brightest, and the last.'"

"Miss Brontë." Mrs. Robinson didn't need to say anything else for Anne to join in harmonizing.

"'Then, chase that starting tear away; come, chase that starting tear away, ere mine to meet it springs.'"

"And so I wish to, Lydia."

Anne daring to look at her brother had to look for him. He had moved from one mistaken place to another and was posed dandy-like behind the small divan where Mrs. Robinson tried to maintain the attitude of being in charge of the proceedings.

"You assume too much ... Mr. Brontë."

The song and partnership between Mary and her governess went on, "'To gild the deepening gloom, if Heaven but one bright hour allow, oh, think that one bright hour is given, in all its splendor, now.'" Anne was torn between the pull of its sentiments, especially of memories never made and an entirely different kind of attraction. Lydia and Elizabeth were also distracted and visibly embarrassed as Branwell leaned over their mother and whispered into her ear.

Mary stopped playing. "What is it?"

Anne stopped her. "Nothing, Mary. Please continue."

"I think you should see what Edmund's up to." There was an uncharacteristic quiver in Mrs. Robinson's voice.

Mary looked up at Anne, tearful over what she didn't need to see. "Don't abandon me."

"Never." At least, Anne spoke of her intention. "Now, go on."

"Thank you." Mary tried to smile as her fingers fell on the piano keys. "'Let's live it out—then sink in night, like waves that from the shore one minute swell, are touched with light, then lost for evermore!'"

"'Then, chase that starting tear away; come, chase that starting tear away, ere mine to meet it springs.'"

Mary and Anne repeated the refrain one last time. Branwell still didn't leave the room, but paced behind Mrs. Robinson ignoring him there. Was he getting up the courage to say something? Anne worried it was what he had already said, inappropriate and incriminating enough in private, absolutely unforgiveable if uttered again in those moments.

"Didn't Mary do well?"

"What? Oh, yes, Miss Brontë." Mrs. Robinson clapped belatedly and briefly. "Well enough for drawing rooms and even parties."

"What else would I want to do it for, Mama? Lydie is the one enamored of the theater."

"Not to perform in it." Lydia stood up and grabbed Elizabeth's hand. "That reminds me, Bessie. I've something to show you."

"Can I see, too?"

"No, Mary." Lydia, dragging Elizabeth by the hand, came over and lowered her voice to speak to Mary, and, less deliberately, Anne. "For you'll tell Miss Brontë before I can."

"Wait," Mrs. Robinson called Branwell, who was also exiting the parlor. "We've had music." She pulled a little volume from the folds of her skirt. "Now poetry."

Even with Anne and Mary still there, Branwell finally sat squeezed next to his employer's wife. They were almost cheek to cheek as Mrs. Robinson flipped the pages and Branwell considered her suggestions. He rejected at least half a dozen poems until one was agreed upon, and he leaned back into his corner of the divan with the book held so close to his face he knocked his spectacles askew with it.

Mary, kneeling on the floor and enticing Flossy to tug-of-war with a rolled-up newspaper, giggled nervously, which inhibited Branwell enough to put the book down.

"What have you been told about playing with the dog in the house?" Mrs. Robinson found a suitable reason to reprimand her daughter.

"Flossy needs to go out before dark." Anne hoped she had offered Mary a means of escape, too.

"It isn't raining, is it?" Mrs. Robinson did her duty by asking.

Mary ran to the nearest window, exaggerating looking out and up, tearful and tenuous. "Not a cloud."

CHAPTER ELEVEN

York, two months later, June–July 1845

Anne drifted in and out of obliging Emily's desire to spend most of the journey pretending to be Gondal princes and princesses fleeing the palaces of instructions to join the Royalists.

Emily's unexpected enthusiasm for traveling didn't waver. Either she didn't notice Anne's mood or, in order to buoy her, was hoping to avoid any acknowledgment of what had brought her sister's spirits so low. Anne felt and appreciated it must be the latter, not convinced she was still tactful enough to spare others the disillusion verging on depression her final months at Thorpe Green had left her with.

The excursion should have been effortlessly exciting for both of them. Other than asking Anne where she thought they should stay and what the essential attractions were, Emily took the initiative of planning their schedule and booking their travel and accommodations. They would arrive early evening to a meal and room at The George, and on Tuesday, after breakfast, spend at least an hour, maybe two, in the Minster, followed by shopping, snacking, and as much sightseeing as time and Anne's stamina would allow. York was one of three destinations for a summer trip first thought of at the beginning of the year. This visit would be the first real holiday Anne ever had there, with the chance to occupy herself as only she — and Emily — pleased, although not the best place to avoid thinking about the Robinsons.

Anne was bothered by so many things these days, least of all the train jolting and choking them most of the way from Leeds, a worse journey than riding the omnibuses from Keighley and Bradford. Even along the roughest stretches, Emily furthered the exploits of Ronald Macalgin, Henry Angora, Juliet Augusteena, Rosabella Esmalden, and Julian Egremont out loud and on paper, undeterred by the compartment's side door rattling as though any moment it would fly open. There was just a slight setback, when, at one screeching stop between scheduled ones, Anne's little case tumbled off the wire shelf above her head and knocked the notebook out of Emily's lap.

"We're coming into York station. Yes. We're passing through the archway," Anne announced less than fifteen minutes later.

"To be continued." Emily looked towards the window to see where they were outside of her imagination that, as Anne could tell from her sister's childlike expression, hadn't let her get away entirely.

***

Their room at The George was one Anne had occupied before. Once the Misses Robinson were considered old enough, their governess' accommodation was away from theirs. At the top and back of the establishment, it provided a savings to their parents in shillings if not embarrassment due to complaints of the girls talking and giggling long into the night. Number fourteen was small and simple without a view of the Minster, but the cathedral's bells could be heard throughout the city.

Anne pushed up the sash window, leaning out a little to hear the skillful change-ringing.

"Don't jump!" Emily caught her around the waist, laughing even before Anne did. "Now if you were Branwell …."

Anne withdrew from the open air and any amusement to sit on the bed that would fit two slim sisters who took comfort in each other's breath and touch. Emily had said the wrong thing, yet Anne didn't expect—want—her to apologize. They must never be sorry for being open to each other. Who else was there to be safely intimate with?

Emily picked up the small cases dropped just inside the door and took them over to the wardrobe, placing them inside and shutting it. She glanced and quickly turned away from its long mirror, only needing to take one step to prop her hands on the bed's bottom headboard. "Perhaps it's not as bad as you think."

"Oh, it is."

"Then you haven't told me everything."

Over dinner Anne said more than she ever had about the impropriety seen, gossip heard, and humiliation felt, which might not be everything but enough for Emily to understand the seriousness of the situation. Especially since their brother had supposedly returned to Thorpe Green even though he was no longer wanted there.

"You think he was already dismissed?" Emily stopped eating and pushed away her plate with what was left of a slice of soggy cottage pie. She continued to sip on a small glass of wine.

"I'm fairly sure of it. Miss Marshall saw Branwell and Mrs. Robinson together in dangerous ways. Also, she overheard Mrs. and Mr. Robinson discussing whether they should pay our brother through July to be rid of him."

"And keep him silent? They don't know our Branny."

Anne nodded, glancing around The George's dining room, at its blue and gold décor, unlit fireplace, low-hanging chandeliers, fringed rugs, and others diners who were also still in dusty street clothes and, no doubt, sleeping in the highest and tiniest backrooms of the hotel. They were the type of people the Robinsons ate later to avoid. Some of them noticed Anne staring. She silently admonished her own rudeness.

"I'm worried, Em." Anne put her hand out to her sister's left arm. "They can't have welcomed him back."

"So where is he?"

"Hopefully, he didn't go to Thorpe Green, but to find other employment before he has to tell Father he needs to."

"Too farsighted for Branny. If in Halifax, he's with Leyland and bemoaning how hard it is to be sensitive and artistic, drinking and drugging because of how he's been wronged. If gone to Grundy, thinking he can be reinstated with the railway, he's deluding himself even more."

"Are we finished?" The waitress was there to collect their dishes.

Anne's reply was demonstrated by her knife and fork neatly aligned across her half-empty plate.

"Summat wrong with food?" The dark-frocked, white aproned and capped young woman specifically asked Emily.

"Not if it was supposed to be undercooked."

"Em," Anne scolded softy.

Emily pointed to the sweet trolley another waitress had rolled over to another table. "I see cake."

"Sponge layered with raspberry cream. Or chocolate with coconut icing. Or—"

"Not for me." Anne immediately thought of how they had already agreed not to have dessert so they could indulge themselves at the confectioners the following day. Her expression must have said it all.

Emily slumped. "I forgot."

"Well?" the waitress began to clear their table.

"My little sister knows best."

Anne waited for their server to walk away. "Hardly, Em. If I did, I would never have stayed five years with the Robinsons."

"Well, at least Branny has given you an out."

"Not the way I wished it to end. I kept thinking the situation would right itself. There was nothing for it but to flee my failure."

"Your failure? What are you talking about? You've had letters from the girls every week since you left. Such is their devotion to you, the best person they'll ever know."

Anne wasn't sure if she felt responsible for Elizabeth and Mary becoming heartfelt and hopeful young women, or for leading them on. "They have such challenges ahead." She expected Emily to mock her pity for any Robinson.

"I wouldn't change places with them."

"I suspect not with anyone, Em."

Emily leaned back, noticing the serviette she had earlier spread on her lap was on the floor. She retrieved it. "I might wish I was you when I meet my maker."

As they left the dining room, Emily noted it was only a quarter to six with hours of daylight left, Anne ineffectively resisting her sister's suggestion they take a walk. Arm in arm they stepped outside of the hotel, hardly at risk of being the only ones at leisure on Coney Street. As they turned onto Stonegate, the heavy foot traffic was more diverse, unhurried and enquiring, fingers pointing this way and that and quite often at the window displays of the shops now closed. Most surprising were the numerous examples of children out with their parents at that hour, in a few cases accompanied by governesses who, too young and too old, reminded Anne of the trials she might have to take on again. In contrast, a number of strolling sweethearts, some probably honeymooners, even showing her what she would never do, seemed right for that bright summer's evening.

Anne followed Emily's lead and walked wide of a well-dressed man watching them pass the Olde Starre Inn. Her sister exhibited no qualms putting a coin in the cup of a blind beggar sitting under the printer's red devil.

Anne nodded to another pair of women who might be sisters or close friends or both, distracting them from their guide's monotonous delivery of facts and directions so they missed the rest of their party turning into one of the many ginnels between buildings.

"Through there." Anne saw their panic, forgiving their lack of appreciation, her understanding almost rewarded when at the last moment before disappearing they looked back and limply waved.

"You may've just spoiled their escape." Emily tilted her head onto Anne's shoulder to let her know she was teasing. "How far shall we go? You look, as Tabby would say, fair knackered."

Anne was tired, but needed a view of salvation. "Since we've come this far, a few steps more."

Emily insisted they stop at the next corner, not to contradict her sister, but to look up at the blue-robed and helmeted statue, sitting with a pile of books and an owl, between the High Petergate and Minster Gates street signs.

"The girls liked her, too. More than the learning and wisdom she represents."

"Never mind them, Annie. She smiles on us. Do you think she knows?"

Anne's interest had already shifted from Minerva to the Minster, as expectantly as she remembered it rising with a creamy glow to calm and even silence the confusion of what had led to it. Its massive construction moved upward, pointing and peaking, lancet windows directing every gaze to its stunning south side gable with its famous rose created by stone mullions, tracery, and stained glass.

It wasn't her intention to go into the Minster until the following day. She couldn't have succumbed to the impulse of that alluring moment if she wanted to, the doors still unlocked only for earlier visitors to leave, a placard outside announcing its closure.

Anne wasn't sure how her sister's first sight of the Minster affected her. Emily silently and loosely folded her hands like she did at church when she didn't want anyone to know whether she was praying or not. They quickly walked back to The George, wrapped around each other, feeling cold with just their summer shawls and because they were overtired and at such liberty away from home.

In their room Anne offered but Emily took the jug down to reception for some warm water. Washed and changed, they climbed into bed and discussed their writing, not for the first time the novels they had begun, and, surprisingly for Anne, Emily admitting she had been copying a number of poems into a separate journal from her Gondal ones. They also talked about what they would do the next day and agreed not to visit Scarborough that trip, because the Robinsons were there.

"I have a feeling Branny went back to Thorpe Green."

"You do?" Anne was glad to feel the warmth of Emily's body. "If so, perhaps at the invitation of Dr. Crosby."

"His shooting chum at Great Ouseburn?" Emily often remembered conversations it seemed at the time she wasn't listening to.

"Yes. Perhaps he'll talk some sense into him."

"No one can do that, Annie. Not even you." Emily gently pulled her sister's neat bedtime plait. "As I'm assuming you tried."

***

The chill of a draughty hotel room and the early morning were soon countered by a walk between Botham and Monk Bars along the city wall from which there were excellent views of the Minster's north side with its tree rich Deanery Park and octagonal chapter house. Anne was slowly warmed and quickly wearied, while Emily had the long lean legs, constitution, and naiveté of a marching soldier who had not yet experienced battle.

It wasn't that Emily ignored Anne's struggle to keep up, but, similar to when she roamed the wilds around Haworth, she couldn't hold back her instinctively animal nature any more than Keeper or Flossy, not even for the one she loved best.

It didn't help that Emily had a long list in her head of all she wanted to do in a day that was in danger of ending too soon to leave enough time to collect their bags from The George and get to the railway station for an early evening train back to Leeds. At the very least their adventure must include the Shambles and its tributaries, Newgate Market, the Assembly Rooms, York Castle and Dungeon, cause one frivolous purchase each, and fulfil the promise of a meal more sweet than savory. Anne was glad her skeptical sister allowed the Minster to be their first necessity. The choir area often closed at noon. Also, because the morning had been open-skied it was likely clouds would roll in by the afternoon; the Minster's interior was even more magnificent when the sun shone.

They made their way to the entrance off Precentor's Court. It rose up to the graceful "Heart of Yorkshire" and even higher in the symmetry of the pinnacled towers framing it that were, as Anne had seen on many a carriage approach, the cathedral's declaration of dominance in the city skyline. She identified the religious tableaus in the arch above the doorway, while Emily grimaced back at the grotesque creatures looking down on all who noticed their immovable presence. The crowding, smells and noise of the medieval maze of narrow streets nearby might have been a hundred miles away as they stepped into the Minster's west transept and found relief in a spaciousness no number of visitors could diminish. They inhaled burning wax and incense and even the dampness of limestone and oak wood, while hearing organ music, whispers, and sighs. Their sights lifted and expanded, the grayness of granite broken by flashes of gold, the purity of marble, candles, and, through the stories windows told, light that floated like dust and shone like diamonds.

Anne didn't assume Emily was experiencing the Minster as she was, but she couldn't imagine anyone visiting there without their steps and eyes wandering reverently. Even children respected its solemnity, refraining from running or shouting as would be tempting in any other structure with such long echoing corridors and soaring ceilings, although, as Anne remembered and reconsidered, being on their best behavior might not have been voluntary. It wasn't her choice to walk the whole of the Nave without her customary sitting for a while, hardly able to keep track of Emily weaving around its north aisle's vaulted columns. They came together at the crossing to the Quire, the large decorative pipes of the main organ gleaming and moaning melodically above its arched passage into the cathedral's east wing. Anne was relieved the section was open to her need to rest and contemplate. Before they went in, Emily insisted they name the sculpted English kings lined up asymmetrically on the screen without reading the inscriptions, proving she was a master of royal genealogy, at least from William the Conqueror to Henry V. Eventually they joined the hushed investigations of the Sanctuary's choir, a lofty pulpit their father would have longed to preach from, the high altar, chapels, and biblical proportions and narratives of the largest stained glass window in the world, as someone finally spoke for all to hear.

Emily still wanted to go to the top of the central tower. Having done it once with Elizabeth and Mary, Anne knew if she did climb its two hundred and seventy-five steps she would make herself ill for the rest of the day and longer.

They agreed to meet in front of the Quire, Anne reserving her breathlessness for the power of prayer while Emily exercised her need to view York and its surrounding countryside.

"Like a hawk pushing the limits of how high it can fly."

While Emily had her say about the experience, especially the thrill of its narrow, dingy, windy, spiraling ascent and descent, Anne was more interested in the interior view of the south transept's Rose Window as mid-morning inspired it to blossom.

They walked in the opposite direction, overhearing other visitors bemoaning the closure of the Chapter House for a meeting of Canons. That inconvenience gave Anne and Emily more time in the north transept to view the massive Five Sisters window comprised of side by side lanceted sections: independent although conjoined, sturdy as lead and fragile as glass, dark and complicated with jewel-like flashes of brilliance.

Anne thought she heard Emily gasp.

***

Missing the six-fifteen train lost their hotel reservation in Bradford. Hungry, tired, with their hair and clothes disheveled from the broken weather that had dampened the second half of their Tuesday in York, they were looking forward to the hospitality their father had experienced at the Talbot Inn off the top of Darley Street. Branwell also had good things to say about the establishment, if for different reasons. During his portrait painting days and many times since it had been accommodating to his self-destructive tendencies. It wasn't until Emily and Anne stepped through its doors and up to the reception desk they discovered their day's journey wasn't over.

"We only hold until eight," a tall cow-eyed male employee told them.

"Our father is Reverend Patrick Brontë from Haworth." Anne hoped for an exception to the rule.

The manager was summoned. He was middle-aged and heavy-set with a trim beard and hoarse voice. "Yes, I know of your father. Always calm and courteous. Unfortunately, we had a gentleman come in on the off-chance. Yours was the only room we had left."

Anne realized, by her sister's lowered eyes and tight mouth, Emily wasn't going to say anything. "Can you recommend another hotel?"

"The fellow who took your room claimed he had tried every one in town. There's always the Lord Rodney in Keighley. You're sure to be accommodated there, if not as agreeably as you would have been here."

"You might just catch the last omnibus," the younger man seemed loathed to offer, his eyes fixed on Emily, realizing his mistake as she responded with a scowl. "You'll have to hurry.

"It stops at the corner of Lower Kirkgate and Darley," he called after them.

How fortunate it did; also useful that Emily could run faster and yell louder than Anne.

***

Alone on Keighley's dusky, misty, sewage-scented streets around nine-thirty, except at such an hour the most familiar in the world to them outside of Haworth, they were thankful for the old lamplighter who escorted them to the Lord Rodney on Church Street. At that point they were willing to accept a chair each in the kitchen to rest on.

They were in luck, not only for a small room on the second floor, but also some cold chicken they were allowed to take up to it. There was little talk between them while they ate, washed, dressed for and got into bed, sleeping entwined and uninterrupted until daybreak when they were as glad of tea and buttered bread for breakfast as the glazed buns they had splurged on at York station.

Emily wondered, "Shall we dare do this again?"

"Not for a few days," Anne answered to match her sister's sarcasm, for she was more than ready to return to Haworth and stay there a long while.

At just after eight on a cool, cloudy but so far rainless second day of July, they stepped out of the Lord Rodney and set off on foot to trek the four miles home by means of Bridge Street to South Street, out of Keighley, onto and then off the Halifax road, always preferring a pathless way forward and back to whatever awaited them.

PART THREE

The flint and steel of circumstances are continually striking out sparks, which vanish immediately, unless they chance to fall upon the tinder of our wishes; then, they instantly ignite, and the flame of hope is kindled in a moment.

~ Anne Brontë, *Agnes Grey*

CHAPTER TWELVE

Haworth, three months later, October 1845

"You robbed me!"

Emily took her tirade to the kitchen, slamming doors, yelling at the dogs, and rattling pots. It was fortunate their father was out and Tabby was almost deaf and knew how to soothe her. Martha was prudent enough not to try.

Anne was exhausted, in part due to the long blustery walk she shared with Emily before Charlotte tactlessly revealed her discovery, not least because she felt the pain of every verbal blow her sisters thrust at each other. Having left Charlotte pacing upstairs to consider what she had done and, no doubt, conclude she wasn't sorry, Anne sat at the bottom of the stairs, a whimpering Flossy leaning against her legs, the dog's long plumy ears comforting to stroke.

Keeper sat just outside the door to the kitchen, his head tilted.

Anne didn't know what to do next or expect inspiration after months of idleness and drama at home, her mind flat and emotions scattered. The summer had been difficult with confirmation of Branwell's disgraced dismissal from Thorpe Green and return there, no dissuading his unrelenting impression Mrs. Robinson would and could welcome him back. He insisted her affection for him wasn't contradicted by her apparent complicity in having him thrown out of the Hall or thwarted by Mr. Robinson threatening to shoot him.

Anne had given up trying to influence her brother except by praying for him.

Charlotte, also plagued with illicit yearning, was finally swayed — by her own reason — to stop writing letters soliciting replies never to come.

Charlotte's prying and Emily's protestations stirred tempers but also temperaments, defining and positioning them like in the old days, the childish days, the best days following the worst days when the clouds that hung over the parsonage were lifted by creative schemes as collective as they were individual. Tabby had long ago decreed the bond between the Brontë girls would never prevent them airing their differences, but always hold them together. As Anne calmed and more pragmatically recalled the argument between her sisters, resistance and solidarity didn't seem irreconcilable.

"She didn't mean it."

"I think she did, Charlotte. The few times I've brought up the subject, she's been against it."

"But she won't really destroy her poems because I now know about them?"

"I'm sure she won't." Anne answered as she wanted to believe. "You see how she reacts to Keeper sometimes and then is generously sorry. Just be patient and don't press her."

"Emily's hysterics turned an accident into on purpose. I'm only guilty of complying with fate."

So it might seem. Alone in the house except for Branwell returned to bed in the middle of the afternoon, the door to Emily's little room left open like the handmade journal on her bed, Charlotte wasn't an intruder but an instrument of destiny. Even allowing for the uncertainty of the circumstances, motives or whether there was some divine intervention involved, Anne was glad such an opportunity fell to Charlotte.

"I understand Emily's concerns and why this is so important to you."

"And to you."

These days it seemed Anne had more in common with Charlotte than Emily. They shared years of going out in the world, the awkwardness and loneliness of living among strangers, the dissatisfaction in working for others, some unpleasant experiences of human behavior, and, as Charlotte wouldn't acknowledge about her youngest sibling, disappointment in love.

Emily had forgotten or, perhaps, never experienced what it was like to silence her imagination because it interfered with duty, or just not hear it over the demands of others. Away from home she became more possessed by it.

By the time Anne was eighteen, having been to Miss Wooler's school where she intended to flourish but instead faced a crisis that weakened her physically and tested her spiritually, she often felt aimless at home. She hoped going away to achieve her own maintenance would also earn her a second chance to expand her intellect, develop character and endurance, find goodly purpose, and show her father, aunt, and, especially, her siblings what she was capable of.

Charlotte's incentive for venturing out might have been formed more by curiosity and enterprise than conscience, but, like Anne, she knew what it was like to be torn between the calling to leave and longing to stay.

What was complicated for her sisters and brother was simple for Emily: there was no going back to working away from home to end up more impoverished. She settled once and for all into the confinement that unleashed her fantasies, escaping change except as she grew taller and stronger and unapologetically herself. "I am as God made me," Charlotte reported Emily's answer to the "silly" girls at the *Pensionnat* who ridiculed her clothes, walk, thoughts, and habits. Anne couldn't decide if such certainty made Emily saintly or blasphemous. According to Charlotte it did the trick in stopping the harassment, so it would seem an enlightened declaration after all.

Emily knew her place and stuck with it without being stuck, like a solitary tree on the moor. She was as violently content, shaped by the wind yet unyielding, in motion without leaving the spot she was rooted in.

Anne could be annoyed with her. At times Emily ruled tyrannically over routine life at the parsonage. Not happy with her sisters attempts at housekeeping, she left little inclination, let alone room, for them to settle at home as she had. Against her better nature and knowing nothing was altogether what it seemed, Anne was a little jealous Emily could choose to be eccentric, never think of being a stranger again, and had no one to please but herself.

Charlotte approached Anne as an ally. "You and I need something like this."

"What do you need?" Branwell leaned on the doorway of their bedroom, his shirt hung open and over his trousers, his eyes swollen. "What do women ever need but to ravage men's hearts and souls?"

"Put that in your novel." Charlotte walked to the door to shut him out.

"Is he writing one?"

Anne wasn't sure Charlotte's nod was in answer to her question. "So you've also been keeping your best musings from me." Charlotte went to the window and began leafing through Anne's poetry, acknowledging how neatly it was written down and, barely reading a few pages, "its sweet, sincere pathos."

Charlotte had come up with a plan, Anne a solution to give Emily a way out to be in.

"Nothing like Emily's, I know. She writes with such skillful abandon. I probably exercise too much restraint." Anne was stirring from futility. "You'll offer some of your own, won't you?"

"I'm afraid adding mine might diminish the project."

"Certainly not." Anne had long ago learned Charlotte's self-deprecation was her vying for praise. "It's the difference yet equality of our work that will make it interesting."

"So we only need Em's agreement," Charlotte begged Anne's diplomacy.

***

"I've never given a thought to being published." Emily's eyes were downcast, her hands rubbing up and down the sides of her skirt.

"I don't believe it. Who doesn't have a spark of ambition? You're just being difficult."

Charlotte was fanning the embers of Emily's temper again. After two days of refusing to be wherever Charlotte was, Anne had finally persuaded Emily to come to the parlor.

"We've been brought all together again for a reason." Charlotte approached Emily with her hand extended.

Emily, sitting stiffly on the sofa, had her most private poetry journal open on her lap until Charlotte walked back to the table with it.

Sitting across from Anne, Charlotte looked through Emily's poems, picking some "wildly melancholy" and "sweetly sorrowful" ones, and then much fault with her own. "Mine are too lengthy. We'll put in fewer of them."

"What about Branwell? Shouldn't we include him?" Anne wondered.

Emily finally spoke up, "No one, especially not Branny, should know we're doing this."

Charlotte laughed. "Doesn't that defeat the purpose?"

"It's your purpose. Perhaps Anne's."

"As I told you, Em, I think it's a good idea. I would rather make a living as an author than a governess."

Emily might have heard Anne's desperation, her own voice softening, "Well, it's an idea."

"How every accomplishment begins," Charlotte instructed.

Emily shook her head and shoulders, making it clear she didn't need the lesson. "If you must, publish the poems. But I'll not be revealed."

"You mean, your name?" Charlotte took off her glasses, unmasking the strain in her eyes.

"Not any part of me."

"*Noms de plume,*" Anne realized with a mixture of relief and regret.

"Hmm." Charlotte nodded. "As much for hiding our sex as our Emily's obsession with being invisible."

"All Gondal references must be removed." Emily knocked off her shoes. "Yours, too, Annie."

"Yes, I realize that."

Emily put her feet on the sofa and her head back. "You need something to do. Both of you. I'm sick of seeing you mope around, one wondering whether she's loved and the other what God wants her to do."

"You might try, Em, but you won't irritate me." Charlotte returned her poetry to her. "Not while I'm so glad we're finally all in agreement."

"I'm submitting, not agreeing, Lotte dear."

***

It was five months since Anne had left Thorpe Green, yet she still felt responsible for the Robinson girls, reinforced by Elizabeth's and Mary's constant correspondence and neediness for her replies. Anne sensed they tried hard not to mention their parents while reporting on the weather, trips, dresses, parties, longings, and boredom, but the elopement of their elder sister that filled a joint letter sent less than a day after it had occurred made the vulnerability of their family impossible to evade. *Lydia might just as well have set the house on fire, for our lives are in ashes because of her setting it into a tizzy and the tongues wagging of all those who shouldn't but do make it their business, shaming us all again, just when a previous trouble was fading too slowly like a bad dream, causing Mama and Papa to accuse each other of things again, leaving us distraught and with little prospects except for the mortifying designs of old men, so while Lydia has done as she pleased we must resign ourselves to being sold to the highest — no, lowest — bidders.* Anne recognized Elizabeth's section, not only by the extreme slant of her cursive, but also her histrionics and run-on sentences. Mary's contribution was more upright and grammatically behaved, informative and discriminating, reflecting the instruction her own judgment received from her sister's actions and, also, as pleased Anne, *from a dear governess' guidance and example. Lydia left on October 20th and was in Gretna Green and married that very night. It shouldn't have come as a surprise. She had been bragging how Mr. Roxby wanted her to run away with him. I thought she might wait until she turned twenty. Of course, she has always been impatient and perhaps felt the opportunity must be seized without hesitation. I don't know if I blame her, although she may have a harder life because of doing other than she was born to do.*

If there was anything to be amused by in that letter, it was entirely due to Anne imagining Elizabeth's reaction to Mary's concern for Lydia's hardship rather than their own. Anne was confident enough of Elizabeth's complaint to make note of how she would respond to it.

Mary wrote in closing: *Even Papa talks of sending Lydia money, although he may never entirely forgive her. Of course, Mama's grandiose hopes for her have been shattered. I also want to marry one I love, but in a manner that doesn't disrupt everyone so. Oh, I long for a happier home.*

The Robinsons' news opened Anne's "why-we-should-go-along-with-Charlotte" conversation with Emily. She was encouraged that Emily immediately responded with the opinion the Brontë sisters wouldn't make such desperate and irresponsible choices "as these Robinson females seem to, although Charlotte has had me worried." Anne heard her cue to bringing up Charlotte's project, even throwing in Tabby's prediction they would stick together no matter their differences. All the while, Emily only offered her back and continued to wash the front hallway floor.

"You work hard to keep the house beautifully clean."

"You sound like Ellen," Emily said without interrupting her robust mopping rhythm. "I'm never sure if she approves of our humble home or not."

"'Scant and bare, yet not a scantness that makes itself felt.'"

They laughed in unison and Emily stopped her work. "She always comments on the lack of rugs and curtains, and that the walls aren't papered."

"Instead 'stained in pretty dove colors.' It's nice to be somewhere so plain and uncluttered again."

Emily turned away to lean the mop against the wall, pulling a chamois cloth out of her pinafore pocket, a scrap of paper falling to the floor.

Getting to it first, Anne knew better than to satisfy her curiosity before returning it. Emily stuck it back in her apron and began to wipe the front door top to bottom.

"There's common ground here, even when we don't all agree. Think, Em, how all three of us have been writing poetry and now even novels. We all need to express our observations of life small and large, and experiences of the heart, mind, and soul. Our foundation of mutual understanding is something to build on, not let crumble."

Emily brushed past Anne to begin dusting the staircase bannister up to the first landing, the longcase clock chiming half-past the morning's final hour. "I don't want you to go away again, Annie."

"Does that mean—?"

"Has Charlotte gone out?"

"She went to the stationers for paper."

Emily almost smiled. "I hope Mr. Greenwood doesn't have to face her unwieldly distress. It's no secret he walks to Halifax especially to have a ream on hand just in case one of those paper-devouring Brontës walks through his door."

"Yes. She wants to get started copying the poems as soon as possible."

"She can start anytime she likes," Emily snarled.

"But what about—?"

"Blast." Emily almost fell down the stairs to get out of sight of Charlotte coming through the front door. She grabbed her mop and Keeper by the collar so he hadn't any choice but to flee into the kitchen with her.

"Watch your step," Anne warned Charlotte of the wet floor. "Did you get what we need?"

Charlotte held up a thick brown parcel tied with string. "Did you?"

Anne was confused as to what she had accomplished. "We'll see."

A few hours later, Emily's acquiescence in the parlor was a relief if not quite undeniable proof Anne should take credit for it. What mattered was Emily was in the same room with Charlotte and talking to her.

When their father looked in on them reciting poetry and exchanging opinions, he saw cooperation and creation, and something like normalcy in his family again.

He smiled and mentioned it was like old times.

"Yet as never before, Father," Charlotte began as if she had more to say.

Anne reacted quickly. "For we aren't children now."

"No, my dears, you aren't." Their father bowed his head and shoulders. "Except as I see you through your mother's eyes."

"I could have told him," Charlotte regretted once he was gone.

"And that would have been the end of it," Emily grumbled.

"Surely he wouldn't stop us."

"That's not what I meant, Annie."

Charlotte addressed Emily's real concern. "Oh, don't worry. I've already been thinking of possible pseudonyms. We could at least use our initials."

"Too much of a hint."

"He didn't say it," Anne declared out of context, going to the door and opening it halfway.

"What?" Charlotte and Emily said, one quickly after the other.

"There's been time for Father to wind the clock and go all the way up. He didn't say what he always does."

Her sisters shrugged, almost in unison. Anne wanted to be glad of their agreement on something, but, instead, was reminded of her last place amongst them, how they still saw her as a helpless girl shaped overly pious, full of causeless worries, simple, timid, tender, and afraid to speak, too ready to believe and willing to admire. She found it difficult to assert other aspects of herself to contradict their view of her as the meekest and mildest creature they had ever known. Up until that moment she wasn't sure she wanted to.

Charlotte stood, waving the paper she had been writing ideas on. "I've got it. And have finally found something useful about Mr. Nicholls."

CHAPTER THIRTEEN

Haworth, seven months later, May 1846

There wasn't any indication the comings and goings of packages over the past months aroused suspicion until Branwell, having overlooked the "C" while noticing "Brontë Esqr.", started opening one. Anne was uncharacteristically aggressive, seizing it before anything more than its delivery was revealed to him.

Laying the parcel on the bed she shared with Charlotte, Anne took responsibility for the paper being torn and its contents spilling out, faulting her own impatience to know it contained the latest proofs.

Whether or not Charlotte believed her, she must have asked the publisher to address any correspondence differently from then on. Fortunately, Emily was unaware the secrecy of their poetry volume was ever in jeopardy, instead obsessing over selecting and editing her poems and examining the proofs that came. She gnawed at her copy like Keeper with a gristly bone, more than once withdrawing to her bedroom, the back scullery, or seemingly out of the house entirely, which set her sisters worrying she would end up burying it.

"If she pulls out, we'll go on somehow," Charlotte told Anne in early March. "After all, the money has been sent and our expectations fully lifted. That's not to recognize our little opus would be much less persuasive without Emily's music."

"She's afraid her poems can't live outside herself. That's why she fought the idea of publication and now finds the preparation and waiting so intense, like giving birth."

"Hopefully, less risk in doing this."

"The only risk is that we'll become better writers and wiser about publishing."

"Not that we might be discouraged? Emily says no one will care for our wordy children like we do."

"Of course, it's possible."

"I've seen your misgivings, too, Anne, when removing Olivia Vernon and Alexandrina Zenobia made your verses more subjective than you ever intended them to be. Unmasking. Unveiling. Even some amount of nakedness. Such are the perils of being published. But there's also a sense of relief, of independence, especially if we can earn our living this way." Charlotte's eyes matched the brightness of her laugh, which pleased Anne. "And as we haven't identified ourselves as female, so our revelations continue disguised after all. Oh, how that cold of yours lingers," she soothingly reacted to Anne's chesty cough. "I feel responsible for it."

"I'm improving. It was my idea to walk to meet you. I know what a long four miles it can be against a harsh wind. When we set out for Keighley, there wasn't any sign of a downpour."

"And I took the old road, so we missed each other. It's all about the choices we make, isn't it?" She seemed to realize what Anne was thinking. "Some accidental, or should I say unavoidable?"

"Perhaps accidental, never unavoidable."

"Oh, Acton, how you shame the rest of us with your responsible nature. I should never have gone away with all this going on, but I had neglected Ellen and didn't want her here with Branny such a hopeless being."

"We're all glad you went." Anne, already sorry she had sounded preachy, was now afraid she would be misheard again. "I mean, you've had your heart's burden." She hesitated, this time wondering if she was intruding too far into Charlotte's disappointment. "And most of the practical considerations have fallen on you: wrapping and sending out our copies, letters to follow up, getting us past rejection, negotiating the cost, and being decisive while Emily and I didn't know what we wanted."

"That reminds me. I must write to Aylott and Jones to insist we do the rest of the proofreading ourselves. The first sheets they sent alarmed me. That they would make such a mistake as having stars 'tumbling' rather than 'trembling' proves delay is preferable to appearing sloppy, incoherent, even absurd. We must examine every single character, let alone every word."

"With each read-through I discover another error."

"I never think what I write is finished." Emily stepped in with her pages a little raggedy around the edges but otherwise intact. "Here, Annie. I give them up to your eye and empathy."

"No, you don't," Charlotte asserted, making the mistake she often did with Emily. "Anne hasn't finished proofing her own."

"I don't mind, Em."

"Of course you don't." Charlotte's cheeks reddened. "Why those Robinson brats continue to plague you with their problems. Why when you take her walking, Flossy runs you ragged. Why Father never thinks you're unhappy. Why Branny expects you won't give up on him. Why—"

"I don't tell you what I do mind." Anne felt the sting of her own words as much as Charlotte's. She took the papers Emily offered, less certainly her wink of approval.

The good sister in Anne was glad Charlotte had finally risen out of the ashes of her Brussels' fervor; the better one, the independent and mindful one, wasn't pleased Charlotte had been reborn an even more calculating creature intent on dominating whomever she had to deal with, especially her own family. Anne's literary wishes might be in line with Charlotte's and her diligence might appreciate her older sister's efforts, but her emotions cautioned that Charlotte's incursions, criticisms, and over-managing were as self-indulgent and, therefore, as threatening to domestic peace as Branwell's intoxications and moods.

Anne questioned Charlotte's wisdom in constantly writing to Aylott and Jones and not only in regard to the poetry book.

In April, almost as if she was losing interest in it, Charlotte inquired if they would look at three fiction works by C., E., and A. Bell. "It is not their intention to publish these tales on their own account," Charlotte read from the letter once she finished it.

"Perhaps you should leave that out," Anne suggested.

"I believe using the word 'intention' allows room for some bargaining if necessary."

"They've already had thirty-one pounds, ten shillings out of us."

"No, Em. Out of the Misters Bell," Charlotte corrected playfully.

"Well, somehow it's shown up in the Misses Brontë's expenditures," Emily's sharp wit confronted Charlotte's impatient humor. "Isn't the point to make more money than we spend?"

"Of course. Eventually. We must aim for our investment of time and talent to pay off in many ways." Charlotte folded the letter, put it into its envelope, and sealed it.

***

On the 7th of May, a package addressed to Miss C. Brontë, containing three copies of the poetry volume without permanent bindings, was delivered. Before long, Anne felt something irreplaceable had been taken away. Only the night before, as Martha brought in coal for the fire to "burn more redly," there had been consensus among the Brontë poetesses of the beauty of the half-waxing moon visibly rising beyond the parlor window. As they settled around the dining table, they continued quite agreeable and, even engaged in lively debate, there was an atmosphere of affection flowing heart to heart. Anne wanted to believe they were finding their way with each other again, towards a more favorable future where they wouldn't be torn apart by necessity but held together by possibility, like being novelists. They were already well on their way with works they had begun to share with each other, even to the point of seriously talking about offering them to the world and equally fickle posterity. Not Emily's words, of course, although she allowed herself a wry smile when Charlotte said it and responded she wasn't sure the world or posterity would look kindly on the shocking tale she was devising.

They were all three brimming with anticipation and accomplishment, certain even Branwell stumbling in on them before he went out to damage himself more wouldn't spoil the pleasantness of those hours.

"I know I've been left out of something. In turn, when my fortune changes, I may do the same to you."

Charlotte didn't look up from writing, as she had announced earlier, to Mary Taylor, who, unlike Ellen, was her confidant on literary matters.

Emily spoke to Anne instead. "Is that Flossy barking?"

"No." Anne's confusion caused her to stand up.

"Not Keeper, either."

Branwell crossed his arms. "You're all so smug in your sudden togetherness. I've heard your disagreements. I'll wager there's more to come."

"Now it's a growling." Charlotte put down her pen.

Branwell cried out incoherently and left.

"No. Let him go." Emily tried to stop Anne from acting on her conscience.

In hindsight, although Branwell refused to hear her and she returned to the parlor within moments, Anne might blame herself for disrupting the cheerfulness and camaraderie of that evening, and days and nights to come. Charlotte and Emily had fallen into a despondent silence Anne replicated as she looked out the window again. The moon, although shifted, was still pure and calm. The hearth was brighter and warmer. No literal death, sickness or pain entered there. However, where was any balm to soothe their thoughts, mirth to lift their mood, all those looks and smiles of fellowship? The evening's conviviality had gone astray with Branwell, no words to console the mourning for their endeavors never to include him again.

As often happened with loss, rather than speaking of it, there was avoidance. Rather than embracing it as mutually affecting, there was stoicism, whether for endurance, indifference, or resignation, so each mourner was on her own. Anne sat separated from her sisters again, verse coming to her so jumbled and sorry for itself she hoped it would as quickly disappear and never be written. By the end of the evening she had roughly jotted it down.

For a few days she had other poetry to occupy her, until Charlotte insisted any final corrections be in the next post.

"Let's get this foolish thing done."

Anne struggled with giving up one last chance to review her poems. "I don't have any revisions as such, but—"

"Anne says my little efforts are perfect, contradicting the notion she always tells the truth," Emily affectionately chided one sister before being cross with the other. "Have you examined yours thoroughly, Lotte? You've spent more time pilloputating and nattering with Tabby in the back kitchen."

"Enough to realize I'm as unhappy with my contribution as I'll always be."

"Your Angria poems are your best. And there are, what, thirteen of them?"

"I've never considered myself a poet."

"Then why did you force this foolish thing upon me?"

"Because I have no doubt you are one."

"A foolish thing?"

"Oh, Em. You know what I mean."

"I know what you mean to make me, or should I say yourself.

"I have all our interests at heart."

"Only, Lotte, as they benefit yours."

Anne, who heard the prelude to yet another argument, decided to leave them to it, surprised no further discord disturbed her already anxious circling of the front garden. The afternoon was warm enough for open windows, but not settled bright or cloudy. A rain shower, now past, had freshened patches of yellow heartsease and quivering bluebells, leaving the grass gleaming and abundant with worms for a blackbird undeterred by Anne's proximity and even Flossy's whining as he was held from chasing it. The bird's charming bravado offered Anne some thoughts about her own limitations. What if she didn't seize opportunity? It was a question which burdened her again with the dilemma of her head siding with Charlotte, her heart with Emily, her spirit aspiring to a higher purpose than mediating family squabbles.

Along with refreshing escapes out-of-doors and the affectionate, energetic companionship of Flossy, Anne found writing a most natural and constant way to seek relief. Her reason became another's, a naively optimistic, determined, almost invisible young woman named Agnes, who composed musings out of *sorrows or anxieties* to acknowledge in a resilient way all those *powerful feelings* that could never be *wholly crushed* and for which solace from *any living creature* shouldn't be sought or expected.

Anne hoped Agnes' story would mark her own passage from a woman of mere occupation to one of true vocation. When she first discovered her sisters were also writing novels, it struck her as remarkable and inevitable, mostly the latter. Their sibling habits and resemblances were like the roots of a tree, some moving away and some going deeper, but ultimately existing to feed back to their source. All except Branwell's, his endeavors withering and exploits poisoning, threatening to bring his family's standing down.

There were still times he tried to spin it differently, waving the issue of the *Halifax Guardian* that had published his poetry in his sisters' faces. He continued to claim he had more to fill a respectable volume and was working on a novel that would reveal a man's heart the way *Hamlet* or *King Lear* did.

Anne didn't expect evidence of those last two literary exertions to be forthcoming. Contrary to Charlotte's accusation and her own nature, she had to all intents and purposes given up on her brother, accepting it was futile to try to dissuade his destructive habits and ridiculous romantic notions. His shamelessness had weighed on her conscience long enough. She couldn't go on feeling responsible for his Thorpe Green debacle.

It was too special a time to let his moods and behavior affect her. She wanted to savor her exciting expectancy, although reminded of the one she couldn't share it with, believing he would have approved how she had gone on.

Agnes knew. *The ties that bind us to life are tougher than you imagine, or than anyone can who has not felt how roughly they may be pulled without breaking.*

***

Not publishers of fiction themselves, Aylott and Jones had sent C. Brontë a list of firms that might undertake the Bells' novels. July was set—by Charlotte—for the submissions to begin. Meanwhile, *Poems by Currer, Ellis, and Acton Bell* was published by the end of May and when Anne finally held one of the thousand printed, she actually cradled and caressed it before carefully opening it with disbelief and utter adoration.

Emily escaped with a copy. Anne also wanted to be alone to examine one. The room she shared with Charlotte was the only place she could do so to insure the secrecy they had agreed should continue. She was forced to listen to her older sister's disappointment with such a thin, unassuming book, its paper not the chosen quality, and stylistic irregularities on the title page.

"What's this?" Charlotte became even more distressed when she discovered the errata slip inserted because of four missed corrections. "And only on my poems."

Still overwhelmed by the look, feel, and implications of the book in her hands, Anne could forgive anything, even her own obedience to Emily's insistence she avoid her Gondal poems and any specific references to the saga of the few she did include. Anne's worry her contribution lacked drama and distinction and would seem too simple and sentimental was for the time being, like Charlotte's fault-finding, minimized.

"I do like the gold lettering on the green." Charlotte closed the copy she had been cynically exploring and turned it front to back to its front again. "The cloth has a nice feel and its size is perfect for carrying conveniently."

"And discreetly."

"Yes, we've been fortunate in not having to hide our extensive reading."

"Here, at home."

"Now, as brothers, we may provide literary temptation to the ladies." Charlotte seemed at last uplifted before taking her desk to the chair by the window, setting it on her lap.

"That's how you get ink on your clothes." Anne offered the protection of the old tea towel she used to prevent such mishaps. Charlotte refused it, already settled into writing. "Who to?"

"Our publisher."

"Not to complain—"

"I've made a list of periodicals and newspapers we need to advertise in, for now no more than two pounds worth. We'll wait for reviews to decide whether we spend more."

Charlotte's publicity requests were sent. Anne's nervous excitement made her ill enough to stay in bed for a few days. Emily's reaction was silence, except for her repetitive demand that the true identity of Ellis Bell never be revealed.

Their father, already brought down to isolation and inactivity by advancing blindness and the prospect of unreliable surgery, was almost told of his daughters' latest venture. Anne expected any day Charlotte would pull out their published poetry while reading letters and the newspaper to him. Anne wished she would, so he might have enjoyed their good news for a little while before events set Branwell behaving more intolerable than ever, the house thrown into turmoil because of his elation over another man's death and then as if there was nothing left for him but to hasten his own.

CHAPTER FOURTEEN

Haworth, two months later, July–August 1846

The first day of rush-bearing was sultry, the church overcrowded and suffocating. Anne could bear the discomfort and even danger to her health for a first-rate concert steps from home. She looked up to her father seated alongside his friend Thomas Crowther, who had arrived the day before to give a Sunday school sermon. Another like-minded ecclesiast, Thomas Brooksbanks, and the head of St. Michael's and All Angels' trustees, Magistrate Joseph Greenwood, were also among her father's companions in the west gallery. Such bright, rational company was just what he needed in that dark, discordant summer.

Emily didn't often show enthusiasm for going to church and was usually loath to enjoy herself in public, but her happy anticipation of Mendelsohn's *Paulus* put on quite a display of smiles and excited fidgeting. The Oratorio was to be performed by an ensemble that included Haworth's own celebrated tenor Thomas Parker along with Huddderfield's Mrs. Sunderland, who, it was reported, Her Majesty Victoria had permitted to be called the Queen of Song. Halifax's musical life had loaned out its principal vocalists Mr. Hargreaves and Mr. Baldwin, along with choir members and instrumentalists.

Also uninhibited by excitement, Anne grasped Emily's hand, hoping she wouldn't mind.

Emily endorsed Anne's effort with a quick squeeze. "I have to catch up with his *Songs without Words* volumes. I believe there are eight now. I only have five."

Finally Anne knew what Emily's birthday present should be, just enough time to send away for it.

Charlotte was seated the next row up, Martha on one side of her, Tabby on the other. The latter was there to observe rather than listen to what was going on, but, as the deaf were liable to do, not quietly.

"No Mester Nicholls?"

Charlotte's shoulders lifted aggressively, forgetting Tabby couldn't hear her answer or just wanting others to. "He's stayed away in protest."

"'Cause how tha' treats em?"

Charlotte was alerted of the gossip by Ellen. Someone had asked her friend outright if the eldest Miss Brontë was going to marry her father's curate. It was puzzling where such a rumor originated, Charlotte, as far as Anne knew, only ever coldly civil with the man. She finally had good reason to dislike him beyond personal opinion when, with other Tractarians in the district, he decided to boycott the concert because its main performer, Thomas Parker, was a Baptist.

Arthur Bell Nicholls was, in a professional capacity, needed more than ever. Anne, still emotionally conscious of what he didn't offer, reminded her sisters of what he did. Emily agreed without an opinion on him one way or the other. Charlotte eventually admitted he was basically a good man who did a good job and any talk of his replacement would unnecessarily add more stress to their father at a time when he was experiencing enough over his and Branwell's afflictions and uncertain remedies.

During the long expressive overture, Anne regretted her brother wasn't there. In bygone days its organ virtuosity would have been to his liking and inspired him in his own talent for the boldly solemn instrument. Listening to the Oratorio might have affected him in that way again: in some way, at least to sober him and heal his wounds, at most to elevate his desires from the sordidness they had fallen into. Anne couldn't help challenge her resignation to his demise with the thought that, on such a warm afternoon with the doors of the church and the parsonage's windows open, Branwell, buried in his room and decomposing in his bed, would hear the magnificent rumbles of redemption and resurrection.

Then, like the music that kept the packed congregation quiet and attentive longer than any sermon could, his life might move on from its intense and dramatic beginning to a more lyrical and contemplative second part.

Such optimism was short lived, as it should be. A few steps and hours away didn't make it possible to forget how Branwell continued, without remorse, to put his family under the command of the chaos that ruled him. Every day his depravity needed attention, not to be rehabilitated but indulged. If his siblings and father didn't spoil him further, and even when they did, he sought the misleading pity of drink and opium, digesting little else and otherwise lying unwashed and undressed in bed feeling sorry for himself. How many chances he'd had to do better, even since Thorpe Green, a year to pull himself together and find employment. As Charlotte rightly noted, to take it and by a fortnight's work be fit for it.

"Instead he does nothing but make us all miserable."

Before Mr. Robinson's death and Mrs. Robinson's dilemma, which Anne was certain was the designing woman's way of getting rid of an unsuitable lover once and for all, Branwell's behavior was almost tolerable. His mood swings and penchant for histrionics were nothing new, his deceit a little more practiced, as was his laziness.

Too much criticism or cold-shouldering could push him to the mercy of their father, who wanted to believe his only son's lies about a debt to pay or a journey to make for an interview and lend him the means to instead continue the abuse of himself and his family.

It happened anyway. Their father hoped for the best when Branwell was absent a few days, but couldn't be protected from his disruptive return. Branwell kicked at the dogs, poor Flossy yelping and running out the open front door, Keeper lunging at his attacker and tearing his coat sleeve until Emily intervened with kinder words and strokes for her dog than brother. Anne didn't know what to do except be silent when Branwell wondered if their father was home. Her brother laughed, then swore as Charlotte bodily barred his way. Unfortunately, their father was already emerging from the shelter of his study and faithfulness, and, realizing the extent of his blindness, found one of Charlotte's arms.

"Take me to him."

"No. He's in a shameful, stupid, aggressive state."

"Am I?" Branwell swayed and smiled, falling backwards onto the stairs.

"Stand up, Son. I'm no longer fooled by your deception."

Branwell tried to get up by himself, giving a pleading look to Emily and then Anne, the first not letting the other give in to it.

"I said stand up."

"My hearing is working, but my legs aren't."

"Where have you been for three days?"

"Where it pleased me, without any pleasure."

"It's obvious what you did with the money I gave you."

"Oh, sir. I suffer … such … wretchedness. I can't resist the temp…ta…tempta…tion to get out of myself."

"I can hardly resist the temptation to tell you to—"

"No, Father." Anne began trembling.

"Well, if you want me … to leave," Branwell stood and spoke with surprising sobriety, "I've made enquiries about situations abroad."

"You haven't any funds. And certainly not sense enough," Charlotte countered.

"You mean like you had in Brussels."

"I'm done with you." Charlotte didn't desert her father, who was leaning on her like a frail old man. She slowly turned him away from what he couldn't change. "Come on. I'll bring you some tea and we'll go through the newspaper together."

"You'd better find Flossy, Annie," Emily provided further distraction from Branwell's unpleasantness. "If he's in the churchyard digging, hopefully he'll not bring back any trophies."

Anne discovered her little dog cowering in a prickly dank corner of the front garden.

***

The voice of Mendelssohn's Christ in three-part chorus rose, not only creating a miraculous sound but haloed light.

Anne wanted to be in that moment. Such bountiful music, the church filled with contemplative commentary drawn from the Old and New Testaments, chorales in the manner of Bach, fanfares punctuating more tranquil instrumentals and vocals. It was quite a trick for the orchestra, even reduced as it was, to fit into the church, the violins arranged around the cellos and violas, the strings in front of the winds, and the brass elevated at the very back. The choir was in front of the instrumentalists, sopranos and tenors on the right, mezzo sopranos, altos, and basses on the left.

Anne glanced up again and again to her father, considering Ellen's opinion of him, for he really did appear extremely honorable with his white hair and his coat's starched collar. He often turned to his companions in the gallery to comment on the music or performers. Anne knew he wouldn't be discourteous by speaking of anything else during the performance. Despite the lack of expression in his afflicted eyes, the other men interacted with him as if forgetting anything about him was changed. He wouldn't want their pity or for them to treat him like an invalid. Even in darkness he saw the light of being a positive influence, as open-hearted and minded as ever, his physical activity curtailed because of his cataracts, but not his mental agility, spiritual journeying, or compassionate campaigning. Charlotte said their father should have been a soldier if circumstances hadn't made him a cleric. Ellen, prompted by her friend's opinion, thought the discipline and selflessness of a military career would have agreed with him.

Even in her twenties, Emily's imagination went wild with the what-ifs of her father inspiring an army rather than a congregation. Anne was glad any inclination he had to enlist only resulted in his commanding the best wooden soldiers to entertain his children.

How long ago that was, not as relieving a memory as it used to be without the brother who was the bright star in the sky of the future: clever, talented, and amusing, a promising painter and poet, with an aptitude for music and making others feel better about themselves. There had been something of the visionary about him, which excited his family and friends while excusing his eccentricities, even deficiencies, most notably naiveté, lethargy, and being too easily discouraged. It might have been better if his sisters hadn't made him the center of a make-believe universe, Aunt Elizabeth hadn't coddled him with rose-colored expectations, and his father hadn't pardoned his initial missteps as part of the maturing process.

Again exalted voices: "'*Sei getreu bis in den Tod, so will ich dir die Ktone des Lebens geben. Fürche dich nicht, ich bin bei dir.*'" Emily understood German better than Anne and didn't need to refer as often to the English translation of the libretto they shared.

Be faithful unto death, as I want to give you the crown of life. Fear not, I am with you.

What if William had still been there? Anne wondered for Branwell but inevitably also for herself. Would she care about poetry volumes and novels, too few reviews and sales, all the times manuscripts were returned, any endeavors that weren't in support of his, any purpose other than loving him? She constantly missed him, but dwelled less and less on what she had been denied and engaged more and more in what she might yet have to offer.

Why did loss destroy possibilities for some and create them for others?

"'*Sie weinten und sprachen. Schone doch deiner selbst. Das widerfahre dir nur nicht*'".

They wept and said. Save yourself. That shall not happen to you.

As the Oratorio's drama neared its end, Anne saw she wasn't the only one wiping away tears as well as sweat. "'*Er hat den Lauf vollendet, er hat Glauben gehalten.*'" *He has finished the course, he has kept the faith.* Emily sat transfixed, her hand grasping Anne's as the soloists, choir and orchestra crescendoed in a powerful double fugue that concluded in silence, a respectful pause requested before the audience gave its verdict. Anne, like her sisters, even Tabby on Martha's direction, and most of the audience, stood to join in the quickly spreading and enthusiastic applause. She was embarrassed by the whistling, shouting, and even stomping coming from the back pews and aisle.

"Forgive them, Anne," Charlotte said. "They live more for the moment than the hereafter."

"Yes. They're heathens like me, even in church." Emily greeted Thomas Parker, who had stepped down from his celebrity with an outstretched hand and observation. "I never expected anything so epic from Mendelssohn."

Except for graying at his temples and cragginess around his eyes, Mr. Parker had altered little since the portrait Branwell had done of him, a gently handsome fellow with a gallant nature and even nobler singing voice that belied his provincial pronunciation. "The word is the Birmingham Festival has commissioned another Oratorio from him. Isn't your brother here?"

"We seem to have lost him," Charlotte answered from behind Mr. Parker.

"He's not—"

"Oh, no." Anne wished Charlotte would control her impulsive wit.

"Ah." Mr. Parker expressed his relief and cleared his throat at the same time. "When he's in the area again, tell him to look me up. I'm at Lower Town, Oxenhope."

"Doesn't fame insist you live somewhere grander?" Emily challenged.

"I insist I not be so famous to need to."

Although he replied to Emily, he looked at Anne, making her feel ashamed because, as she convinced herself, he should have been asked to supper at the parsonage. Her father wasn't up to visitors and Charlotte and Emily were already bidding Mr. Parker good evening, agreeing with Tabby's complaints about the heat. Anne hadn't any choice but to let go of the hope of talking to the celebrated tenor regarding York Minster, where, she had read, he often performed, the first time at the age of thirteen. She dismissed herself from his attention to follow her sisters, instead hurrying past them out of the church that had emptied quicker than it had filled a few hours before.

***

Charlotte didn't hide her concern over her youngest sister dealing with their father single-handedly, even for a day and a half, Emily enlisted to accompany her to Manchester to talk to an Oculist about his worsening eye condition.

"His obstinacy is sure to frustrate your well-meaning. You must insist he doesn't go up or down the stairs on his own and he takes meals, although he'll say doing so little means he doesn't need to eat much and a cup of tea will suffice. He'll be critical if you don't read to him at the right pace: not too fast, not too slow. And he won't be fooled if you skip over articles in the newspaper. I think he can tell by hearing you flip a page too soon. He might want to dictate a letter to you and will not be happy if you make a mistake and waste paper copying it over. Just don't tell him if that's the case. He won't want you to hang around him otherwise. Well, I don't need to tell you how he values his privacy. Still you must hold vigil for him doing anything that puts him in danger. And, of course, keep Branny away from him."

With hours of traveling by foot, omnibus, and train ahead of them, her sisters set off very early, even before their father was awake. Within half an hour he had dressed and groped his way down to his study. Anne, remiss in one duty, fulfilled another in bringing him breakfast, Martha having darkly brewed his tea, boiled a rasher and an egg, and cut bread in strips for dipping. Flossy followed Anne into the room and, to her mistress' surprise, when the affectionate little dog jumped onto his lap her father actually patted his head before gently returning him to the floor.

At first it seemed caring for her father would be without more mishap than his navigating the stairs on his own and the newspaper getting a little wet when the postman rolled it around the mail. It was almost noon and Anne was glad the rain held off until her sisters were on the train from Leeds to Manchester. Her father wanted to know what was in the post for him, which allowed time for the paper to be separated over the back and seat of a chair in front of the kitchen range. Tabby's recollection of the news on fire—not because of what was written in it—prompted Anne to shut Keeper and Flossy in the back kitchen. She asked Martha to bring the paper to the study as soon as it was dry.

Opening letters and reading to her father was a simple, immediately rewarding task. If he gave her high marks, perhaps Charlotte would allow her to do it more often. Anne wished he would open a window, her chest tightening and causing her to choose between reading and breathing. She thought she was over the worst since her asthma had been aggravated by the concert and continuing high humidity. She coughed once, twice as sometimes worked to clear the congestion, but couldn't stop a full-blown attack.

"My dear, my dear. This is not right."

"I'm … sorry … Father," she managed to say.

"No, my dear, I am. Go to your bed."

"But … the post … paper …."

"I shall live in ignorance as well as blindness today."

"I'll be all right," she was able to get out in one breath, immediately suffering the consequences of doing so.

"Oh, Miss." Martha came in with the reassembled and stiffly wrinkled newspaper. "I tald ye t'change yer damp frock."

"You were out in the rain?" Reverend Brontë stood.

"No—"

"Sir. Hap'n at door when post cum." Martha crumpled the paper even more as she put her arms around Anne consumed by coughing to the point of doubling over.

"Doesn't sound good." Branwell appeared, his father spared the clear sight of him barefooted and looking like he had slept in his clothes from the night before, but not the smell of his sweat and cocaine and whiskey breath. "What do you need me to do, Father? Read you the paper? In a bit of a state, isn't it?"

That was the last thing Anne heard before being shut out of what went on between them, thinking she had failed Charlotte in the worse way, saying so to Martha.

"Oh, Miss Anne. Calm yersen. Soon as I git tha abed, I'll find cause t' lok 'n on em."

Once in her room, Anne resisted Martha's attempt to help her undress. "I'll just lie down for a little while, Martha. Don't close the window. It's stifling."

"I hear yer father tellin' me to."

Anne felt weakened not sleepy and was about to pull a book from under her pillows when Martha returned to assure her Branwell was "very nicely" discussing the news with her father.

"That's—" Anne started to identify a soft whining.

"Cum, lad," Martha's entreaty brought Flossy very obediently and slowly into the room.

Anne readied herself for the dog to jump onto the bed. He sat at Martha's feet.

"He also waited outside the door?"

"Aye."

"How did you get him to do so?"

Martha took something out of her apron pocket, Flossy's wiggling indicating his patience was about to give out.

"Bacon?"

"Rev'r'n Bronty dunna eat."

"I don't know, Martha," Anne tried to seem stern but couldn't help smiling. "How will I ever again persuade him to do anything without bait?"

Martha laughed softly, her face reddening, her openness always relieving. "Oh, Miss Anne. I knowd—he knowd—how tha lik t' spoil em."

Anne couldn't disagree, patting the bed, Flossy understanding the invitation with a bark, leap and scuttle up to lick her face.

"Nay, Flossy."

"It's all right, Martha. His warmth and loving can only help me feel better."

Once Martha left, Anne lifted the spaniel to the side and on top of the covers, a copy of *Poems by Currer, Ellis, and Acton Bell* replacing him on her chest. As she did almost daily, Anne examined and read through it and the decent, even encouraging reviews on slips of paper that marked her three favorite poems, one of Charlotte's, two of Emily's. She had copied them from now scrapbooked clippings taken out of *The Critic*, *The Athenaeum*, and *The Bradford Observer*. Between scratching Flossy's ears and reminding herself of the accomplishment of the poetry volume, she might, at least until Charlotte returned, ignore the parcel sitting on the dresser. It had been delivered that morning, more accurately returned yet again, its wrapping well-worn and address crossed out and replaced by another too many times to hide its history of rejection.

CHAPTER FIFTEEN

Haworth, one month later, September–October 1846

"'Early to mid-evening. Tuesday,'" Anne began reading the latest letter from 83 Mount Pleasant Street, Manchester, even before she closed the front door, "is … tomorrow."

Emily rushed out of the kitchen with her hands wet and red, probably from scrubbing something. "Tomorrow?"

"I thought it might be soon, once Charlotte dismissed the nurse."

"She never liked the woman."

Anne could tell by Emily's squint and lip biting she was considering what had to be done in the next twenty-four hours.

"The journey will exhaust him." Anne held her attention on what Charlotte had written. "Although they're hiring a Hansom from Leeds train station." She expected Emily, practical Emily, penny-pitching Emily, to disapprove.

"Good. Rather expense on our father's pocket than his health and comfort."

"Yes, of course." Anne was once again reminded not to second-guess Emily. "Father's eyesight is continuing to improve, but he must stay quiet and out of strong light." She read silently to the end of the letter. "She's anxious to work more constantly on her new manuscript."

"Should be a reason for her to stay away longer."

"She seems to think it will be better at home now the Robinson drama is no longer Branwell's business."

"Convince him it isn't. At least he's gone for a while. Forever, do you think?"

"I'm not sure we should hope so or not, Em."

It was good he was in Halifax. They didn't need him to notice their expectancy, disappointment, and frustration in reacting to the post delivering only silence and denial to their latest enterprise. Waiting for what never came nudged them back into their literary shells where ambition was unnecessary but inspiration might console them. For Emily there was the refuge of Gondal, always ripe in her imagination and eagerly consumed, never left to decay. For Anne, returning to writing shaped out of inexperience and fantasy offered a disguise her conscience continued to nag at her to remove.

For the time being, Anne kept up the charade. She had already written several more Gondal poems and knew Emily had, at least, finished one. On numerous evenings in the parlor the two of them worked on companion pieces, which excerpted read like a scripted dialogue between them.

Anne: "'A younger boy was with me there, his hand upon my shoulder leant; his heart, like mine, was free from care …'"

Emily: "'They had learnt from length of strife—of civil war and anarchy—to laugh at death and look on life with somewhat lighter sympathy.'"

Anne: "'We had wandered far that day o'er that forbidden ground away—ground, to our rebel feet how dear. Danger and freedom both were there—'"

Emily: "'It was the autumn of the year; the time to laboring peasants, dear: week after week, from noon to noon, September shone as bright as June.'"

Anne: "'He bade me pause and breathe a while, but spoke it with a happy smile. His lips were parted to inhale the breeze that swept the ferny dale, and chased the clouds across the sky ….'"

"I think the Bell brothers should give a recitation at the Mechanics Institute."

"You might get away with it, Em." Anne had seen her sister dress in their brother's clothes to walk the moors and even hunt with more virility than Branwell ever did.

"Good t'ear ye two laugh," Martha said when she brought in an unsolicited supper of cheese and toasted crumpets.

"Have some with us, Marty."

"Thank ye, Miss Emily, bot nay." Martha bowed out before any insistence embarrassed her further.

"I wasn't surprised by *Wuthering Heights*," Anne told Emily the last evening they had the house to themselves except for Martha and Tabby, who enjoyed their intimacy almost as much as they did and, therefore, supported it. They had put down their pens and their stocking feet up as was usual for each: Emily's on the sofa and Anne's on the hearth's fender that had cooled in the hour since they decided to let the fire go out.

"But you were astounded." Emily stretched out one of her legs to prod Anne's arm with her toes. "Weren't you?"

Anne tried to grab her sister's foot. Emily sat up before she could. "I soon realized it was like nothing else ever written. And not for the faint hearted."

"I would never write for the faint hearted. That's why I knew you would bravely read it. Charlotte thinks my little rascal Heathcliff is preventing any publishers taking on *The Professor* and *Agnes*."

"We both wish we could write like you, Em."

"You shouldn't wish to be anything like me." Emily scowled, sat up abruptly and bent over to look under the sofa. Even the sister who idolized her and understood her beyond comprehension was sometimes too much company. "Come on." Emily dropped the shoes she had seemed so desperate to find and pulled Anne out of the rocking chair.

"What?"

"It's time for Mendelsohn."

"On the piano? It's almost eleven."

"Who's to mind?"

Since Charlotte and their father had been away, Emily couldn't be stopped from opening the windows in almost every room and occupying herself on the cottage piano in the Reverend's study any time she pleased. Yet, Anne, who rarely went out of the house without Emily and then only into the front garden or the church to refresh the flowers by the pulpit, hadn't heard Emily playing, not even the music she had given her for her birthday.

"You've been practicing. But when?"

"In the wee hours, as lightly as I walk about."

"Oh. That explains—" Anne didn't reveal her entire thought, standing to the side and holding the flickering light that illuminated the sheets Emily hardly needed to look at. She wondered how in the dark of a new day, with a candle placed precariously on the corner of the piano's lid, Emily managed to follow the score well enough to commit it to memory as well as perfecting by heart how gracefully and unpretentiously it sang without words. Anne heard it then, as she had in her dreams, something of William in its wordlessness, something of herself in its longings, something almost tender about Emily, which, except in her constant forgiveness of Keeper, might otherwise never be admitted.

***

As they set out to meet the hired Hansom wherever along the way they happened to, Emily needed to do something with her nervous energy and Anne wanted to purchase paper from Greenwoods as a homecoming present for Charlotte.

"We might see something at Number Eighty-three for Father, too," Anne thought out loud.

Moving towards nightfall in late September, the steep, cobbled Main Street was almost deserted and had begun to slicken as the air mingled coal smoke with fog. They descended arm in arm, whispering their thoughts about the smell and how Haworth appeared more depressed than ever, agreeing another day soon they must be sidetracked from their comparative privilege down dirt paths to visit the poorest cottagers.

Haworth's narrow, dingy alleyways always made Anne uneasy and it didn't help when Emily described unearthly presences lurking in them. *I know that ghosts have wandered on earth. Be with me always — take any form — drive me mad!* Anne was reminded and once more uncomfortably comforted by a line from *Wuthering Heights*.

"Oh, Em. What makes you so wicked?"

"I suspect the same deity that makes you so good."

Most of the shops already had their window shades down and door signs turned or were in the process of closing, as John Greenwood was, although he waved them in.

"He's one of the few around here who pretends to welcome our peculiarities," Emily remarked before he could hear her.

There wasn't much customer space in the shop's front room. It was cluttered with fixtures for newspapers, periodicals, and pamphlets that included sermons, their father's often among them. There was also a mishmash of cabinets, some glass-topped for writing and drawing implements, two wide ones serving as props to a board that made a counter, others with their doors removed to provide shelving, the smaller ones for bottles of ink, the larger for reams of paper. What was new, at least to Anne's eyes, were framing and printing samples on the walls, similar to those in the front display window. Selling papers, as Mr. Greenwood called it, was just a sideline to wool combing, oil stains on his long canvas apron and rough hands, wisps of yellowish fiber floating around him like a slightly tarnished angelic aura.

"Paper fer Miss Charlotte?" Mr. Greenwood bent down behind the counter to come up with it, dusting it off. "Surprise t'see ye two in village this hour."

Anne explained as Emily ignored his question to look into one of the display cases. "Oh, I just thought. We might miss the Hansom while we're in here."

"Nay if'n door be open a bit."

Anne made sure it was. Mr. Greenwood wrapped the ream further in brown paper and bristly string. "Great news 'bout yer father."

"We want to purchase something for him, too."

"A journal? Ready fer when his eyes be. Just got sum nice uns." He reached to the end of the counter.

"Yes—"

"No," Emily grunted.

"Why not?" Anne hoped her benign tone apologized for her sister's brusque one.

"A new dip pen. That's what he needs. When I was dusting his desk, I saw the state of the one he has. The nib is split and handle splintered."

Not for the first time, Mr. Greenwood proved himself a conciliator.

"What 'bout journal an' pen?"

"Yes. We could—"

"No, Annie, we can't be so extravagant."

"Pen's on me."

"Oh, Mr. Greenwood," Anne wanted to gratefully accept his offer, but not to provoke Emily's disagreement again.

He moved from behind the counter towards the case Emily had been leaning over, her hands sliding off so he could open it.

"What about this 'un? Turn'd walnut, brass nib. Ah'll throw 'n couple of pencils fer Miss Charlotte. She seems t'use lots."

Emily didn't agree or disagree, her eyes lowered, her mouth terse as she stepped to Anne's side. She was intimidating until she relaxed and spoke as sweetly as she could, both her sister and Mr. Greenwood mesmerized by her unpredictability. *"Merci, monsieur."*

Anne didn't think Mr. Greenwood could look more delighted, but was immediately proven wrong.

"I'll be sending down some of the best buttermilk bread you've ever eaten."

The man didn't seem to realize he licked his lips or, like Keeper, Flossy, or Tiger, didn't care he did. "Yer bak'n has tha' reputation, Miss Emily." He began to hand them their purchases, but refused to take the money Emily offered. "I ken yer good fer it." Still he held onto the packages. "Ye lasses go meet yer father an' sister. I'll tak these up t'parsonage. Is som'un thar?"

"Martha and Tabby." Anne felt weepy. "How kind you are, Mr. Greenwood."

"Martha is the one with ears to hear you knock," Emily added. "The dogs won't let her ignore it."

"She wouldn't." Anne followed Emily out, wiping her eyes in the brief window of opportunity when neither her sister nor Mr. Greenwood would notice.

"Watch yer step, lasses," Mr. Greenwood called after them.

He was right to warn them, the air markedly colder and the cobblestones even greasier than little more than half an hour before. They worried the Hansom wouldn't be able to make it all the way to the parsonage, slipping backwards a real danger for horses and wheels. Their father might not have the strength to walk even halfway up that devil of a street. What was their option if he couldn't? Emily offered some ideas, Anne too breathless to do more than nod in response. He might wait in the Fleece Inn, off his legs and out of the cold while Emily went for John Brown, or they could enlist some strong if less than sober help from the public house. Either plan became redundant when their concern was substantiated and relieved by the sight of an unknown man, because of his uniform presumably the Hansom driver, and Mr. Nicholls, in his thick tweed costume, holding Reverend Brontë up. His arms were around their shoulders, his feet barely moving.

"Where's Charlotte?" Anne wondered.

The mist and street's sharp drop left their older sister out of view for a few more moments.

"She's coming. Like a little pack mule." Emily started to run with a sure-footedness Anne couldn't manage.

"I told them to leave the luggage on the Hansom. I could've gone back for it," Mr. Nicholls murmured, hardly lifting his heavily browed eyes as Emily flew past.

"Thank you, Mr. Nicholls." Anne didn't even try to keep up with her.

"What an ordeal." Charlotte dropped the bags she was carrying, except for the well-traveled writing box she kept under one arm. "And my toothache acting up again the whole trip."

"Mr. Nicholls must have been returning from his usual afternoon visits around the parish."

"No, Anne. He claims he came upon us deliberately 'because he had thought of such a problem arising.'" The second half of her answer mimicked the Curate emphasizing consonants to hide his Northern Irish accent.

Emily had picked up the baggage. "Does it matter? Ellen isn't here to make more of it than his interest in impressing his employer."

Charlotte grunted and, as Anne attempted to, took one of the cases from Emily.

Even without anything to physically carry, Anne trailed the others, acutely aware, as if in slow motion, of the climb she was making, the narrowness of the street and the nearness of neighbors she hardly knew, their lives closing into the dim lighting of cramped residences above and between Haworth's main businesses. A window here and there remained open and offered cooking smells and the drone of conversations, amiable and angry and indifferent, as families often were. Further up she passed the apothecary and, hearing raucous even threatening voices, half-expected Branwell to come stumbling out of the Black Bull.

He was currently a problem for Halifax's public houses, hopefully not the Ovenden Cross on the Keighley Road where he was lodging and, by his own report in the one letter he had sent home, turning the head of the proprietor's eldest daughter. Anne was of two minds about whether she wanted him to court any eligible young woman. It might signal he was moving beyond his obsession with Mrs. Robinson, but also that he was now set loose to ensnare and potentially damage an unprepared and, more critically, unsuspecting female. Anne hoped there was someone to advise Miss Walton to view a man's attentions dispassionately until she was sure of his sincerity and worth, knowing full well Branwell would soon enough prove himself insincere and unworthy.

First study; then approve; then love, Anne thought of something she must write down as soon as she could.

The trudge up the hill was less than half a mile. Anne felt as if she had traveled all day like her father and Charlotte and was upset the church bells were out of sync with the tower clock, chiming at least ten times when it couldn't be later than seven. Her pace quickened past the graveyard even without Emily to animate its shapes cast blue in the twilight or the wind rustling leaves yet to be cleaned up along the curb of the Sunday School where they often accumulated from nearby trees. As Anne turned into the side gate of the parsonage's front yard, everyone else must have already gone inside, Emily holding the door open for her and Mr. Nicholls as he emerged from the house.

"You won't stay for supper?" Anne also assumed no one had asked him.

"I mustn't impose. Your father is tired. I'll be back tomorrow to catch him up on parish business."

"Yes, yes," Emily didn't even try to sound civil, walking into the house and kicking the cases she had dropped to move them further inside.

Anne stepped up to the stoop her sister had vacated. "Thank you again, Arthur. What would we have done without you?" She dared to be so familiar because she felt sorry for him. She knew what it was like to be employed without consideration, needed yet resented, having to do one's best while always aware of being replaceable, involved—at least admittedly so—for no other reason than professional reputation and financial compensation. "Good night."

"Good night, Miss … Brontë."

She might have succeeded in buoying him a little. Charlotte and Emily would have claimed it was arrogance that set Mr. Nicholls' shoulders high as he walked away. He didn't have far to go, a minute to the door of the Sexton's house where William had also boarded. Mr. Nicholls was as excellent a curate and as honorable a man, as good looking as William, too, but in a darker fashion and without his cheerfulness and charisma. Mr. Nicholls pouted and pontificated too often, was easier to ignore than take notice of.

Anne had begun to consider the folly of women enticed by the least reliable of men because they were the most desirable. Besides the initial lure of handsomeness, if a fellow wasn't a flatterer or adept at light discourse, his good sense, respectability, sufficient income and even compatibility might not be enough to recommend him for study, let alone approval or love. When Anne thought about her own heart's longing, mostly untold and certainly unfinished, she considered herself fortunate not fooled. Then again, she would never know for sure.

CHAPTER SIXTEEN

Haworth, two months later, December 1846

Debts must be paid, *upon the wintry breezes borne*. The last clause of Anne's thought was borrowed from her own poem reflecting the comfort of Christmas music and now sadly suited to the choice her father faced between losing more money or honor. It must be done, he said over and over after the Sheriff's officer left, Branwell hanging his head and vowing he would be better before turning away with a fragile grin that confessed it was a promise he couldn't keep. That was how Charlotte described the scene to Anne still in bed because of a cold her sisters had gotten over quicker. As was expected, it had set off Anne's asthma and after over a week still interfered with her normal routine and progress on a second novel.

"Of course his debts must be paid." Charlotte sounded unconvinced, standing at the window, looking out.

The thought of what would happen if they weren't stoked Anne's fever and deepened her shivering. She pulled the covers higher.

Charlotte also shuddered. "Do we suddenly live in the Arctic?"

"I can't remember such a dreadful December." Anne's heart disagreed, her lungs expressing her distress.

"Oh, dear."

Anne wiped her mouth with a handkerchief embroidered with red chevrons that hid what was faintly mixed in the phlegm she had coughed up, probably due to the bloody nose she'd had earlier that day.

"Branwell has recovered enough, even from his lack of funds, to go out for the evening, so he doesn't need the excuse of a cold to sleep in until it's dark again."

"How's Father?"

"His cough is harsh and lingering like yours. He sits in his study for most of the day with a blanket over his shoulders because of the draughts, breathes in steam from the broth or tea Martha or Emily bring, and sips at it. Just when he was almost his old indomitable self, he hasn't the strength to chew."

"Bed would be a better place for him."

"He balks at the suggestion. 'Five weeks was enough of that.' At least he's recovering in more pleasant surroundings now."

"I thought your rooms were comfortable."

"They were in terms of furniture and carpets, the wallpaper once pretty. As were the draperies until they became a constant barrier to fresh air and natural light. We burned through a lot of candles, as substantial an expenditure as tea, bread and butter, and even the beef and mutton Father enjoyed as he began to feel better. I would have liked to explore Manchester a little. At least I got out to buy paper for my novel."

"It seems without distractions you made good progress."

"I guess it's true everything happens for a reason. I think even my wicked toothache helped during the day when the nurse took care of Father, dear Jane my only distraction from it." Charlotte walked over to her writing desk that had relegated a wooden hairbrush and a few jars to the back of the dressing table. She opened it, rubbed at the stains accumulated around the ink bottle from her pen dripping, blackening her fingertips as well.

Anne always kept a rag handy to immediately wipe up any spills; no wonder Emily teased her compulsion to put everything right so it was never wrong.

Charlotte spread a sheet of paper, as far as Anne knew the same one she had, for the last few days, been writing and scratching out on. She expected Charlotte to sit, take up a pencil, and add something to it. Instead she soon left the paper unattended and unfolded. "Yes, while in Manchester this story overtook me, pouring out of me for hours without hesitation. Now I struggle with each paragraph, slowed down almost to the point of stopping and even giving up."

"Your plain Jane would never forgive you."

Charlotte offered the smile her sister was looking for. "I need a smarter title. I'm not good at thinking of them." Charlotte was back to the window, her face pressed against it. "The sky looks like ice. Well, everything is frozen as if to never thaw. I can't get warm or remember I ever was."

"It will pass." Anne wondered if her exhaustion ever would.

"Are you too cold? Too warm?" Charlotte felt Anne's forehead and undid the top buttons on her sister's nightdress. "Is the plaster uncomfortable? Is it burning you? I told Tabby not to put in too much mustard seed, your Branwell skin so sensitive. She said that was why she used egg white instead of water. It's been almost half an hour. It should come off."

"Yes. Please."

"Of course. You must complain first. Really complain. But you won't. Even if I get on my knees and beg you to."

"We have to endure some things to enjoy the blessings of others."

"I admire you, but cannot imitate you. You're heroic."

"Only in childish stories and places that are made-up."

"Don't let Emily hear you say so. Gondal is the world to her."

124

"She knows it no longer is to me."

Downstairs the dogs were barking and Charlotte decided the postman was to blame. Removing Anne's plaster could wait. Just about the time Charlotte would have reached the front door, Emily began shouting a dire warning to Keeper. The great beast of a dog had probably attempted an escape for another unfettered romp through the town or even out on the moors. One destination would bring complaints, the other put him in worse danger on such a blustery, bone-chilling day, the snow deeper than the length of his legs and his nasal sense of direction could handle.

"Has our package been returned yet again?" Anne wondered as Charlotte walked into their room with a severe frown, before she saw there was only a letter in her hand. "Perhaps good news."

"Could a letter from anyone with the surname Robinson be so?"

"Oh, not for Branny?"

"No. You. Now, shall I remove that plaster?"

Anne thought Charlotte took much longer than was necessary, in slow motion pushing her nightdress sleeves down her arms and its bodice to her waist, unwrapping the towel from around her bosom and back. Charlotte insisted on applying a little of Rowland's Kalydor to blotchy patches on Anne's breasts, the bottle close at hand for Charlotte was always trying to improve her complexion. Anne was grateful, more so when Charlotte finally gave her the letter from the Misses Robinson, the first for over six months, and left her alone to read it.

Anne was conflicted in receiving it: happy to hear from Elizabeth and Mary and sad to find out they had left Thorpe Green for good, even though that was likely why they were allowed to write to her again. They professed to be afraid *their dear friend and confident Miss Brontë* would think they had *fallen off the face of the earth, which wasn't so far from the truth while they recovered from their papa's death.* They wrote mostly with affection for their mother, of her grief and worry that found little relief until *everything changed with an invitation to Great Barr Hall near Birmingham.* They didn't acknowledge any errors in their mother's behavior more grievous than *her eagerness to have them marry expediently and the sooner the better,* and seemed eager to relocate and live with *ailing cousin Catherine and her rich highborn husband* in the hope—as Anne read between the lines—expediency, youth, love and ever-after happiness would find them there and satisfy all concerned parties.

"Branny mustn't know they're writing to you again," Emily expressed what Anne already realized.

One letter could be hidden, even two or three, but there was another from Mary and Elizabeth nearly every day. Fortunately, Branwell no longer looked for the post to change his life, hangovers and the darkness of his mood and bedroom also keeping him out of the way of its delivery.

A few days before Christmas, the weather was stormy enough to delay the postman by hours. Branwell, finally coming downstairs, was the first to the door.

Anne, who had found the strength to dress and was combing Flossy in the back kitchen, heard Emily curse and the click of her heels. By the time she followed her sister into the front hall, Branwell was holding a battered package.

"No C. Bell Esq. here," Branwell told the postman, whose expression was as frozen as the rest of him.

"Thar's never been a question afore."

"Perhaps there should have been." Branwell took the parcel and closed the door.

At least no letters. Anne felt half-relieved.

Branwell wrapped his arms around the package as Emily approached him. "I think I know what you're all up to."

"Think what you like. And know it's none of your business." Emily waited for him to give it to her.

"Who is this C. Bell Esq.? A relation of Mr. Nicholls? Or a pseudonym for him? Are my sisters part of something he doesn't want our father to know about? Or John Brown, why he has it delivered here." Branwell bounced the package in his hands. "It's heavy, like a manuscript." He examined its addressing. "Looks like it's made the rounds of publishers. A poor curate's salary doesn't stretch to using new wrapping each time. Probably some over-blown thesis on ridding the world of Baptists. Or, at least, women who dry their laundry over gravestones."

"Don't be ridiculous." Emily tried to wrestle the parcel from him.

Charlotte came out of their father's study in a rush. "Give that to me."

Branwell did as he was told, looking as if he was about to cry.

***

The weather continued frigid and snowy after Christmas. Although Anne was feeling better, her sisters followed their father's orders confining her to the house, prohibiting her from housework, and insisting she take a long nap in the afternoon. Some days she was ready to do so, others she hoped having the bedroom to herself might enable her to write more than a few guarded responses to the Robinson sisters. Often she was frustrated, wondering if she had it in her to write another full-length fiction, dwelling on the disappointment of a mere two sales for the poetry book compounded by multiple rejections of her first novel. Writing a second was like struggling out of a chrysalis: instinctively responding to the need to be free from it, then deliberately pushing against its confines to stretch it into transparency and break it open. Still at the emergence stage, she wasn't wholly convinced she could survive outside of it, but maturity was pulsating within her, insisting on showing itself as no one expected.

Her new literary work had yet to unfold its wings and find its strength. Writing came in fits and starts, and when it wearied her in a way sleep couldn't remedy she began to reread Ann Radcliffe's *The Romance of the Forest*, moving through it slowly and without concentration, although she knew it merited more engagement. On New Year's Eve she put it aside when she noticed Flossy had moved from the bottom of the bed to the windowsill. He sat sideways to mournfully gaze on the world beyond that was also off-limits to him while the temperature stayed in the minuses and the snow piled in feet rather than inches and whipped around without mercy.

On the wall was a painting Emily had done of Flossy running on the moors, the lift of his wavy ears, tail, and legs implying he might fly like the merlin hawk up and out in front of him. On an evening in August, defined as such in Anne's memory by the ochre and blue of the sky and rolling purple hills, Emily had captured Flossy's impetuosity to set it free for all time. What a contrast to the last daylight hours of 1846, artist and subject cold and restricted to imagining liberation. Patience was required, first Flossy's as he struggled to please his mistress by keeping still, then Anne's as her pet's best intentions didn't conquer his restless nature.

No matter his fidgetiness, Anne experienced her usual pleasure in drawing because it calmed her and ordered her thoughts. She managed a decent depiction of Flossy before he left his window pose and the room. Setting her art box on the nightstand, she sat on the edge of the bed to use the sketching block on her lap, first draping the eiderdown over her legs and feet. Even fully dressed she was chilled to the bone. On the canvas Anne's imagination and brush redesigned the window, adding a curtain hooked high to one side and a warmer outlook. Eventually Flossy returned to the room. Anne observed him stalking and scratching at overwintering bugs, rolling on the braid rug between the bed and the dresser, and briefly posing at the window again.

She spent the next hour on the painting, coloring in his darker curls and smooth cavalier face and the shadowing of his white underbelly.

"You're right," Anne said once the light and her impulse to be other than convalescing started to fail and Flossy had long since curled up on the bottom of the bed. "It can be finished another day."

"And another year." Emily entered the room with something wrapped in a serviette, tapping Flossy's nose to let him know what she thought of his begging.

"It's warm and smells sweet and of currants." Anne accepted Emily's gift. "You've made bannocks."

"It's New Year's Eve, after all."

"I haven't even made an effort."

"It appears you have." Emily examined Anne's painting without touching it. "A bold likeness."

"Like trying to capture a fly." Anne leaned over to stroke Flossy, who glanced at Emily sideways, his jowls slavering and a paw reaching up.

"You don't fool me." Emily folded her arms. "You're more in love than frustrated with that little bugger of a mutt. Now, won't you try the bannock?"

Anne unwrapped it in her lap, admiring it: a golden-brown, crusty hillock made of pastry and dried fruit that crumbled compactly as, not long out of the oven, it should. Finally, she broke off a piece.

"If you don't smack your lips," Emily winked, "how will I know you're enjoying it?"

"Anne keeps us all wondering." Charlotte was in the doorway. "Is the party up here? And with the best society, our little society." She took a portion of what was left of the bannock. "The safest society."

"Has Mr. Nicholls come?"

"Yes, Em. He has." Charlotte sat at the dressing table, looked into its mirror, lifting her hand to a straying strand of hair, leaving it to hang disobediently after all. "To see Father." She stood up and moved around Emily and the bed to sit on the side she slept on. "There are many who wouldn't have minded if Mr. N. hadn't returned from visiting his family in Ireland. So Martha told me."

"It's a good thing he did come back, with Father ill again." Anne closed her paint box and laid her artwork on top of it.

"Why are we talking about him? Curates come and go." Charlotte couldn't hold back her compulsion for cynicism and ambition. "We're on the threshold of a new year and need a strategy to succeed as we didn't in the last one."

"No one wants our poems or stories," Emily raised her voice and Flossy jumped into Anne's arms. Anne buried her face in the embrace.

"You're still writing," Charlotte accused.

"If I am, as always, for my own satisfaction."

"Well, it doesn't have to be a living for you. And you don't need to see a way out of the mist."

"Maybe you should stop trying so hard to," Emily snapped.

"What choice have I got? What have I done these thirty years? Life is passing and I'm earning nothing, doing nothing."

Anne seized the opportunity to move past Charlotte's earlier insensitivity. "You've taken care of Father through his darkest days and operation, still read to him and help him write his sermons and articles.

We wouldn't have our poetry volume without you and might yet see our novels published because of your efforts. Ellen idolizes you. And your Jane Eyre is something."

"As is your Agnes." Charlotte picked up the portrait of Flossy.

"And your Helen." Emily sat on the bed next to her youngest sister, stroking Flossy still on Anne's lap and sleeping with one eye open.

"Ah, Helen." Charlotte put the painting back on the nightstand. "Poor Helen Burns. Short-lived but memorable."

"I meant Anne's brave new heroine."

"You've named her Helen, Anne? We're prisoners sharing a cell. How could I not know?"

"Aye, our Annie is cagey." Emily laid all the way back with her hands behind her head. "So I shame things out of her."

Charlotte laughed. "Like this?" And leaned towards Anne, stroking her hair. "If you care for me at all sweet baby sister, what's the title?"

"Not sure yet."

Charlotte kissed Anne's cheek. "Where does it take place?"

"Yorkshire."

Charlotte hooked Anne's arm, pretending to twist it. "Will it have a happy ending?"

"Will yours?"

"Perhaps. But not a conventional one."

"The Bells aren't conventional writers," Anne felt a little pride to say.

"Whether to oblige the public or yourself." Emily frowned and closed her eyes. "I know what I choose."

"Those who read *Wuthering Heights* will know."

"Doesn't look like anyone but my forgiving sisters will, Lotte."

"Jane will do more than endure, I think." Anne was feeling herself unfold, the blood rushing to the tips of her fingers, ideas testing their wings. "So will my Helen. Do you remember Mrs. Collins, the wife of a local curate who about six years ago came here to ask Father's advice? You were at home, I think. It was just before I started at Thorpe Green."

"Her husband was a bad egg, wasn't he?" Charlotte tentatively remembered.

"A drunkard like our Branny."

"Except, Em," Anne was saddened and inspired, "Mr. Collins wasn't only abusive to himself."

"Give our brother time."

"No, Charlotte. Branny doesn't mean to cause us pain."

"He does all the same. So what of Mrs. Collins?"

"Father told her to leave her husband. And she did, taking their two children."

"He told her to break the law," Emily added matter-of-factly.

"To save herself and her girls, body and soul." Anne knew she didn't have to justify, especially not to Emily. "Which she did, admirably."

Charlotte puffed in disbelief. "That's what your novel is about?"

"A basis for it. Many women, otherwise sensible women, act on what they want the truth to be when it comes to whom they marry. They are too often encouraged and agree to indiscriminately give themselves away rather than be unchosen. They are fooled into believing they can change men by wily or enticing or romantic love, or just shaming them with loyalty no matter what. How ridiculous, how ruinous is this notion that girls and women aren't supposed to think as much as feel, learn rather than be ignorant, speak as well as listen, lead rather than uncritically obey. What convenient fraudulence convinces them femininity is all they have, and their intelligence, sense, will, and talents must be nipped in the bud because such things are unattractive and, worse, unnecessary? Over-protected, under-educated, choices made for them by the highs or lows of their circumstances and prejudices of their guardians, many of our sex don't recognize danger, not even when they are thrown to it and are left defenseless against the consequences of their husbands' bad judgment, vanities, and vices. Even spinsters, especially as they waste so much of their youth hoping not to be, frequently fall under the dictates and failings of men. We've been lucky to have a father who has steered clear of folly and considered the edification of his daughters as important as that of his son, not seeing us as possessions to be bartered off but as vibrant persons to be as God intended rather than any mortal man desires. The only drawback to that, if thought as one, is that we have to take full responsibility for what we do and chose and cause. We are the navigators of our destinies, which requires us to be fully aware of what we're about."

"That's more words than I think I've heard you speak in the last year, Annie," Emily teased in all seriousness. "Maybe the last two."

Even Anne was surprised by having so much to say. Such a speech should have exhausted her. Instead, she was exhilarated, the struggle, the wait, the trying out her wings bolstering her, exciting her.

"But," Charlotte's eyes gleamed although she frowned, "what is the novel about?"

"Drunkenness, debauchery, infidelity, and absconding in defiance of the law," Em pronounced every word with a relish one of her little rascals might have. "From what she's told me."

"I hope you're joking." Charlotte also spoke as if Anne wasn't there. "Those are unsuitable subjects for our little sister, don't you think?"

"Not for Acton Bell," Emily reminded that, as they were and sought to be published, the Brontë sisters didn't exist, "as he has yet to reveal himself."

As was often the case, Anne was glad to be left out of her sisters' verbal jousting, although Emily was watching her and might even hope for a surprising challenge to Charlotte's opinion. Anne would have to disappoint her closest sister for the moment, not far enough into her new writing project to effectively declare, let alone defend, its content and intent. She had to explore it more herself to understand where it was coming from and why she was compelled to go on such a difficult journey through the depravity of human behavior in her writing as well as reality. She might be easier on herself and others by satisfying appetites with an entertainment easily digestible and offering a final course of happily-ever-after, as Charlotte thought more suitable. Except it wasn't what she wanted—was compelled—to do.

Anne looked at Emily, who was still lying back, her eyes closed again, and Charlotte meticulously and then redundantly cleaning her glasses with her skirt as though she was loath to look up. It was a scene to be grateful for, framed as it was by their physical togetherness, which Anne never took for granted. She only had to think of her mother stolen from even any recollection of her, and Elizabeth and Maria, Aunt Branwell, Godmother Firth, Martha Taylor, little Georgina Robinson, and, effected by the softness of Flossy stretched across her lap, many dearly departed animal companions. Of course, there was also William, whom Anne grieved for like she did her mother and long-lost sisters, without any or enough memories to fill the spaces death left. The difference was with the loss of her mother and sisters there were no feelings to hide. William had been a phantom in her affections even while he lived. Cholera stole away all wishing and her heartache settled in wondering, refusing to bury the anticipation of him walking through the door, glancing her way, approaching her disbelief to speak so only she could hear.

"At last. I think he's going," Charlotte said and stood in reaction to the men's voices downstairs.

Emily sat up with more weariness than she had shown prostrate on the bed. "Poor Mr. Nicholls."

"Doesn't he have more sense than to let our father stand in the cold?" Charlotte was already in the hall, clapping her hands when the Reverend Brontë could be heard bidding his curate goodbye and shutting him out.

Flossy followed Charlotte and Emily downstairs. Anne felt abandoned, not so much by them but the promise of her youth. The painting she had begun of the spaniel didn't satisfy her and she put it away. She didn't know when or if she would finish it, not with another novel to write, as long as she felt clear-headed and strong enough to pursue its truth and convey its moral, every moment dedicated to it. *Agnes Grey* had found its way in moments and corners, through interruptions, irritations, and anticipation, a little too timid in its expression, brief in its storytelling, and uncertain of its objective. This new work was something else entirely.

PART FOUR

"Adieu! but let me cherish, still, The hope with which I cannot part."

~ Anne Brontë, *The Tenant of Wildfell Hall*

CHAPTER SEVENTEEN

Haworth, ten months later, October–November 1847

Anne and Emily agreed they would not bring Charlotte down from her good news because their first novels weren't yet published.

The best scenario would have been the acceptance of all their submissions by the same firm at the same time to be released conjointly. The beginning of summer ended the pursuit of a publisher for *Wuthering Heights* and *Agnes Grey*, if less than satisfactorily with Thomas Cautley Newby's request for fifty pounds to produce them. Once more *The Professor* left Charlotte rejected.

After sulking for a few days, Charlotte became available to Emily and Anne as they struggled with Newby's proposal. As Anne expected, Charlotte wasn't about to refuse a little ego boost from her sisters' doubts they could deal with such things without her.

"We resolved not to pay to see our novels in print. And here we are about to do so."

"Sometimes resolve must be adjusted, Anne."

Four months later Charlotte was caught up in her own achievement, a time frame of little more than eight weeks in which *Jane Eyre* was finished, submitted, accepted, proofed, and gone to print. Not a farthing was sent to her saviors Smith, Elder and Co., and they paid her an initial sum of one hundred pounds with an option on two more novels.

"Small compared to what others are receiving, so I made my weak complaint. In the published fiction world, I'm a first-timer. However, I stood my ground on doing a third revision."

The unveiling was saved for their parlor hours. They sat around the table while Charlotte unwrapped six boxed sets of the triple-decker first edition of *Jane Eyre*, requesting her sisters help inspect all eighteen books.

"Rather drab." Emily said what Anne was thinking. Still Anne protested by causing a gentle collision of their feet.

Charlotte visibly and audibly scowled. "The publishers are anticipating a high demand, especially if it isn't overpriced."

"A book may be richly bound but poorly filled. At this point, Anne and I would be glad to see our novels presented in any way at all."

"It's something you admit to wanting to be published," Charlotte was quick to reply.

Emily left the table and plopped herself on the sofa where Tiger waited to be acknowledged with a push or a pat. When the latter occurred, the cat put its head down, curled even tighter, and purred loudly.

Anne held one of the volumes of *Jane Eyre* in front of her and carefully bent back its cover. "Like drawing open plain brown curtains to discover a vibrantly colored day with such an engaging outlook there's no doubt it will continue so."

How could Anne not think of her first "girl" and wonder whether she would be clothed more elegantly than Jane or as plain in cloth-backed gray-boards with little trim. As the months since proofing dragged on without a sign from Newby other than him giving his word to break it, would *Agnes* make a public appearance at all?

Anne continued to have faith, although she was more prepared for betrayal than before she knew its look, how it spoke and maneuvered. She had written *Agnes Grey* as a reaction to her inaugural governess experience with the Inghams, but, also, as an instructional reflection. She had meant to bring less naiveté to Thorpe Green and the writing she did in the limited free time allowed her there. She had soon discovered — or rediscovered — it was easier to live with wit and wisdom, to maintain a pensive cheerfulness or, at least, a philosophical viewpoint, through imaginary encounters rather than actual ones.

The passages of Agnes had brought Anne through insecurity, loneliness, worry, wavering, weariness, and grief. Agnes' story had helped Anne navigate a life that wasn't hers but needed to be traveled with enough involvement for learning and growing towards the best purpose of the one that was. The challenge was not to lose sight of the destination she hoped was ahead of her: to do the most good she could in the world before she left it.

The journey of someone who never existed was at times more real than Anne's own, its importance to her not diminished by how few knew of it. Even if the book never made it to the presses and fifty pounds was lost or required legal action to retrieve, nothing would change Anne having conceived it and carried it full term. No matter if Agnes was stillborn, lived for a few years or many, she was the offspring of Anne's desire to write with more purpose than being clever with words and entertaining. Instead, to produce a calm, undistracted, useful, and benevolent child who, if anyone did encounter her, would whisper a few wholesome truths to make them wiser and kinder, and open their minds and hearts.

***

An afternoon trudge into the sooty, stagnant air of Haworth was the result of Charlotte suggesting Anne take a break from stooping over her desk.

"You lead too sedentary a life, little one."

Anne straightened and rubbed her eyes, wishing she could feel less guilty about doing anything but writing in Helen's diary. Even a few hours away felt like she might never return to it.

"Time to rest your mind and exercise your limbs. Perhaps you'll converse as well as walk with us."

"Good idea, Lotte."

"I'm shocked you think I finally had one, Ellis."

"Keeper and Flossy need a good run."

"No. Don't excite them. They can't come," Anne commanded as she stood. "I only agree to going out for better work than I'm doing here."

She assumed her disgruntled sisters knew what she meant. They could have no doubt when she pulled them into the kitchen to each fill a basket with whatever food—bread, cheese, flour—could be spared and some—tea, butter, eggs—that couldn't. There wasn't any argument left in Charlotte once she was following Anne out the front door.

Emily, on the other hand, lagged behind. Standing on the front stoop, she made one last protest a proclamation, "The moors are in an ideal state for November: crusty but snowless, blustery but bright."

Anne agreed but not to change her mind over sacrificing a little of what made them more fortunate than many of their neighbors, in particular those mill-hands and wool combers who were accomplices and victims of a three-month-old strike. It had threatened a long while before August because of a depression in trade and the inflation of food staples, the masters refusing to pay higher wages to those laboring in the mills or a better price for what was produced at home. Their father supported the stoppage. He had little patience with those who could afford to relieve hardship not recognizing their duty to do so. Anne felt a strong affinity with his benevolent beliefs and actions, enough to dismiss the danger to her health. It was, after all, minimal compared to those who lived and worked in cramped quarters with poor ventilation, the business of oiling and jigging, drawing and roping producing good strong yarn but also intolerable heat and noxious fumes.

During the strike, Anne and her sisters were spared the hell-like conditions essential to the daily combing of around thirty pounds of wool that barely kept these Haworthians fed. With caldrons and broitches idle, the small dingy dwellings were frigid. Without the wool to justify its use, what coal there was in store wasn't for heating except to boil water and cook.

For the most part, the welcomes the sisters received were also chilly. Emily mumbled it was because they hardly knew what to make of Reverend Brontë's plainly odd daughters. Charlotte blamed Branwell's behavior, which, no doubt, was the talk of the parish. Anne preferred to think it was because the wool workers and their families hadn't much choice but to accept whatever assistance was offered.

She was pleased both her sisters took her lead and tactfully left some provisions, sitting down in the kitchen when they were invited to and knowing not to linger when they weren't. There was little to talk about, which pleased Emily who was only socially available to any animals she encountered: in one instance a scroungy couple of chickens, in another an emaciated caged rabbit, otherwise as half-starved cats and dogs. Charlotte tried too hard to initiate conversation, her intellect overshadowing her compassion. Anne was most comfortable with the elderly who seemed to appreciate her leaning over to quietly greet them and touch their cold veined hands. She was nearly as easy with the younger children who responded with large eyes and shy voices to her squatting down to ask their names and ages. Older siblings stood stiffly and looked on; their despondency broke her heart. More than one sick baby did, too.

Before they had achieved Anne's goal of visiting every strike affected family, the emptiness of their baskets overruled her thinking it was still early enough to call on a few more.

"Our well-meaning words alone won't help them."

Charlotte couldn't be faulted for putting the practical aspect of charity over indulging the conscience of the charitable. Emily walked faster than Charlotte was able or Anne wished to. They caught up to her in the cobbled square at the top of Main Street that, depending on which way one turned, peddled drugs or drink or salvation.

Emily was standing next to Branwell, aggressively holding onto his arm.

"Tell your crazy sister to let me go," Branwell begged, specifically of Anne.

"Go on home, Annie. As you can't help seeming sympathetic."

"None of us should bother with him, Em," Charlotte concluded, putting her arm around Anne's waist to prompt her to resume walking.

Branwell tried unsuccessfully to keep Emily's hand out of his coat pocket, coins spilling onto the pavement.

"Where do you get them? Not from Father. Not anymore. You haven't done a day's work in a year and a half and before that it doesn't bear thinking what you were up to." Emily caught her brother by surprise as he straightened after picking up the money and, unchallenged, except for him stamping his foot, pulled something out of his other pocket, this time not about to let him own it again. "I'm sure the apothecary won't give you more credit."

"A doctor prescribed it for my tremors."

"He didn't lend you money for it." Charlotte took the bottle from Emily, uncorked it and sniffed its contents. "Your Dr. Crosby is a mere contrivance for you to get it from the old quarter."

"Oh, Branny," Anne finally spoke up, "if I had any hope left for you, it was that you were done with her."

Branwell looked from one sister to the other and then bowed his head before turning away for the unforgiving familiarity of "his corner chair by a blazing hearth" just steps away in the Black Bull.

"Why would she still be sending him money?" Charlotte asked as they continued home. "For amusement or intent?"

"Both," Anne didn't hesitate to reply. "Mostly to silence him."

"She doesn't know our brother well then. He's too weak to be vengeful."

"He has a heart that welcomes pain." Anne was more emotional than she wanted to be. "He walks into temptation like a storm he hopes will blow him away."

There was a quiver in Charlotte's voice, too. "He's useless against deviousness. If he's flattered, he's defenseless against the motives of the flatterer. He's been too much petted. He admits it. If that's made him vulnerable, then we're all instruments of his downfall."

"Not me." Emily didn't look back at her sisters.

"You can't get out of it that easily," Charlotte tried to joke.

"Watch me." Emily walked even faster into the thickening fog.

Charlotte hooked her arm through Anne's, possibly sensing she was about to go after Emily. "She's running from her own hope of saving him. Let her make peace with the impossibility of doing so, as I think we both have."

Anne didn't contradict Charlotte. She wanted the discussion of Branwell to end, at least for that evening. When they returned to the parsonage, Emily was already in the kitchen, cloak and gloves off and apron on. She ignored her sisters as she stirred the mutton stew bubbling on the range, scolding Martha for not doing so and letting it scald on the pot's bottom.

Charlotte covered her mouth and nose, unable to hide her revulsion to burnt food. She turned to leave the kitchen and almost ran into their father.

"Charlotte, do they know you've written a book?"

Her nausea seemed forgotten. "Of course they do, Father."

Emily nudged Anne. "She told him. Damn her."

"I heard that, Emily."

"Sorry. But—"

"So you know *Jane Eyre* is quite good. And accomplished at a profit, not expense."

Charlotte was beaming. "Oh, you like it."

"Yes, I do. I'll read more tomorrow in natural light."

Charlotte took his arm, even stroked it. "My sisters aren't far behind me."

"Writing novels? Should I pretend to be surprised?" Reverend Brontë playfully scratched his head. "Also to be published?"

Emily leaned over Anne's shoulder, "You knew she was going to tell him," before sinking into one of the kitchen's chairs.

Anne didn't acknowledge Emily's accusation. "Yes, Father, soon. In joint volumes. As Ellis and Acton Bell. By a different publisher."

"I hope yours does as well by you and Emily as—"

"Smith, Elder and Company," Charlotte sounded as if she was speaking of a lover.

"Does Branwell know?"

"Not that we are or will be published."

"He mustn't find out, Charlotte. It's good you haven't used your real names."

Anne and Charlotte followed their father into the hallway, both finally removing their cloaks.

"Where have you been, my dears?" he wondered as he walked towards his study. "I hope you bundled up better than it appears and were wearing your pattens."

"Obeying Anne's need to feel useful," Charlotte quipped.

"Oh?"

Anne wanted to explain without seeming self-satisfied. "I felt we … I … had been neglecting our out-of-work neighbors."

"Ah. You took them food?"

"We did. Hardly enough."

"Enough for Tabby to complain."

"I'm sure we could spare it, Charlotte," Reverend Brontë put his hand on the doorframe of his study, "and Tabitha didn't mean to sound uncharitable."

Charlotte's face reddened as she crossed her arms behind her back.

"Nor did you, my dear."

"Of course not, Father."

"But what can we do for their ailing?" Anne felt so inadequate. "They haven't money for the doctor."

"We'll do what we can and more. The five books of Moses tell us 'the poor shall never cease from the land', so we're called on to 'open our hands wide to relieve them.' My girls have done so today and many other times. And I'm proud of them for that … but not just that. In many ways they lighten my burden of paternal failure."

He may have sensed Anne's desire to throw her arms around him, a poignant pause turning into urgency for him to shut himself in his study.

CHAPTER EIGHTEEN

Haworth, five months later, April 1848

"I have to tell you," Charlotte interrupted her reading and Anne's. "I don't like this one as much as *Agnes Grey*."

Anne waited for Emily to differ, but her sister didn't react as she squatted in front of the hearth to poke at its failing fire.

"Not only has it been such trouble for you to write, when published it will bring you more. It will lay you bare."

"Then what difference could Smith and Elder make to it?"

"They might—I know you don't want to hear it—suggest how to smooth it over ... tone it down ... make it more palatable ... more—"

"Entertaining?" Anne wasn't asking for a reply.

"At least recognize Newby is a shuffling scamp."

"She does," Emily admitted listening, "but not without giving him a chance of redemption."

After months of being upset by Newby's negligence, Anne could finally smile a little at all the red marks in her personal copy of *Agnes Grey*. She told herself the best remedy was to move on with a polite yet unyielding expectation of a better result next time. Charlotte continued to argue that Newby had proved himself unreliable and without conscience, and since the success of *Jane Eyre* had stimulated Smith and Elder's interest in future writings of its author's "brothers", the choice Anne should make was obvious.

Why didn't Anne agree? The long delay in the release of her and Emily's novels had been exasperating. Then Newby rushed them into print and, although Anne carefully labored over final corrections, overdue Agnes was born with defects that couldn't be hidden. The results of Emily's expectancy weren't much better. Messrs. Smith and Elder had managed *Jane Eyre's* entrance into the world as promised, with little inconvenience to Charlotte, no noticeable pain, and as near-perfect an offspring of her literary efforts as could be expected.

The case for Smith and Elder was persuasively made. Yet Anne knew all along she would persist with Newby to obviously resist Charlotte's influence. She anticipated her oldest sister harassing her up to and beyond the day she sent *The Tenant of Wildfell Hall* off to 72 Mortimer Street, London.

"I worry about both of you. Em, you haven't said a word about the response to *Wuthering Heights* and hardly more about your next one, which doesn't seem to be progressing at all."

"I never wanted to publish and will not again."

"You knew *Wuthering* was a strange book, but 'not without evidence of considerable power,' as one reviewer put it. And another," Charlotte continued from memory, "'Impossible to begin and not finish; quite impossible to lay aside afterwards and say nothing about it.'"

"Unlike *Agnes Grey*."

"So, Anne, is the coarseness of *Tenant* your response to the lack of attention gentle Agnes received?"

"It was conceived before I knew Agnes would be received or how."

"I don't criticize your effort. But your subject choice is a mistake. You're too driven by this need to torture yourself, like some kind of penance."

"I've witnessed the degradation human behavior can fall to."

"Oh, Annie." Emily was barely audible. "If only you had stayed safely here."

Anne didn't need Emily's prompting to wonder. What if she hadn't lost her innocence to the torments of Blake Hall and deceptions of Thorpe Green? What if Gondal fantasies and a little of her girlhood at school were the extent of her worldly adventures? What if her conscience had confined itself to home and church responsibilities, visits to the poor and sick with practical and prayerful offerings the extent of her reaching out beyond the protection of family? Why would she write novels if only age, love, and death changed her? Poetry would be enough, a more natural and satisfying means of expression. It suited her pensiveness and piety, could be composed in isolated moments, and reflect without analyzing. Poetry was a solitary art; even when read by others, its author could go unnoticed. It was perfect for disappearing into.

Novels wouldn't leave their authors alone. They needed much attention and were complicated things, requiring names and places, themes and tensions, plotting and resolving, and so much in between it was difficult to keep track of where they were going. They were crowded with words and at the mercy of grammar, hard to give up on when months, even years, had been lost to them. Long works of fiction were hard to persevere with, no guarantee anyone would ever read them, or, if they did, with interest and forgiveness.

However, Anne had found a stronger part of herself through their invention. If nothing else, she had achieved independence—cautiously in the first, and, according to Charlotte, irresponsibly in the second—from the Anne Brontë created by circumstance, inhibition, and expectation.

Emily claimed being published was the end to her writing at will. Anne was just beginning to do so.

"But you hardly appear to be enjoying the process, Anne. You might be happier otherwise employed."

"I've tried that and—"

"No, not as a governess again. But, considering your violet eyes, soft hair and complexion, neat figure, and giving nature, you might yet marry.

"You'd flare at anyone telling you that."

"They won't. I'm squat and plain and selfish. If you didn't hide away brooding over your writing, you might have Mr. Nicholls' attention. I recall once you knew how to make yourself obvious."

Anne sensed Charlotte was trying to goad her into a confession.

"Although I don't think he's good enough for you. For any of us."

Anne was tempted to quote a declaration Helen made early in *Tenant*: that there were very few men she would consider marrying and of those few it was likely she would never meet them or they wouldn't be single or, if they were, none would be willing to marry her.

Or, as in Anne's story, something sudden and merciless would make all the above seem frivolous.

As different as they were, her novels were both confessions and platforms, heart to hearts and a way for her to be a philosopher, hopefully, without too much preaching or lack of good storytelling. In the little mention *Agnes Grey* had received, Anne had already been accused of over-coloring. If that moderate volume was seen as an exaggeration of characters and events she knew were possible, then Charlotte was right. *The Tenant of Wildfell Hall* would receive a harsher reception. Yet Anne thought about its publication with less anxiety than she had *Agnes Grey*'s. She would rather expect its instructive intent could be understood, the honesty with which that instruction was conveyed accepted as necessary and, therefore, applauded.

Criticism was expected, but Anne couldn't recall any as damning as Charlotte's. If only Emily would come to the book's defense as she had with *Wuthering Heights*. The only reason Anne could ever wish she hadn't written *Tenant* would be the irreversible loss of her sisters' support. Writing was as much of a bond between them as blood. It might be as different as they were, often done when they were physically separated; all of them at times, Emily like a lion with her cubs, guarding its privacy. Yet there was no mistaking the kinship in its strengths and weaknesses, oddities and independence, partiality to escapes, wild winds, and open views. Writing and talking about their writing inspired them, and defined them, at least to each other.

"I fear you'll never recover your optimism."

The problem was Anne couldn't allay Charlotte's concern. The completion of the novel had left her exhausted and distrustful. There were scenes in it that had been more difficult to write than she thought she had a steady enough voice for. Why was she so driven to relate the worst ways men and women were attracted to each other? Why hadn't she stayed within the influence of William, a good man with a sunny mind and warm heart, a bit of a tease and something of a riddle, but with an abiding sobriety and conviction, and a brightness of spirit like a candle that never burns down? Anne had reflected her feelings for him in Agnes' for Mr. Weston. Only a few years later she refused Helen any real sweetness in love, even in its freshness and first tastes. Was that because Anne could never know for sure whether cholera had deprived her of matrimonial bliss or Heaven had saved her from its impossible promises?

Just considering such a query, like a mirror held so near a face defects were more evident than agreeable features, tempted her to put *Tenant* aside.

She continued with it, acknowledging those blemishes she had witnessed, letting them blister before they healed. If ever they could. The errors and abuses that marred the best expression of human nature—love—were too close to her, her own brother wasted by them. It was hard not to take a jaded view with such a tragedy in sight.

She had her doubts within the unwavering of her faith. She believed providence had designated her an observer and given her a quiet skill to extract lessons from what she saw. There was truth to be told, warnings to be issued, patience and prudence to instill in young women like Mary and Elizabeth Robinson, their constant letters about suitors, engagements, breaking off engagements, and longing for happily-ever-after pushing Anne on page after page, holding her pen to its purpose. She subscribed to the idea that it was better to expose the rough roads certain choices led to, rather than, for the sake of being agreeable, cover their pitfalls with flowers.

Anne was ready to let *Tenant* go to Newby's, the critics' and public's chancy treatment of it. She was weary, but with an unfamiliar sense of accomplishment in her growth as a writer and a woman who had moved beyond naïve notions of adventure and romance. She had written her future into another objective. What Charlotte called brooding over her work was her determination to convey hard truth rather than soft nonsense. Anne was compelled to show corruption and bad character as it really was rather than disguise it as amusement and imply recklessness ever offered real rewards, pleasure was a substitute for good judgment, and Godlessness a way to avoid consequence.

"You'll do what you will." Charlotte patted the manuscript, pushing it towards Anne. "I guess I don't want to admit your stubbornness."

"It's not stubbornness."

"Oh, some higher purpose, I suppose."

"There isn't any higher purpose." Emily, lying on the sofa, turned her back to them.

Anne didn't want to admit being rankled by either of her sisters. She still loved them devotedly and wouldn't go so far her own way she couldn't return to stand with them. She had awakened to the idea of not indulging their moods by compromising her vision and truth, a rebellion begun before *Tenant*, at first measured, since unstoppable. It hadn't done her harm as Charlotte declared, hadn't sunk her into sensitivity as if it was quicksand, but pulled her out of uncertainty, setting her on solid ground, strengthening her steps up the steep way ahead of writing and living with unwavering conviction in her own perceptions and objectives.

Charlotte stood up, "I won't say I told you so," and went to look out the window, although it was almost dark.

"Of course you will," Emily spoke again to the sofa's upholstery.

Anne wanted to believe they were on edge with each other due to the fatigue of writing, being published, and realizing there was nothing they could do to turn Branwell from disaster. Also, they had been cooped up too long, having been nowhere and seen no one who might amuse them, surviving another winter and early spring of sharing colds, influenza, and contention. The spring had begun wet and chilly with the usual thick mist and low clouds. Views from the parsonage were often resigned to remembering and imagining. Increasingly, there were days offering a vague sense of the front garden, Sunday school row, graveyard and church tower, and, at the back of the house, a still-wintry tree marking the threshold to a wider, wilder world. When the sun did break through, usually early morning or late afternoon, there was a burst of warmth and clarity, the grass glistening and the outlook assuming nothing ever changed but the seasons.

"I think what we all need is a long aimless walk," Anne tried to sound more convincing than she felt, "and be as we once were."

"Can we?"

"Perhaps, Charlotte. If we clear out our heads and simply enjoy ourselves."

Emily finally sat up as if with something to say, but remained silent.

Charlotte came back to the table and sat down. "Only if it's warm enough. Your chest is still very weak."

"It seems it always is."

***

The next day they waited until late morning to set out, once Charlotte decided the rest of the day would be fine. Starting on the path between the chapel and the cemetery, daffodils flowered in bunches around some gravestones except for single droopy ones here and there, violets less obvious but noticed when they were looked for. Noisy starlings mobbed the sky over them, yet it was possible to hear doves cooing. Keeper and Flossy ran on ahead, Emily surprisingly acceptant of her dog's disobedience when she ineffectively whistled him back. Anne let Flossy go without any command, ready to indulge her precious pet who was fatter than ever but no less mentally active. Charlotte, Emily, and Anne were also less agile up the steep hill that took them to the edge of their civilized world. Even Emily, who had always been athletic, struggled with the incline and against strong gusts, winter lingering in the wind's might but not its touch that was warmer than expected. The previous autumn was also still evident, its browns mingling with the effect of weighty snow and ice and the emergence of spring, last year's flattened countryside resurging in fresh tuffs of grass and mounds of heather. It was a familiar rising and falling journey with gates to go through, broken walls and stiles to step over, and bridges to cross.

Around and far beyond them, millstone grit created beautifully bleak views. Sunlight and shadows, like caressing hands, slid over the land and the full coats of sheep Flossy was already too tired to chase.

"Come here," Emily finally commanded Keeper to her side for that reason or another.

Anne carried her squirming little dog a little way before announcing she couldn't do so for long. "You both go on. Flossy and I will rest a while at the waterfall and then make our way home."

"Let's all go down there."

"All right." Emily's compliancy was more surprising than Charlotte's.

For a few moments a full reconciliation between them seemed viable. They stood arm in arm looking into the shrubby, mossy gully washed by winter's thaw and spring rain streaming off the moors, blue light casting it as fantastical as their imaginations had once been. If they were to continue on, there wasn't any choice but to follow each other precariously down an uneven and slippery path, water rushing, splashing, and, eventually, falling steeply and musically towards the beck it was destined to join, song birds adding their voices and the rhythm of their wings.

There wasn't anywhere to dryly sit, early spring the only time of year when the waterfall moved more noticeably and louder than the wind. They decided not to linger, the sky darkening with clouds they hadn't counted on but, as any living thing that knew the moor was wary of its kinder moments, they understood were always about to blow in.

"Pull up your hoods. Wrap your chest and neck, Anne. We're about to get very wet," Charlotte directed and admitted the folly of her earlier prediction.

"Often rebuked yet always returning," Emily said in a language all her own. Anne knew what she meant.

CHAPTER NINETEEN

London, three months later, July 1848

Anne reached the last step up, turned and looked at how far she had come. She hadn't made a grand entrance, although the staircase was one: three-to-four-people-wide with crimson carpeting, bordered by smooth porphyry columns, and glowingly lit by suspended Grecian lamps.

Her expectations for the evening had been to simply enjoy the relief of a crisis averted and, by no later than nine, try to settle in a strange bed after going almost two days without real sleep. There was the possibility of visitors to be entertained in a remote corner of the Chapter Coffee House lobby. She and Charlotte made themselves ready just in case. Charlotte resorted to a dose of sal volatile for her headache before they fixed each other's hair and changed to appear less limp and crumpled if still provincial in high-necked, dreary dresses.

They had nothing better to wear, not in their luggage or the world. When had it ever been necessary for them to have large-skirted, off-the-shoulder gowns, gloves more than half the length of their arms, and jewelry other than a small cameo pin or locket necklace? At least, as they ever admitted to each other.

Their evening was redesigned by Mr. Smith and his sisters' insistence the Misses Brontë attend The Royal Italian Opera in Covent Garden with them. Charlotte decided to dismiss her headache and accept.

The stylishly outfitted and graciously mannered Smiths never made Charlotte or Anne feel unequal to their company or the excursion, and continued generous and amiable in their carriage where Mr. Smith Williams had been waiting. Even disembarking off of Bow Street in full view of London society promenading across the theater's main plaza and through its front portico didn't alter the kind demeanor of the Smiths and Mr. Smith Williams. They did their best to shield their guests from scrutiny and, especially, unfavorable opinion. No matter, Anne couldn't help feeling travel-worn, awkward, and poor. It was difficult to read Charlotte's reaction. She was probably reminded of Brussels and uppity girls who thought, because their clothes and lineage and prospects were finer, they were superior to her, and how in intellect, resourcefulness and resilience she had proven they were not.

When it came to society's segregation according to birth and wealth, Anne, as in many other issues, erred on the side of humility and restraint. Charlotte, like Emily, tended to jump to indignation without considering where she might land. Even badly bruised, it was unusual for her to wish she hadn't. These days Anne didn't always regret her oldest sister's compulsions. After all, they wouldn't be about to step into a box of a grand opera house if Charlotte's rage at Newby's lying and manipulations hadn't sent them off to London on the spur of the moment.

What a journey they had undertaken with only a few hours preparation and no time for planning around wet weather, if such a thing was possible in the West Yorkshire climate. John Brown was able to find a lad with a cart, who for one and six took their small trunk to Keighley Station ahead of them. They had something to eat and drink before they set out with their father's blessing once they had addressed if not allayed his concerns about them walking into the threat of rain and traveling to and being in London alone.

"We've done it all before, Father," Charlotte reminded him with a squeeze of his hand. She forgot—or was afraid to weaken her argument—Anne had never been to London or even out of her home county, except lured on long walks to the edge of Lancashire's piece of the Pennines.

Anne almost backed out when her father bowed down for a kiss on his cheek and she realized Emily was no longer standing behind him. Another opinion of Anne's leaving came from Flossy, who sat on her feet, leaned against her legs, and looked up with begging eyes. Keeper could be heard barking in the back yard, the way he did when Emily played fetch with him, possibly an explanation of where she had gone. Anne caught a glimpse of Branwell on the stairs.

By then Charlotte was adamant they must be on their way. "Even now I'm not sure we'll avoid a soaking or catch the six-twenty train from Keighley to Leeds, which means we'll miss the overnight to London and our plans will be in disarray."

Impulses not plans, Anne thought but knew better than to remark, already preparing herself to be understated during the days ahead. The last time Anne had been *en route* with Charlotte, she was a sickly, uncertain, inexperienced school girl. Much had changed, but Charlotte still thought she knew better and expected Anne's compliance.

As the parsonage door closed, Anne could hear Flossy whining and their father telling them to take care. Once out of Haworth they walked quickly, pinching their cloaks tighter over their bonneted heads and around their bodies, not for warmth as the air was hot and heavy, but to prevent their hair and clothes from being messed by the wind that blew in spotty showers before they were half an hour towards Keighley. At first Anne pretended not to mind the rain. She became uneasy when lightning branched through the sky over Oakworth Down, flashing more frequently as it came closer, eventually in a vivid cloud-to-ground strike no more than half a mile ahead.

A few moments later there was a thunderous explosion, almost as deafening and threatening as the Crow Hill Bog burst of their early childhood that had tested their budding trust in nature. Anne remembered the sound and shaking, although she was only four. Emily was six, Branwell eight, Charlotte away at school with Elizabeth and Maria. Nursemaids Sarah and Nancy had led them off the common and too many miles across the moors, eventually recovering some sense of responsibility as the sky blackened. By the time the rain was a torrent and the earth quaked, they were safely sheltered.

Now there was only Anne to be sensible. "Perhaps we should turn back, Charlotte. There are those worrying at home. In London no one is expecting us."

"Impossible. Our things are already at the station. And our minds set on this mission."

It wasn't a reasonable answer in terms of walking into a storm, likely without a chance to change for the long nocturnal trip, but acceptable if Anne thought of London as she imagined it, the urgency of putting things right, and meeting with the best of publishers if not so much with the worst. She could endure traveling in a damp and disheveled state by putting the consequence of her writing over that of how she looked. She couldn't disagree with Charlotte's impulse to make truth a priority and even found some amusement in assuming a good part of her sister's motivation was to, as soon as possible, put paid to the rumor, which had gone all the way to America, that Currer Bell had anything to do with the creation of *Tenant*.

Anne's own indignation at Newby's deception had already begun to ease into excitement for what the next few days would bring. Besides managing Charlotte's moods and taking care of business, the physical boundaries of her world would be expanded and her identity as an author unveiled. She anticipated what she would see and feel in London: the magnificence and malevolence, and the ordinariness that might be the most compelling. She wondered whether there would be enough time there or too much. Like York Minster and Scarborough, would she long to return, or, like Cowan Bridge, Mirfield, and Thorpe Green, not care if she ever did?

Anne wished the trip was less of a "mission" and more of an adventure for her sister. At least Charlotte gave in to extravagance as Anne on her own probably wouldn't have, purchasing first class tickets from Leeds to London. Even in a plush upholstered and carpeted carriage that was private much of the way, Anne couldn't sleep, nor did they talk more than was necessary, Charlotte dozing on and off. There wasn't enough light for reading or air for breathing. It was an express train, no stops for exercise other than standing up and pulling down the window to be no wiser about where they were. Hour after hour, through dusk and darkness, Anne occupied herself by remembering passages from the Bible and enjoying the idleness, composing scenarios for her living and writing to come. Finally, weariness prompted her to close her eyes and try to sleep. She did, until Charlotte's voice disturbed her traveling with William, a loving and lawful companion, his hand holding hers, her head on his shoulder.

"I'm getting a headache. It's the humidity. No doubt both will get worse in London."

Just as it seemed the night and train journey would never end, they were headed into the sunrise. Mist and steam screened the passing countryside that, from what they could see of it, was fairly flat and distantly forested. The dawn wasn't yet fully realized when they arrived at Euston Station. At barely four-thirty in the morning it was, as they expected, lonely and menacing, and the same must be true of the streets beyond the depot's Doric arch. They were glad the promise made at the ticket booth in Leeds allowing them to remain on the train until seven, while it was pulled off the main track for cleaning and reloading with coal, was honored.

At last there was enough daylight to read—or write, Anne attempting to make a little progress on the forward to the second printing of *Tenant*, a response to the critical complaints and utter misrepresentation of the novel since its publication in late June.

"What's that?" Charlotte asked.

"Nothing of consequence."

Charlotte didn't inquire further, Anne considerately and selfishly submitting to her sister's need to stay quiet and nurse her head while she could.

***

The doors to the elegant box Mr. Smith had reserved finally opened and so did a view of one of the most famous stages in the country, if not the world. Anne could hardly contain her amazement as she sat next to the pale, mildly-whiskered, middle-aged Mr. Smith Williams, the closest thing to a gentleman escort she'd ever had. Her own reserve welcomed his. He waited for her to settle before softly expressing hope she would enjoy this particular performance of *The Barber of Seville*, one he had seen already and found excellently executed and amusing. No matter how appropriate a companion Mr. Smith Williams was, Anne's attention wistfully strayed to a revived and even smiling Charlotte. Sitting between Mr. Smith and his younger, similarly dark-haired, dark-eyed sisters, she was the center of their attention, Mr. Smith proving himself to be a firm, intelligent man of business, and charming.

"Please, call me George."

Even without his request, Anne suspected she was witnessing the securing of an important relationship for her sister, certainly for Charlotte's mind and ambitions, whether or not her heart. As much as she tried, Charlotte couldn't hold her hands still on her lap, her glasses reflecting the red glow of the theater, her posture struggling to appear disinterested in this newfound partnership. Anne felt some jealousy but, knowing how much Charlotte needed to be acknowledged and accomplished, it was mixed with relief and even joy so she didn't experience any guilt.

"All right, my dear?"

Anne had little choice but to acknowledge the sigh Mr. Smith Williams had obviously heard, if only to answer him with a nod, which seemed to satisfy him. She realized Charlotte was looking at them. *How do you always stay so composed and evasive?* Charlotte might have wondered if Mr. Smith's sisters hadn't been seated between them. Anne wasn't sure it was to her benefit to be so versed in hiding her feelings, but rarely was she ready to reveal them, whether afraid others wouldn't take them serious or she would too much herself.

My nature was not originally calm … I have learned to appear so by dint of hard lessons and many repeated efforts.

Her words put into Helen's voice were her latest attempt at being heard, yet, even in writing, all she had felt and learned and practiced was misunderstood.

Enjoy yourself. Don't worry about critics or how you must answer them, or Father or Emily or Branwell … or anything to disturb the wonder of this unexpected adventure.

She didn't think Mr. Smith Williams was reading her thoughts but wanting to witness her enthusiastic participation in the custom of applauding for the conductor as he danced into the pit, took his place and a bow, and turned to prompt the orchestra's tuning up.

There was some movement behind the curtain, the footlights burning brighter as Anne focused on the stage. "This is beyond my dreams. Beyond what I deserve." She lifted her hands to her cheeks flushed, as Mr. Smith Williams might assume, with pleasure and embarrassment, but really just the warmth and closeness of the theater.

"Oh, Miss Brontë, you're more than worthy to be here." Mr. Smith Williams was prompted by Anne's admission to make one of his own. "I think you're a perfect companion for attending the opera, for I suspect you understand how music—"

"'Kindly bids us wake. It calls us, with an angel's voice, to wake, worship, and rejoice.'"

"How lovely," reacted one of Mr. Smith's sisters. "Your own words?"

"Yes," Anne answered spontaneously, then realized Mr. Smith leaning forward.

Charlotte could no longer behave as if she wasn't listening.

"So you're a poet?" the other sister joined the questioning.

"For her own amusement." Charlotte seized the moment of Anne's hesitation.

"George doesn't publish enough poetry."

Mr. Smith's pretty sisters seemed satisfied with a conversation among themselves. "Well, I suppose novels are more saleable."

"Shh," scolded their brother, for they were the only noise in the theater moments before a brash chord swung the conductor's arms into calculated motion, the music he directed scampering, surging, echoing lyrically, and fading into a long pause counted by his baton.

"The curtain is going up." Charlotte sounded relieved.

The stage was set as an empty public square, the overture resuming and finding a melodic momentum in the violins, which the brass interrupted and the woodwinds revamped into a more jovial theme and rhythm of anticipation, finally crescendoing with a cavalier potency.

Anne turned to Mr. Smith Williams. "I can't believe I'm here."

"Believe it, my dear," he said without the nervousness or difficulty in expressing himself Charlotte had ascribed to him after one meeting.

"The amazement is ours," Mr. Smith said, no doubt puzzling his sisters even more regarding the identity of their guests.

"That you've managed to release my sister from the bondage of propriety is enough to admit the miracle of this evening, this entire day," Charlotte had the last word as Count Almaviva entered from the back of the stage, unfolding and reading a letter that set him singing to his heart's delight.

Miraculous or not, it was fortunate the publishers of *Jane Eyre* had so quickly adapted to the Bell brothers turned Brontë sisters. If anything, the reason for that trip to London offered great doubts about how Currer and Acton would be received physically manifest in skirts rather than trousers. That morning, after resting for half an hour, washing, pinching some color into their faces, and breakfasting, Charlotte and Anne left their lodgings in Paternoster Row for an unannounced appearance at Smith, Elder and Co. They considered what they had just spent on a cab and would have to for their return to Euston Station, and in frugality and curiosity embarked on a long disorientated and distracted walk. Later they discovered it could have been ten minutes instead of an hour. Despite ending up sore-footed and red-faced, they didn't regret the roundabout way that took them past the domed delight of St. Paul's, the medieval towering of St. Mary-le-Bow church with its authoritative bells, the imposing Bank of England, and too many bookshops and stationers to ignore or visit.

"Here it is. How many times I've written 65 Cornhill on correspondence." Charlotte tripped up a few shallow steps and put out her hand to a heavy wooden door that opened without her touching it.

A neatly bearded man with a substantial package stood aside so Charlotte and then Anne could enter the large bookshop. Everyone else inside was male, in various sections of the shop, and it was difficult to tell customers and staff apart. Charlotte didn't hide her irritation, which Anne guessed was really terror at what they were about to do, scraping her heels as she went up to the counter and pressed hard on its bell, once, twice, and then again. A young man approached and looked surprised at Charlotte's request, hesitant to confirm Mr. Smith was in. He left them for longer than Charlotte thought necessary, the wait filled by noticing some of the books on display as ones Smith and Elder had sent them as gifts, and browsing piles and shelves for others, a few they were interested in purchasing.

"Except we can't spare the money. If we wish to get home."

"Well, we'll make a note of them to send for." Anne strayed from her sister, noticing a sign announcing the botanical section. She heard:

"Did you wish to see me, ma'am?"

"Mr. Smith?"

"I am. What can I—"

Although Anne didn't see her sister's next move, she guessed on hearing Mr. Smith inquire, "Where did you get it?"

Charlotte had revealed her possession of his last letter to Currer Bell.

"Anne? Oh, there you are." Charlotte was waving her glasses in the air.

First they were introduced to a room behind the shop structurally only large enough for a desk and a few chairs but spaciously lit by a sizeable skylight, and, after a flurry of questions hardly pausing for answers, to Mr. Smith Williams, the firm's co-owner and chief reader. Surprise kept Mr. Smith talkative and his colleague quietly in the background. As was assumed and would soon be proven, disposition was also a reason for the difference in the men's reaction to the two women with minimal resemblance to each other except for their accents, some mannerisms, outdated wilted dresses and hairstyles, and anger with Newby. Charlotte spoke more than Anne, but not without looking for her youngest sister's opinion, proceeding as she thought best anyway.

She not only convinced Mr. Smith and his partner of her and Anne's innocence in Newby claiming three Bells were one, but also to purchase the remaining stock of the Bells' poetry volume from Aylott and Jones.

"Smith and Elder would be so much more effective at selling it."

Charlotte accepted Mr. Smith's invitation to his house on the condition her and Anne's identities weren't exposed to his mother and sisters. The awkwardness of otherwise explaining his acquaintance with two Quaker-like spinsters should have killed Mr. Smith's plan. Instead, he expanded it into a dinner event with a few literary associates like William Thackeray and George Henry Lewes.

"I have to stop you." Charlotte stood up, acting badly, wringing her hands, wiping her brow, and pretending she didn't notice her bonnet had fallen to the floor, not even as Mr. Smith Williams picked it up and gave it to Anne who hadn't taken hers off. "As much as we would like to meet Mr. Lewes and, especially, Mr. Thackeray, we revealed our true identities to you in faith they will remain unrevealed. In our authorship we must remain gentlemen."

"Of course, of course," Mr. Smith Williams echoed himself. "Of course."

Mr. Smith finally sat down behind his desk, shaking his head, obviously not resigned even as he spoke, "Pity."

"Otherwise, our sister Emily—"

"Emily? Ellis?"

"Oh, no." Charlotte didn't often admit saying something she shouldn't, but the panic in her eyes acknowledged she had given away what Emily valued most.

"Where are you staying?" Mr. Smith smiled persuasively. "I insist you shift yourselves to my house in Bayswater. I'll pay the cab and any charges you've already incurred."

"That is kind." Anne stood up, surprised Charlotte followed her lead, feeling a little uneasy as her sister stepped towards her. "But we've made this trip of our own volition and return to Yorkshire tomorrow. We couldn't impose on you and your family in any way for such a short visit."

Charlotte reached out for her bonnet and put it on with a tug on its ribbons.

***

Anne didn't regret refusing Mr. Smith's hospitality, although a brief stay grew longer with each new temptation to sample London's attractions. Their nightly retreat to the Chapter Coffee House offered a few relieving hours away from being Mr. Smith's "country cousins" or not knowing how to present themselves without raising suspicion they were hiding something. Fortunately, Sunday and Monday, as busy as they were with a church service at St. Stephen's, exhibitions at the Royal Academy and the National Gallery, walking in Kensington Gardens, dining grandly at Mr. Smith's and having a simple tea at Mr. Smith Williams', even a less than satisfactory visit to Newby's, weren't as exhausting as their first day in London.

It was after one o'clock in the morning when they returned from Covent Garden to their accommodation. Another dose of sal volatile made Charlotte nearly comatose moments after she crawled into bed. Anne didn't mind. She also shut her eyes, hoping to continue the dreamy sights, sounds, and even scents of the opera house: the height of its domed ceiling and perilous dangling of sparkling smoky chandeliers around its towering tiered walls of velvety-draped boxes. One not only allowed her a privileged view of an outstanding performance of a Rossini creation but, also, in a way she knew she would never regret, moved her closer to heaven.

A certain fragrance from that Cinderella evening was the last thing Anne enjoyed before she finally fell asleep. Her short, discreetly mended gloves weren't laid on the dresser with her sister's equally worn out ones, but on her pillow where she could inhale the delicately floral perfume the slightest touch of the Smith sisters' fingers had transferred to them.

CHAPTER TWENTY

Haworth, two months later, September 1848

Reverend Brontë had gone out. The message wasn't for him but, on hearing Branwell cursing and stumbling around upstairs, he insisted on knowing whom it was from and what it was about.

"I must warn Mr. Grundy."

"He knows what to expect," Emily mumbled, coming out of the kitchen. "As we all do."

Charlotte stopped their father to wrap his scarf higher and tighter around his neck, make sure his coat was completely buttoned and he put on his gloves. She didn't do the same for Branwell, who left about half an hour later dressed sloppily and not warmly, his hair uncut and uncombed, a hollowness about his cheeks and dullness in his eyes.

"Too late fer sum, but I'll nay let tha catch thy death." Tabby embraced Anne's shoulders from behind and closed the front door to also prevent her watching for Reverend Brontë's return.

He went straight to his study, ignoring his daughters gathered in the parlor. Anne had hoped he would intercept Branwell and turn him around, yet wasn't surprised her father returned alone. As Tabby hinted, it was too late, even for forbearance, faith, and unalterable affection, to bring Branwell back to emotional and physical health.

Only his spiritual recovery was in question now and Anne wondered if she had fictitiously foreshadowed what the answer would be.

"I hope Grundy or someone will bring him home." Anne finally couldn't keep her concerns to herself. "It's such a cold, wet night. Falling out there could be the end of him."

Neither of her sisters so much as looked up.

Charlotte had long since withdrawn from "the subject of Branny" to the point of rarely speaking to him. Emily's dealings with him had become mainly practical "for someone had to be." On those fewer and fewer occasions Branwell found enough energy and coins or, like that evening, the generosity of a still-tolerant acquaintance, Emily made sure she was available long after midnight to unbar the door and let him in, get him upstairs and into bed with as little commotion as often was impossible. Anne wanted to help, but Emily wouldn't let her to do anything but remove his boots. Otherwise, she could only watch her sister get thinner and thinner and less and less effective in shielding their father from his son reeking of liquor, opium, and vomit, and using language they might have never otherwise heard. Anne couldn't talk Emily out of sitting in Branwell's room, but, since the fire, their father was likely to relieve them both and, when he thought no one saw, lay beside Branwell, even putting his arms around him and pulling his son's blotchy face to his chest.

The air upstairs was still a little smoky, in Branwell's room a near tragedy also evident in scorching on the bed's head and posts, and burn holes in the carpet. The book apparently dropped from his hand as a candle tipped over had somehow escaped catching fire but not water damage, left on the side table inadvertently as evidence of sibling generosity and timing. It was the volume of Tennyson poems Charlotte and Anne had brought Emily from London, loaned to Branwell one day when he seemed almost lucid and ready to revive his old self. A few hours later Anne was curious what he thought of it, knocking his bedroom door without getting a response, opening it to a pungent haze through which she found him senseless, the bed linens beginning to burn. She tried to move him, begging and shaking him, and, with no choice but to disturb her father, shouted for help.

Charlotte was soon on her way up, followed by Emily carrying a large pitcher of water always ready in the kitchen. Charlotte took it to leave Emily free to pull Branwell away from the flames she doused into sizzling and dying.

All three sisters lifted their bewildered brother to his feet.

"Hey," he yelled, struggling against them. "Hell is finally as it should be."

"We'll take him to my room," Emily decided. "The parlor and little sleep will do for me until his is fit again."

"No. To mine." Their father used his authoritative voice and height to take over wrestling with Branwell. "Would you kill us all, son?"

Branwell quickly realized whom he was up against. "I never meant—"

"Damn it. We've kept you out of debtor's prison. And nursed your self-inflicted wounds. And had to live with your shame as if it was our own. Your carelessness has gone too far this time."

"You're right, Father. It will be better when I'm gone."

***

Dr. Wheelhouse had heard about Branwell wielding a carving knife in the back room of the Black Bull, along with the insane explanation Branwell believed Francis Grundy's invitation to dinner was from Satan.

William Brown brought Branwell home about ten-thirty. Anne saw how her brother was better and worse: silent and compliant, his mouth slightly upturned with a little drool from one corner, his eyes meeting hers affectionately before rolling back, his legs as useless as a scarecrow's.

William Brown handed Anne the knife that belonged in the kitchen not her brother's pocket. "I found em on his knees b' Sunday school with a smile a happier, healthier fella moot muster."

It was hard to watch William cradling Branwell in his strapping arms. It was years and moments since her brother had ascended the stairs two or three at a time to frustrate his sisters encumbered by skirts and modesty, except for Emily who had never hesitated to prove she was more than his equal and not just because her legs were longer.

Through the pounding of her heart, Anne heard the few grateful words he weakly spoke to the man who had returned him to the love of his family.

"He knows he'll die soon," Emily recognized hours before Dr. Wheelhouse made his pronouncement.

That night even Charlotte admitted she was, at least, trying to forgive Branwell. "Despite the strain he put on us, we've accomplished much and still look forward. I'm even writing a new novel. But how can I forget the fun I had with him, the pride and hope I had in him, the talents of his mind and hand, how time and again he might've taken the right path, how—?"

"I put him on yet another wrong one. The most misleading of all."

Was Charlotte even listening? "How can I forgive what's been wasted on him?"

How could Anne not blame herself when, knowing she would hear, Branwell wished he never met the one who stole his heart, respect, reason, and, as it was becoming all too obvious, future? How could any of them know the extent of his weaknesses before they manifested in such a way as to irreversibly ruin him and torture them all, and, in Anne's case, prove she had done more harm than good by trying to help him?

Anne pushed her thoughts in a higher direction. "There might be joy and fulfillment for him yet, if he'll try to receive it."

"Even our father seems to have given up on his eternal salvation."

"I don't think so."

Anne wanted to feel as sympathetically close to Charlotte as they were in the flesh sitting on the bed they shared, both in their nightgowns and caps but neither making a motion to get under the covers.

Emily walked up and down the hallway, as it seemed for hours, to the drone of her father praying, which was a little comfort to Anne. Even covered with blankets Charlotte complained she felt cold. She said she was going to throw up but never needed the chamber pot for that purpose and finally fell asleep. Anne couldn't and, needing something to do, assumed her father hadn't interrupted his vigil at Branwell's bedside to wind the long-cased clock.

Emily was leaning against the door frame of the room where, Anne hoped, father and son might bond in dying as they hadn't in living. Emily's eyes were closed, her mouth moving, her words muffled, Anne making them out in their repetition.

"You've killed yourself ... you've killed yourself ... you've killed yourself ...."

"Oh, Emily," Anne reacted softly, walking towards her sister, knowing she wouldn't be able to comfort her. She had to try. "He may yet recover."

"You don't believe such nonsense."

The expectation of another skeptical reaction sent Anne to the clock, the action she could take to keep it going, and the struggle with her own faith she didn't want anyone, especially not Emily, to witness.

"Oh, luv." Tabby startled her into dropping the winding key, but immediately relieved her of holding back her tears.

They hugged. Tabby was grown more bosomy in a frill-less, high-necked nightgown, her face becoming redder. The old woman wiped a billowing sleeve across her face, allowed herself a few more sniffles, and walked up to Branwell's room, stroking Emily's arm before she went in.

"He sleeps quiet," she reported, touching Emily's shoulder this time, reaching out to take Anne's hand. "Rev'r'end be restin', too. Y'uns shuld get sum sleep."

Emily shook her head and went downstairs.

Tabby noticed Martha was in the hallway and waved her back to their little room. "Need tha up early, Missy."

Charlotte was also awake, sitting in bed with the covers pulled to her chin, questioning Anne, panic in her eyes.

"No change." Anne slid in alongside her, lying on her back, which wasn't comfortable. She needed to listen for what she hoped she wouldn't hear.

It was the unexpected Charlotte responded to first. "What's that? It's not—"

"It is."

Emily usually performed the first movement of the *Moonlight Sonata* nimbly with soft dynamics and reflective expression, letting it rise and fall like a singer's perfect breathing and articulation.

That night, just past the new moon, too far from old joys, too close to last wishes, one of the darkest nights of the month and their lives, her playing was labored, hesitant, even harsh, as broken as all their hearts were.

"Must she make it worse?" Charlotte grumbled, lay down and curled sideways.

Anne didn't know how long Emily stayed at the piano before she finally dozed off all too aware of what she would wake to.

***

Whatever went on between Reverend Brontë and his son before that last Sunday in September sunrise might yet or never be revealed, but the relieving result was known. Following Charlotte into what had once been Branwell's studio for pursuing the artistic and literary promise of his youth, Anne no longer saw him failing but, instead, opening himself up to the devotion of his family and Maker. She no longer felt left out of what was assumed to be her father's overnight appeal for her brother to recognize how he went wrong and repent. Branwell's earnest plea for forgiveness at the sight of her and her sisters offered more proof his demons had finally been exorcized.

Then Anne saw her father standing slumped and disheveled in the morning's gray light, looking like he was shouldering a burden heavier than any before. Was she witnessing his regret as she was feeling her own also in opposition to a true believer's relief in the saving of a wayward soul? Her father was more practiced in compassionate detachment, especially at the deathbed hearing confessions, offering absolution and an easier departure for the final journey, while assuring those left behind it was for the best. Anne hadn't any memory of how he dealt with the loss of her mother and sisters. He had solemnly and respectfully eulogized Aunt Elizabeth and Curate Weightman, but Anne never saw him shed a tear for them. Now her father's spiritual conscience was visibly overwhelmed by what was only natural for him to feel. Given a choice, would he not rather keep his son imperfectly on earth than guide his premature passage to heaven?

"I need to talk to John," Branwell could barely be heard.

It happened the Sexton was in the kitchen, as Martha claimed, unsure of whether or not he wanted to see Branwell.

The door closed on their exchange. When John Brown emerged he was embarrassed by having to wipe his eyes. Charlotte wondered out loud what Branwell had said to him.

"'Thirty-one years 'n I've done naught gret nor e'en good,'" John obliged before acting as sorry for himself as for his dying friend. "Five pennies worth a gin. See now. I dun em no fav'r."

The hallway clock had just struck nine when Reverend Brontë called Charlotte to join him at Branwell's bedside and directed Anne to go quickly for Emily, Martha, and Tabby. Anne wasn't prepared for Emily's emotional inability to walk up the stairs without the young and old servants' assistance, although her sister managed to ask Anne to get

Keeper and Flossy.

Anne found them closed up in the back kitchen. One look at their questioning expressions overruled her doubts about bringing them upstairs because her father and Charlotte wouldn't approve. She carried Flossy, while Keeper tiptoed behind her and sat just outside Branwell's room where Anne also commanded Flossy to stay. The little dog immediately flattened on the floor with his head on his paws and whined until Anne stroked his ears and kissed the top of his head, a reason to delay her approach to her brother's dying.

At first it wasn't what she expected. Branwell was propped up a little, his face too flushed, shivering another sign he was feverish. He was conscious of his father leaning over him, possibly of his sisters standing side by side at the bottom of the bed, probably not that holding Emily up was one reason their arms were interlocked.

Branwell began praying softly. It was the miracle Anne was hoping for: her brother persuaded and allowed to leave the world peacefully.

"Amen," Branwell echoed his father.

Tabby stroked his thinning hair and let him squeeze her hand.

Martha abruptly left the room weeping. Charlotte turned away as though she wanted to follow her, instead closing the door on Keeper and Flossy.

Calm resignation gave way to convulsing, Branwell grimacing horribly, a sound coming from his throat that wasn't speaking but not choking either, his torso writhing, his arms and legs thrashing violently enough for Emily to forget her own frailty and help Anne, their father, and Tabby hold him down. All Anne could think was she didn't want death to come upon her like that, fiercely tearing her from life and frightening everyone else, too. She immediately regretted her selfish response to her brother's final moments and, instead, lost herself in what was left of any earthly interaction with him, fortunate that he grew quiet again, so it was only necessary to touch his arm, not restrain it, and feel the coolness of his cheek when she kissed it. She stepped back in case Charlotte or Emily had a similar need to bid him farewell, not knowing whether or not they made any motion to before he lurched up and held his chest, gasping and gurgling in his father's arms.

Reverend Brontë gently let Branwell slip out of his embrace and began another prayer, his hands steadying themselves around his son's, his head bowed, kneeling more a matter of necessity than supplication as the bed supported him.

"My boy, my boy. My only boy."

Tabby straightened the bedclothes around Branwell and centered his head on the pillow. "Dear lad. 'Tis bet'r now."

Charlotte took off her glasses and added, "For life couldn't give him happiness." She moved towards her father, leaning over and reaching out to him, but Tabby stopped her.

Emily only responded to scratching at the door. Anne didn't react quickly enough to prevent her, not from letting the dogs in, but collapsing on them, bewildered Flossy almost crushed before being rescued by Anne's distress as she was by his need to love and be loved in return.

CHAPTER TWENTY-ONE

Haworth, three months later, December 1848

It wasn't the best time for visitors. Emotions were drained and spirits low, nothing to share as a family but grief and apprehension. How could they nicely entertain others? Charlotte suffered migraines and didn't write any letters for a week after Branwell died. Their father eventually fought off the bad cold that affected them all, including Tabby whose constant napping, heavy wool shawl, socks, and mittens, and sipping of cider toddies were effective remedies, for her, at least. Emily got worse, her cough persistent and obviously painful, her breath short, complexion ashen, and weight loss approaching what was feared to be irreversible. She continued with her usual routine: doing anything—other than writing—to stay indoors. She hadn't left the house since Branwell's funeral, except to go into the yard to use the privy and tie up Keeper or bring him inside. Despite her over-the-years lecturing that fresh air was the best medicine, any suggestion she take a walk, even a short one on a rare fine day during that wet autumn, seemed an affront to her.

No one was surprised she grew angry at the idea of a doctor examining her.

As far as her own health, Anne didn't think she was sicker or for longer than she had been before, although Charlotte's nagging concern caused her to wonder if sharp pains on her left side indicated something more serious than asthma aggravated by a cold. She didn't want to refuse the two youngest Robinson sisters' request to come to Haworth. If anything, and secretly, she was flattered they couldn't be put off.

"As soon as they heard about Branwell, they wanted to come."

"Also, because their mother remarried." Charlotte took the letter Anne never intended her to read. "I'm sure Lady Scott, as she's finally become, can't be bothered with what they do now." Her frown turned into an exasperated laugh. "They want to bring their carriage right to the house?"

"It would be difficult for them to walk up the hill."

"They'll never want to do those breakneck turnings again."

"So, may I tell them yes?"

"Check with Father. No." Charlotte thought of something. "Pretend they didn't give notice."

It could hardly be said Mary and Elizabeth called in passing. Certainly, Emily didn't believe it when Anne acted surprised at John

Brown announcing that halfway up the village the horses pulling their vehicle had refused to take another slippery uphill step until he and his brother calmed, persuaded, and guided them all the way to the parsonage's gate.

"Oh, Em. I would love for you to meet the girls."

"I don't exist."

Anne wasn't sure she trembled at seeing Mary and Elizabeth again or because of Emily's vanishing.

The entrance of the young women was like a sudden change of season, a burst of spring on the threshold of winter, a flurry of greetings rather than snow, a disturbance that warmed the house rather than chilled it. Brontë black and gray, long faces and taciturnity were interrupted by color, excitement, and chatter, although not disrespectfully. Mary and Elizabeth offered their condolences delicately and sincerely. The parsonage's plain hallway was suddenly decorated with velvet and soft wool, rich shades of purple, royal blue, and plum, as well as ribbons and ruching, braid and embroidery, and pleasantly scented by a mixture of lavender and rose. Between them Anne and Charlotte took the women's large-collared three-quarter-length capes, veiled bonnets, lace mittens, and the bakery box Mary was carrying. An elegant capping of Mary's perfectly side-ringleted coif confirmed her marital status. Elizabeth's hair was pulled severely down her cheeks and back into a small bun, as if, with a broken engagement behind her, she relished looking old-maidish.

Despite their growth in the last three and a half years, Anne was prepared for the Robinson sisters to behave like the overindulged, frivolous girls she had been so exasperated by and forgiving of. Charlotte insisted on freeing Anne's arms for more hugs and kisses the visitors were impatient to give, and was only burdened by the Robinsons' outerwear for a few minutes before Martha took it from her. "Put their things carefully over the chair in the Reverend's study. And make sure Tiger isn't in there to lie on them."

Charlotte also ordered the visitors. "Go on. Into the parlor that's been vigorously dusted and where there's a blazing fire as though you were expected."

"Will you join us?" Mary asked.

"What? Of course not. Except to bring in some refreshment. Fortunately, Anne made sandwiches as lovely as those we had in London, with egg anyway, watercress hard to come by this time of year. Did you know we were there last summer? Went to the opera? And the Royal Academy? And Kensington Gardens?"

Anne stiffened and lowered her eyes.

"How stupid of me. My little sister must have—"

"No, Charlotte."

Elizabeth hooked Anne's arm as they went into the parlor. "There's so much to catch up on. What a neat little dining room, which, I assume, also serves for sitting." She touched the fringed cloth Anne had put over the table to hide the ink stains, candle wax burn, and "E" carved into it. "Although I remember you said you took most of your meals in the kitchen along with your old servant Tabby who fed you suet puddings and scary stories." She looked back at Mary who was following them. "Mrs. Clapham, pull in your skirts and petticoats, otherwise they might bury our dear Miss Brontë. She looks like she needs to eat those sandwiches and the cake we brought all herself."

"Don't talk to me like I'm a child, Bessie. After all, I've done what you haven't." Mary adjusted her clothing as Anne settled next to her and put a caressing hand on her arm.

"Only because I did what you wouldn't." Elizabeth looked around, realizing her choices for sitting were the little rocking chair or at the table.

Anne stood up. "Please. You're my guest."

"No, she's fine there." Mary gently tugged on Anne's sleeve to bring her down to the sofa again. "I'm doing fine cutting a superior dash to the Keighley elite. I relish their envy."

Elizabeth laughed and moved towards the window.

It was too soon for Mary to be married. She was very young, not yet of legal age. When the desperate girl had written she was vehemently unwilling, Anne wasted no time in advising it was prudent for her to wait until she knew Henry Clapham better and was sure they cared as much for each other as her mother did for his supposed fortune. In contrast, Elizabeth was no longer engaged to a man she hadn't any affection for. Anne felt she had done some good, but also worried such a headstrong girl might be resentful now both her sisters were wed and, even worse, think Anne's counseling was influenced by spinsterish spite. Seeing Elizabeth's vitality, optimism, and glowing eyes, even hearing her playful sarcasm assured Anne that was not the case.

"I'm a horrible host letting you stand, Bessie."

"Oh, it's fine, Anne. I sat for hours on the journey here. Longer than my sister."

"You'll not go all the way back to Lichfield today?"

"No. I'll stay at Aireworth House tonight." Elizabeth went to fully open the door Charlotte, back first, pushed on as she brought in sandwiches and cake, followed by Martha carrying a tray weighing heavier with a teapot, cups and saucers.

Mary pulled at her ringlets. "You said you'd visit for at least a week."

Anne took advantage of Mary's distraction to get up and move beyond her reach.

"We'll see." Elizabeth didn't look at her sister. "It depends on whether Henry makes me feel welcome."

"That depends on whether you remind him how he deceived us."

"I'll leave that to you, sister. It makes no difference to me."

"He's related to Haworth's Sugdens and Greenwoods," Charlotte declared as she and Anne arranged the refreshments on the table. "I'm sure you know."

"Unfortunately." Mary spread out her skirt's fullness, flapping it so the fabric shimmered.

Anne was disappointed in Mary, not due to her having made a hasty and—as she too freely admitted—unhappy marriage, but because she pretended to find satisfaction in exhibiting the same superficiality with which her mother had designed the match.

"Coming so near to being mistaken myself, although Mr. Milner's wealth, high connections, and business acumen are real, I know I must be useful, whether I marry or not."

Anne nodded, remembering Elizabeth's declaration had once been her own.

"I'll begin by pouring the tea."

Elizabeth gave Anne the first cup and Charlotte, who seemed to have forgotten she meant to leave, the next. She insisted Mary get off her "delicate duff" to fetch hers. Martha portioned the cake, putting a piece and sandwich on each plate she offered. She shook some coal out of the scuttle into the fire, curtsied, and hurried out.

Anne sat at the table with Elizabeth and Charlotte. Mary returned to the sofa until she realized joining the others was preferable to juggling a cup and plateful.

"Aren't we missing someone? Your sister Emily? I was looking forward to meeting her."

"She's very ill," Charlotte answered Elizabeth without hesitation and further explanation.

"You always said she had the strongest constitution of you all."

"So it was, Mary." A bite of cake along with one drink coming too soon after another caused Anne to cough, harder and harder, and tip over her tea.

"What's wrong?" Mary leaned towards Anne in the next chair to put her arm around her.

"Oh … just … a stitch."

"They see it's worse than that." Charlotte used one of the cutwork napkins to soak up the spilled tea.

Anne thought how she must get it and the table covering to Martha before Emily saw how badly both were stained.

Elizabeth filled Anne's cup again, suggesting she didn't eat more cake as it was disappointingly dry. "I imagine Emily makes better. You must complain to your baker, Mary."

Mary didn't answer, withdrawing the uppity version of herself for the rest of the visit. Anne was heartened Mary's basically good and hopeful nature wasn't completely lost to disappointment and cynicism. She was equally pleased by Elizabeth agreeing to stay at Aireworth House for a week, maybe two, and promising to try to get along with her brother-in-law.

"Well, if I don't succeed, it won't be my fault," Elizabeth added, grinning and winking specifically at Mary.

"I doubt that, Bessie." Mary smiled and frowned, Anne understanding too well why they simultaneously resisted and needed each other.

Charlotte hadn't remained in the parlor, although Anne noticed her peeking in, alerted by the tap of her spectacles against the slightly open door. Charlotte would expect Elizabeth and Mary to do most of the talking, with Anne not having much to say, especially as she couldn't— wouldn't—reveal anything about her new vocation. Charlotte wasn't as furtive in participating in the young women's leaving, although Anne stole her sister's best excuse and fetched Mary and Elizabeth's coats and bonnets before she could.

Charlotte loosely hugged the young women. "I hope you'll visit again as it buoys Anne so. I think it's a grand idea she meet you in Scarborough this summer."

"Lydia might be there, too, if Harry is performing," Mary sighed as she spoke. "That's where we usually get to see her."

Anne said only that she would think about it, her hesitation to make any promises not because she didn't want to. One after the other, Elizabeth and Mary held her tight, wiping their eyes, and leaving her happier and sadder.

***

Should she tear the harrowing death drawing out or throw the whole journal into the fire? There was more than one disturbing sketch in it. Anne had hidden the book in her underclothing drawer since discovering it while going through Branwell's possessions within a week of his passing, Charlotte too ill to help and Emily refusing to acknowledge there was anything of him remaining. Anne's immediate reaction was for no one else to see it. She was determined to dispose of it as soon as she could, yet, even having many opportunities, she waited months to take advantage of the kitchen being empty of servants and sisters.

The content of Branwell's journal wouldn't come as a surprise to

Charlotte and Emily, but, as Anne had been the one to find it, she might spare them the reminder of how they had long-suffered his degenerating imagination and hallucinating rants. Their father must never be subjected to it. Charlotte had regained her health and strength and was the backbone of the family again, if less dictatorial than she had been, at times almost gentle in her fussing over her sisters. In the case of her own health, Anne felt she succeeded in easing Charlotte's anxiety a little by blaming her delicate constitution always subject to one impermanent winter ailment or other. It was becoming more and more difficult to see any light at the end of Emily's consumptive tunnel.

"Em so ill takes the sunshine out of the world. For her to be so determined to act as if she isn't, well … doesn't she realize her life is as precious to us as our own?"

Was it what Charlotte confirmed and inferred that pushed Anne to finally hold what seemed like her brother's Last Will and Testament towards the range's coal embers? Emily was in the parlor where Charlotte was reading from Emerson's *Essays*, a recent gift from Mr. Smith Williams. Martha had the afternoon off and Tabby was resting in her room. Anne was shivering, desperate to do something, if just symbolically, to rid the house of the morbidity that continued to threaten it, knowing hesitation would suck time from the chance she had. Giving way to such a destructive impulse went against her better judgment. Despite the heat from the stove, she felt she was turning to ice, as unable to move in the present or affect the future as she was to change the past. She couldn't breathe, either, not in the way she was used to, struggling to release air from her lungs, but as though there was nothing left of life to inhale.

She heard a thump and once again her brother's demise was out of her hands.

"Anne?" Charlotte was in the room. "Are you—what's this?"

Too late Anne saw her sister picking up Branwell's journal, flipping the pages, shaking her head, curling her lip.

"I wondered what happened to this. How he continues to torment us."

Just in time Anne realized Charlotte was going to do what she hadn't. "No."

"I thought—"

"I was tempted. But it's not right. We may censure our own work, but not another's."

"Exactly." Emily wheezed, shuffling into the room without the strength to pick up her feet, slipping into the narrow space between her sisters and the range for no obvious reason. Anne caught her as she swayed towards it, Emily's bare wrist hitting it.

"Oh, no." Anne panicked even more because Emily didn't react to being burned, and tried to convince her to sit at the table while Charlotte rushed out to break some ice from the barrel in the yard.

"No. No. I must—" Emily only took a few steps before reaching towards her younger sister, looking as if she had never suffered greater shame than at that moment. "Please. I need ... the privy."

Charlotte had already returned and took Emily in her arms.

"Grab Tabby's coat from the scullery."

"There isn't time, Anne." Charlotte hurried Emily out to the two-seater in the blustery yard.

Emily's diarrhea became chronic. She decided it was purging the sickness out of her. Charlotte said she might be right, but, like Anne, must have seen that, along with Emily's constant sometimes violent coughing, shaking spasms, gasping and severe pain, it was draining her of any likelihood of improvement. Charlotte wrote to a respected physician in London, but his answer was too vague to be of much help and the medicine he sent was refused by Emily anyway. Helplessness once again overruled normalcy, hope losing another battle with despair. The east wind cut in whenever the front or back doors were open, always wheezing through cracks around them and the windows, the reason the shutters were kept closed, day and night almost indistinguishable.

Nothing prevented Emily rising at dawn. She wouldn't accept help to straighten her bed or get dressed no matter how long it took before every lace was tied and button done, or fix her hair, or go down the stairs even if she had to sit to descend them one by one. Determined to carry on with a domestic routine which had given her the freedom to be who she was in simple and extraordinary ways, she moved through the house looking for what there was to hold on to and rest against, depending upon inanimate objects rather than flesh and blood for support. She won most of the arguments over what she wasn't well enough to do, except when Tabby barred her from rinsing, wringing, and hanging laundry. It was sheer will that gave Emily any temperamental and physical strength at all, for she only consumed a little tea and the softest part of a bread slice once, not more than twice, a day. She must have realized she couldn't disguise the betrayal of her body, but, excluding frustration and anger, continued unresponsive to the humans around her. In contrast, Emily had evolved from any power struggle to a constantly caring relationship with Keeper, who she still changed her expression for, spoke to, slipped her thin arm over, and, when she sat on the rug in front of the parlor hearth, used as a backrest.

The sicker Emily became, the more Flossy followed her, getting hazardously under her feet but somehow never tripping her. Martha said it was because as she was leaving them Emily was walking on air a little more every day. Haworth folk were known for their bluntness and peculiar lore. Usually Anne welcomed the contrast to her own circumspection and realism—her Irish-ness might normally play along, while her Aunt Branwell conscience relished the relief. However, to hear Martha or anyone else speak freely and inevitably of Emily dying angered Anne more than anything ever had, not due to her refusal to see what was happening to her beloved sister, but because quiet preparation allowed for a miracle, while outright fatalism did not.

***

"'Powerful'. 'Interesting'. 'Coarse'. 'Brutal'. 'Morbid'. Do we write with any such adjectives in mind?" Anne had been reading through the reviews of *Tenant* she had collected, portions aloud to Emily, especially those that might stir any fight left in her. "Or go through the tormenting process of writing a novel for 'reveling in scenes of debauchery'?"

Emily was quiet lying sideways on the sofa in the parlor. Since Anne had repositioned the pillow borrowed from one or other of their beds, Emily's head had slipped to bow against her frail neck. Her torso was curled so her length was contracted, no definition to her arms or bosom within the sleeves and bodice of her dress, no movement under its skirt since Anne had lifted her sister's skeletal legs up more than an hour before.

Anne wondered if Emily was still pulled by the brutishness and beauty of the moors and the similar punishment and reward of writing. Did a look out a window or opening of a door remind her of what she was missing, and new Gondal rascals or Heathcliffs or Catherines find her imagination receptive? Anne longed for one more conversation with her, whether playful or intense, one more chance to agree, argue, and confirm they were good for each other's inspiration, intellects, and souls. Anne ached for one more meeting with the Emily who was wiry but robust, strong like a man and simple like a child, her head full of logic and fantastic stories at the same time, her choices uncompromising, as were her passions. If only Emily's life could return to being routine and yet so exceptional, filled with writing brilliantly while she was bread making or sewing or everyone else was asleep, making music like a perfect lady and rambling the Pennine way like a free and easy lad.

Instead, Anne had to helplessly watch as Emily continued to disappear through those December days and nights. On that Monday evening, a week before Christmas, her stillness, half-open eyes and mouth, and leaning towards resignation indicated there was only one way she would be released from consumption's captivity.

Anne was jarred out of her lament by Emily making some effort.

"The dogs, the dogs," Emily muttered, unable to hide the pain she was in as she got up.

"Oh, I'll tell Martha to—"

"Feed them. I must feed them."

"Charlotte," Anne cried out, meeting her in the hallway as she came out of their father's study.

"What ... is it?" he wondered from within his refuge.

"Nothing. Anne called so loudly because she didn't know where I was."

"Ah. I thought—"

They left his unease to address their own, following Emily through the kitchen into the abruptly cold passage leading to the scullery where Martha turned from some task at the same time Emily stumbled and fell against the wall.

Emily refused their help to recover her position. "I must ... give ... dogs ...."

"Oh, Miss. I wuldna let 'em starve."

"You think I would?" Emily snapped as she grabbed the bowl of scraps from Martha.

"Let me get you to bed," Anne offered once Emily had emptied it. "I'll comb and plait your hair."

"You know I don't care how I look." Emily had begun holding her throat when she spoke, its raspiness getting worse. "It's too early. I'm not ready."

Emily lingered in the parlor until ten, then made it up to her room as stubbornly and slowly as she had fed the dogs. She refused the stone bed warmer Anne carried and closed the door on her younger sister who wanted to, at least, make sure she managed to change into her nightclothes without falling again, and, at most, sit on her bed and have that longed-for conversation, even if it hardly needed words.

Around nine their father had looked into the parlor with his usual advice before going to bed himself. He got as far as winding the clock before going back down to his study from which, as far as Anne knew, he hadn't emerged.

Emily coughed on and off throughout the night. Charlotte didn't move or make a sound, although, like Anne laid beside her, it was likely she didn't sleep much either.

The clock struck five and Charlotte sat upright. After a few moments of remembering what her panic was about, she threw the covers off and swung her feet to the floor. "How will we bear it?"

She shivered out of her nightgown to dress in more woolen layers than were necessary for staying indoors. When she returned over an hour later, the aura of winter accompanied her despite what she held in her hand.

Anne was sitting in Emily's room waiting for her to wake, having already checked that she might yet do so. "Wherever did you find a sprig with flowers?"

"Exactly where I dreamt it would be." The thawing heather Charlotte laid on the pillow touched Emily's cheek without any effect other than making Anne even sadder because she realized and regretted what wasn't happening.

Emily's eyes opened but didn't acknowledge a parting gift, her urgent rising knocking the heather to the floor.

"Surely not, my dear." Charlotte struggled with how to restrain her when it looked as if any part of Emily would break with more than a touch. "Let me, at least, put a shawl around you and socks on your feet."

Anne was already holding both. Unable to extend or lift her arms, Emily let Anne drape the shawl over her shoulders, but her feet remained bare as step by difficult step she left that little room of childish play, wild imaginings, and secret scribblings only dying had grown her out of.

Charlotte did what Anne wanted to do and put an arm around Emily's waist to help her down the stairs. Anne grabbed Emily's simple barber comb.

Emily didn't resist being taken to the parlor, Martha quickly responding to the request for a fire, Charlotte going to get more coal while Martha lit it. Emily insisted on sitting at the table and asked for her sewing box, which Anne knew was in the kitchen.

"Let me tidy your hair first."

"I'll do it myself. Go. Get my sewing."

Anne reluctantly handed Emily the comb, assuming Martha understood to remain in the room while she was gone.

"If she couldn't make out the heather, she can't see to sew." Charlotte, dirtied and weighed down by the loaded coal scuttle she needed both hands to carry, followed Anne back to the parlor.

"What's happened?" Anne rushed to Emily collapsed in front of the hearth, Martha using the poker to drag something out of the fire just beginning to flame.

"Oh, Miss Anne, Miss Charlotte, she culdna hold it. I culdna save it."

All was soon calmed for the sake of Emily panting like the dogs on a long walk on a hot day and the Reverend who just after noon returned from a morning errand. He smiled to see Charlotte writing a letter. Anne was on the sofa with Emily and using their mother's silver rose-budded brush to untangle her hair at last. He need not know Emily's comb was badly charred with some of its teeth melted away—or why. It wasn't so easy to conceal Emily sitting only because Anne was holding her upright. Nothing but despair came between him and Emily unable to lift her eyes, keep her head from wobbling with even the gentlest brush strokes, or her boney hands and the knees below them from trembling uncontrollably.

The long-case clock announced midday, the front door bell adding a thirteenth chime.

"That'll be Mr. Nicholls. We have some parish business to discuss. But ... this is not the time."

"No," Emily whispered. "But if you send for the doctor, I will see him now."

Charlotte met Mr. Nicholls in the hallway, telling him to go for Dr. Wheelhouse.

"Anything. Anything, my dear."

Everyone knew what Emily was really giving in to. It didn't matter Mr. Nicholls was obedient or the doctor was attending another patient in Stanbury and took hours to get there. Emily didn't need one's benevolence and the other's expertise, and, as Anne ached to admit, not even the company of her already grieving father and sisters.

They wouldn't be sent away. Instead, Martha and Tabby brought Keeper and Flossy in, the dogs not needing any command to lie down, only a soft "shh" to stop whimpering. Tiger had been curled on Emily's feet for the past hour, no one minding his constant purring. Dick's chirping ceased the moment Charlotte covered his cage.

The room was crowded with waiting and emptied of hope. In the end, Emily was too weak to protest any prayers and tears or prevent Anne's caresses and kisses.

CHAPTER TWENTY-TWO

Haworth, one month later, January 1849

Anne walked around the parlor arm in arm with Ellen, their conversation about anything but recent sorrows or Dr. Teal's consultation with Reverend Brontë, which had gone on for almost an hour. Ellen should have been the best companion to have at such a time. Her rosewater fragrance, sparkling eyes, signature sausage curls, and pretty clothes, even sympathetically gray and black, perked up a somber household. Her kind temper, optimism, and uncomplicated thoughts refused to acknowledge the worst that could yet happen.

Ellen thought Anne looked well, mentioning her pink cheeks and how chatty and companionable she was. What was well-meaning also reminded Anne why she was flushed, had been talking too much, and was afraid she would fall without her friend's support.

At last Charlotte was bidding Dr. Teal goodbye.

Reverend Brontë came into the parlor for the first time since Emily had passed away. He rarely made it a place for being with family. There were Christmas dinners, except last December; for obvious reasons, no one had an appetite for making more of it than the kitchen could accommodate. Anne's memory went back much further, as Charlotte had created it, to when she was only four and their father had called in all of his children and, one by one starting with Anne, had each try on a mask and answer a question. He had lifted her onto his lap and wondered what she wanted most.

Age and experience, Charlotte told her she had said.

Anne didn't doubt it. For a long time she couldn't wait to grow up. Now all she wanted was to grow older.

Her father stood by the fireplace, one hand on the mantle, the other reaching out to Anne. She wasn't ready for why he wanted to embrace her or had so little to say.

"My dear little Anne," he murmured into her hair.

Ellen reacted with a hand to her heart. "Oh, no."

Anne hid her face against her father's chest as long as possible. She need not have worried he and Charlotte would notice her reaction. They were looking anywhere else, likely thinking of their own fear, desperation, and shaken faith, of what they had to go through again.

Anne didn't judge them harshly. She understood the selfishness of loss.

Charlotte touched Ellen's arm. "You must return to Brookroyd. Dr.

Teal thinks there's the possibility of contagion."

"What about you?"

"Anne and I will no longer sleep in the same bed. But, other than that, we are in this together."

***

Dr. Teal was a respected Leeds physician, a specialist in treating consumption. His services cost more than Dr. Wheelhouse, additional expense incurred when, with the consent of Reverend Brontë, he consulted a doctor in London. For those reasons, if not only for those reasons, Anne accepted he was someone to trust and submit to. She never blamed or outwardly doubted him as she endured blistering compresses applied to her side, foul cod liver oil and carbonate of iron, which only increased her nausea even a milk and vegetable diet didn't relieve. At first everything prescribed weakened her more and more, especially inactivity, which often meant staying in bed and feeling entirely useless.

Anne's cough was worse at night, also disturbing Charlotte who won the argument about which of them would sleep on the small bed John Brown brought in from Emily's room after it was disinfected with vinegar and baking soda and its mattress aired. The morning was the most normal part of the day for Anne. She would get up and go downstairs, try a little tea and thin porridge or a boiled egg, brush Flossy, listen to Tabby's commentary on all she knew or assumed to be going on in the neighborhood, watch Charlotte awkwardly knead dough and chop vegetables, all the while Martha toing and froing to take care of other tasks. Emily was rarely spoken of but always present, especially when Keeper crouched under the table and whined, Martha whistled, or Charlotte wiped her hands to adjust her glasses rather than pull paper and pencil out of her apron pocket with an idea that couldn't wait.

Around midday, if he wasn't needed elsewhere, Mr. Nicholls would take the dogs for a walk, a kindness he had been offering for months. After a number of terse refusals, he no longer asked Charlotte to accompany him.

Feverishness returned to Anne by the afternoon, usually not immediately incapacitating. She might spend an hour or two in the parlor struggling to read or write, looking forward to Flossy's return, afraid her eyesight and inspiration never would.

A few days after Dr. Teal's verdict, while—as Charlotte put it—she occupied Emily's chair, Anne shakily scratched out a reply to one of the Robinson girls' letters.

She was very upset with herself for dripping ink on it. "I must not waste paper like this."

Charlotte cautiously held out a pencil, knowing how much Anne hated using one.

Anne didn't refuse Charlotte's offer. She wouldn't intentionally do or say anything to put her sister or father through the powerlessness they had experienced with Branwell and Emily. Instead her most constant answer was to submit and withdraw.

Some days depression blocked every possible route to getting better. Others she willed a way to continued faith in the advice of good doctors, her anxious family and friends, and what she read and wanted to believe. There was the chance Godbold's Vegetable Balsam might succeed as cod liver oil had failed. At least it was better tasting. She hoped to try hydropathy or Mr. Smith Williams' suggestion of homeopathy. The cork soles from Ellen warmed her feet so well Charlotte ordered a pair for herself, and Miss Nussey promised to send a respirator that might be just the thing to help Anne breathe easier.

Anne intended to be as submissive, patient, and piously enduring as was expected, and if she ever veered off that path to do so privately in prayer and poetry. Combine the two, as she had begun to do using her muddled emotions, a half-sheet torn from an unlined notebook and Charlotte's pencil, and she had a hymn, a plea, a plan for recovery one way or other through God as she had discovered Him in her heart long ago. *O let me suffer and not sin, be tortured yet resigned.* She closed her eyes and found Him again in the glistening sun, every little flower, the wilderness of the heath, and the vastness of the sea. She opened them to Flossy's devotion and knew He hadn't deserted her.

Still let me look to Thee, and give me courage to resist the Tempter till he flee. She wanted to be brought back to life but more importantly to the consoling creed that would sustain her whether she was to depart the world sooner or later. *Thus let me serve Thee from my heart, whatever be my written fate.* She was sure she was too frightened to write anything worthwhile. Words seemed of little use when her outlook was so limited. Then she remembered the letter she had recently received from Reverend David Thom of Liverpool in praise of her affirmation of universal salvation. It was such a comfort to have her most passionate beliefs shared by a truly benevolent and thoughtful mind, especially as he and others like him would continue to spread the doctrine of God's goodness and forgiveness when she could not.

Anne had written back to Reverend Thom at the end of December, satisfied with their brief correspondence. *Accept my best wishes on behalf of yourself and your important undertakings, and believe me to remain with sincere esteem yours truly, Acton Bell.* Since the confirmation of her tubercular consumption, she was plagued with wondering if she would ever hear from him again.

Despite her *secret labor to sustain with humble patience every blow, to gather fortitude from pain, and hope and holiness from woe,* panic affected her like the phlegm persistently building up in her lungs and obstructing her breathing. She should be calmed and comforted by the intimacy with God awaiting her beyond the veil, and those other reunions her heart longed for. Instead, *crushed with sorrow, worn with pain,* dying loomed in front of her like a wall. It blocked out the light, prevented any onwards movement, an unrelenting barrier to all she yearned to achieve. She could accept she would never marry or have children, but not, at barely twenty-nine, that she was nearing the end of all her possibilities. *For Thou hast taken my delight and hope of life away.* She thought of her sisters Elizabeth and Maria, who died without planning to. She had been told her mother agonized over leaving her children, but nothing of William's regrets. She could imagine her aunt anticipating heaven in the midst of unbearable suffering, and needed no one to convince her Branwell was as unprepared for dying as he was for living. Emily had barely differentiated between them, performing both with stubborn independence.

For Thou hast taken my delight and hope of life away. For a moment, Anne wasn't sure whether she was writing to face the loss of her worldly existence or Emily's. She continued to feel closer to her departed sister than anyone, not to discount the good, caring one she still had in the flesh, but because no one but Emily had ever loved Anne's contradictions more than her certainty.

I said so with my bleeding heart when first the anguish fell.

***

"I've never known anyone as patient in illness, so courageously cheerful."

Charlotte, rarely patient or cheerful, was relentless in her care of Anne, to the point of being annoyingly attentive and even experiencing a sore throat and chest pains.

"I hate to see you devote so much of your time and thought to me, Charlotte. What about *Shirley*. I'm sure she's neglected."

"She can wait. When you're better I can be Currer Bell again."

Charlotte was not one to choose resignation over "doing something, anything." Her first impulse after Dr. Teal's verdict was to whisk Anne away to somewhere warmer, which, in January, would have to be to the south of England or even the continent. The scheme was, not surprisingly, rejected by their father. Dr. Teal agreed it was a foolish idea due to the strain of travel and because home and rooms of even temperature were safer.

"You must go on writing," Anne lifted her voice to disguise her despondency, "no matter what."

Anne wanted to heed her own advice, if only to finish what she started. As the month moved into its middle, her need to write couldn't overcome her worsening eyesight, inseparable movement and pain, feverish shivering and sweating, and nausea spoiling her appetite, vomiting often a result when she did eat. She coughed as Emily had in her last month, blood spotting her handkerchiefs, collars, cuffs, and pillow. This might be it, Anne thought, far sooner than had been professionally suggested. No one told her outright a cure was impossible. Instead, the talk she heard was of effecting a truce with or arresting the progress of her illness. If only she had been enduring the worst to feel better.

She would probably make it to her birthday, a sad one even without the forecast of it being her last, missing Emily's special presence and parkin, although it was unlikely Anne could keep cake down. Would there be another chance to mark Valentine's Day reminiscing over a card of lace paper and satin ribbon, embossed flowers and a little bird in an egg-filled nest, and the mystery of what *Anne, dear, sweet Anne* really meant? Should she not look ahead to Easter or, if she survived into April, would she be well enough to witness another spring's slow greening, resilient flowers, sweet lambs, nest-hunting curlews and lapwings, low-flying grouse, peacock butterflies, and the gushing of Sladen beck and waterfall? Like Emily, would she be denied one more opportunity to sit on the stone chair shaped by the elements, the ages, and God?

Would she ever be active with Flossy again, with Charlotte's help, at least, take him for walks and call him back from chasing shadows and sheep?

Was there any hope of her reaching the sands and waves of Scarborough once more? Planning to do so in summer when the Robinson sisters holidayed there might have been a good idea if she wasn't already so ill. She was determined to hang on until May, the latter part when warm days were expected and the laburnums and lilacs were in bloom. Beyond that June was often cold, July thundery and rainy, and time even less on her side. From what she had read a change of climate, especially to sea air, could prove beneficial for the consumptive condition if undertaken soon enough, but once the disease progressed too far such action could do more harm than good.

May, late May, was the time she was called to go. "Ellen could accompany us. Not as my nurse—of course not. But as a companion, for you, Charlotte, as much as for me."

"It seems strange you wish to travel when you're out of breath going up or down stairs, unable to eat properly, and weakened by the effort of dressing. To be sick in a strange place, at a strange table, in a strange bed, doesn't seem preferable to being at home."

"A few weeks ago you wanted to take me away."

"I was panicking, not thinking."

"Anyway, Scarborough isn't strange to me. I always feel I belong there."

"I wish I could find such a place."

"Perhaps it will affect you the same. Anyway, with you and Ellen I would be among friends. We might book rooms at Wood's Lodgings."

"We'll see."

Anne guessed what Charlotte didn't say in resistance and wanted to pursue the discussion, but the excitement she felt at the thought of returning to Scarborough quickly wearied her, which in turn brought on stabbing pains in her side, a spell of coughing, a need for Charlotte to get her to the kitchen and a bucket, and the realization that planning anything was ridiculous as she struggled to make it through another day.

***

"She seems better. The January thaw may have helped. I think we may yet hope."

Anne overheard Charlotte talking to their father. If he made a reply from the depths of his study, she didn't catch it.

"Perhaps Dr. Forbes should come after all. You know Mr. Smith offered to pay for his services and travel from London. And Mr. Smith Williams suggested homeopathy as—"

"No."

Anne went nearer the room, standing to the side of its door, which was slightly ajar.

"I don't wish to be placed under such an obligation."

"Not even if it offers hope to keep our Anne with us?"

"If I thought another doctor or homeopathy or any other method not yet tried had a better chance of healing her, I would not need charity to pay. No. I fear it may only impose more trouble on her."

"You're so resigned?"

"Only to the Lord's will, which will save her. If not for this life, then the next."

"I cannot be so passive, Father."

"I know, Charlotte. So you take good care of her. That is your way of faith."

Anne didn't tell Charlotte she was in agreement with their father. Which didn't mean she had given up on medicinal mixtures—other than cod liver oil. She still wanted to try recommended therapies and looked forward to revisiting Scarborough and her writing. By January's close it seemed Anne's own end, for whatever reason, even consumption's trickery, had been deferred. She felt well enough to use ink and work on an unfinished poem as if it was the beginning of her life as she always meant to live it: *more humble, more wise, more strengthened for strife, more apt to lean* on God's love than away from His will. Meant only for her eyes, she crafted and corrected the lines and verses that had come out of *a dreadful darkness* and *bewildered mind.* In a calmer body she found the brightness of faith and clarity of thought to add hope where there was none, abundance when all seemed lost, and, in winter's brief respite, warmth in her heart for when the frost returned.

CHAPTER TWENTY-THREE

Scarborough, four months later, May 1849

Anne sat by the window in the double-bedded room of their perfect situation on the Cliff, happier than ever to have the sea in view. Charlotte came in and suggested shutting out its salty breath. She didn't insist, because Ellen, already there unpacking, was convinced and convincing it was best to let their sister, friend, and patient do exactly as she wished.

"Remember what you wrote to me, Charlotte? That fresh air, if not too warm or too cold, may stimulate her."

"Temporarily. Only temporarily. Its therapeutic effect soon weakens and can even be misleading."

"You also thought the worst about the journey. Despite the delay, it proved fairly easy and, undoubtedly, raised dear Anne's spirits. Has she not already coughed less and smiled more, eaten better, enjoyed shopping and sightseeing, and satisfied, as her Godmother Outhwaite willed, her heart's … desire?"

Anne guessed what word Ellen's hesitation avoided.

"I've also seen how it's weakened her."

Anne was afraid Charlotte's fretting would confine her to Wood's Lodgings. She may have had little choice but be assisted train to train and getting in and out of carriages by unfamiliar masculine arms, and concede the need for hiring a bath chair to take her from The George to the Minster where, even with her companions' help, she couldn't walk farther than the first row of chairs in its nave. Yet she still held out hope she would more freely experience as much of the more pleasant aspects of her Scarborough past as she could in her moment-by-moment shortening future.

***

The next day, after a visit to the Baths and a light dinner taken in No 2's good-sized sitting room, Ellen revealed her skill at fixing Anne's hair to appear slightly curled from under a new pale-blue, chiffon-veiled, straw-flowered bonnet. A satin neck ribbon and lace gloves were the only other evidence of Anne's patronizing one of the most fashionable establishments in York City. It was Ellen's favorite, normally far above any Brontë's budget. However, £200 recently bequeathed to Anne by her Godmother meant respectfully refusing Miss Wooler's offer of accommodation in her house overlooking the bleak North Bay and, instead, enjoying rooms on the prestigious and sunnier Cliff as well as certain other extravagances.

Fanny Outhwaite's generosity couldn't prevent Anne running out of energy to shop more. It hardly mattered. With her arms, chest, and waist reduced to the size of a child's, Anne doubted she would have found a woman's frock to fit. She was more disappointed her sister didn't go beyond half-heartedly looking for new clothes and accessories for herself.

It seemed Charlotte couldn't chose anything but to worry about Anne.

Anne was still alive enough to realize a costly new bonnet would make the Thorpe Green summer holiday muslin dress she had worked for weeks to take in, look shabby. She had forgotten to bring the parasol purchased during her London adventure when the weather had been unsettled. A bamboo-handled one with a hand-painted rice paper canopy, bought from a vendor loitering outside the Bath House, was lighter and prettier. As long as the wind wasn't as strong as Anne knew the sun reflecting off the sands could be, it would be an aid rather than a hindrance.

"Is it your side again?" Charlotte noticed Anne wince as she wrapped the Chinese silk shawl on loan from Ellen tightly around her sister's shoulders.

"No, no." Anne stopped short of saying she felt better than she had in weeks.

She only had herself to blame for the new pain, mostly in her right arm, having asked Charlotte and Ellen to leave her at the Baths, the attendant on duty assuring them she would safely soak in the Spa waters. That meant Anne walked the five hundred yards back to her accommodations alone, chilled with sweating as she reached and unlatched the gate into the Wood's Lodgings front garden.

Anne had lost count of the times she had expected to end up on the floor at home and willed herself to stand and even take a few steps to where she could sit. She needed the same strength of body and mind as she pushed on the gate when she should have pulled it open, hitting it hard as she went down.

A moment later she was facing the housekeeper Mrs. Jefferson, who was too late to help as Anne had already gotten up.

"Please don't say anything to Charlotte or Miss Nussey."

Mrs. Jefferson lent a hand to brushing off Anne's skirt. "But your sister's been waiting for you, watching for you, if not from the front door then through one window or other."

"She would have rushed out if she saw what happened."

"Of course."

"Please don't tell them."

"I won't, Miss."

Mrs. Jefferson kept her word. Anne was certain because otherwise Charlotte wouldn't have accepted Anne's grimace at the touch of her arm as normal discomfort from her illness.

"Can we go now?" Anne didn't conceal her excitement.

As Charlotte wouldn't her misgivings. "I still think you should rest and go down to the beach tomorrow."

Anne felt her chest tighten, but didn't—wouldn't—cough or even lift a hand to her mouth as a reflex. "I can't wait."

"She's all ready for it." Ellen handed Charlotte a straw bonnet lifted from her own baggage.

Charlotte took it, shaking her head, her glasses not hiding her distress as she put it on.

Ellen tied its navy-blue ribbons into a perfect bow under her friend's chin, then stroked Charlotte's shoulders. "And now you are, too."

***

The tide was out, the afternoon as fine as Scarborough ever offered, except to be warmer for swimming or wading in the sea. Anne stayed with her companions until they reached the beach. Charlotte and Ellen didn't want to let her go, but were helpless against Anne's will and legs strengthened by her need to get away from what held her back. The sands cushioned and eased her walking down to the donkey-pulled traps once a cause of pity for those who, because of age, disability or disease, had no other way to enjoy mobility up and down the South Bay shoreline.

"I need some help," Anne was loath but forced to say to the Heathcliff-like lad who chose her before she had a chance to employ another. She also unwillingly groaned as he lifted her onto the seat of his brightly painted little vehicle.

"Yer all bones, Miss." He was soon sitting beside her, surprising her again by laying a small woolen blanket over her lap. It was ragged and smelly, but instantly warmed her legs.

He picked up the reins. Anne noticed he also had a whip in his left hand.

"A gentle drive, please." Anne couldn't be sure of the lad's compliance until he put the whip away. They began to move along at a pace that didn't jolt her body or feel rushed.

After about five minutes the whip was in his hand again. "This ain't a funeral, ole girl." He cracked it across the donkey's hind quarters.

The donkey stopped and kicked up her back legs. The lad lifted his arm to strike her a second time.

"Stop it." Anne grabbed the reins, the blanket sliding to her feet. If she couldn't be his equal in physical strength then in will. "Get off. I'll drive myself."

"'Tis my cart 'n my beast. Well, my da's."

"You—he—might own one but not the other. Not God's blessed creature."

"Well, suit yersen." He jumped down. "It'll cost ye mar."

"Why should it? To reward your cruelty?" Anne was almost in tears, leaning perilously forward to stroke the donkey where the boy had hit her. "Don't you know it's wicked to beat her? How would you like it? What if it was done to you?"

His eyes told her it had been.

Imagining his story, she struggled with continuing to scold him, but, also, realized an opportunity to make him more empathetic. "Animals live and feel as we do. You must remember that in how you treat them."

He mumbled his reasons for needing Millie to go faster, not so much now, out of season, but when the crowds came and he lost business to other boys who sold two even three rides to his one. Anne told him he might charge a little more for customers who wanted or even required a slower ride.

"You might specialize," she concluded, not sure she had talked him into anything the offer of an extra penny would have also achieved.

"No, Anne, you can't." Ellen was running up from the water's edge.

"I can. And I will." Immediately Anne was sorry she sounded so cross with her friend. "I'll be fine."

"You won't go far? Not out of sight."

"Once up and down."

"Tha'll tak 'n hour or mar wi' Millie," the boy remarked.

"If it does, there'll be another coin for you. Oh, here comes Charlotte." Anne barely tugged the reins and Millie lifted her head, braying as she began to walk.

Anne didn't feel guilty escaping. She had saved Millie and herself from the dominance of others for a while and thought driving the cart might show Charlotte the holiday was doing her good. In truth, Anne was moving away from the exhausting fight to survive towards surrendering to the precious time she had left. The curve of the bay was all hers. A beautiful sparkling headland lay ahead. The dip and lift of gulls and equally roguish clouds were almost indistinguishable as was the sea sounding near and far. She couldn't stop thinking about what came next, mulling over questions soon to be answered. Was dying like closing her eyes without the choice to open them again? Would vision be gone or just different? If it was like falling asleep, would she be as unaware of the precise moment it happened, not knowing it had until she came to in another way of being? Or was the transfer between life and death like getting off one train and moving to a different platform to board another, not for a change in direction or destination, just to continue? Would she slip away from everything or everything slip away from her? Would nothing matter but the state of her soul? What if there wasn't a consciousness she could still recognize as her own, or any at all? She couldn't fathom extinction: to be without feelings or thoughts, to be nothing. She might be just one among many, but never nothing. Except as her brother had teased, as she hoped he had been teasing.

Would pain or peace see her out? She might have an idea of what it was like to be short of breath, but not without it completely. As she watched Branwell and Emily take their last, it seemed the hardest thing they had ever done. Anne wanted dying to be welcome and welcoming, releasing and promising, like driving along the shore that afternoon and how she had tried to steer her life, her hands on the reins but faith guiding her progress.

Graying Millie might be slow but she was wise, going gingerly one way and then the other, staying above the wettest sand that could swallow enough of the carriage's wheels to necessitate a cry for help. When they did stop, it was because Millie decided to. What some called a dumb animal Anne appreciated as a special creature of God's making, who sensed Anne's need to pause and reflect in some semblance of solitude.

Anne thought of Lily, her Scarborough friend in passing. Their correspondence had ended too soon and Anne never made inquiries as to why Lily had gone silent. Perhaps she would see her soon. She waved to Charlotte and Ellen waiting with the donkey boy. There weren't many goodbyes left to make. Home—the touch, the sight, the sounds, the smells, its memories and those yet to be made, its isolation and inclusion, its agreements and arguments, its reverence and scandals, its joys and sorrows—was done with her now. The last time she saw Tabby, the old woman scolded her for leaving them and forgave her with a hug. John Brown busied himself with loading their cases on the gig waiting in Church Street, eventually wishing her well with a wipe of his eyes accepting she wasn't. Mr. Nicholls was discreet about the private word she'd had with him a few days earlier regarding keeping William's memorial plaque polished and not giving up on gaining Charlotte's affection. He was also something of a savior as he steadied her father stumbling back from embracing her shoulders and kissing her cheek. She had made her weepy farewells to Keeper, Tiger, and Dick the canary. The years and last days adoring and being adored by Flossy turned into last moments when Martha, tears streaming, carried him out and handed him to Anne already seated in the chaise.

"My dear, dear little man. What a love we have." Anne buried her face in his silky fur, caressing his underbelly, ears, and tail, kissing each paw, holding onto him until Charlotte and Ellen were squeezed with her and the driver said they had to go if they were to catch their train to Leeds.

When Anne looked ahead again, the gypsy boy, Charlotte, and Ellen were approaching. The lad roughly grabbed Millie's bridle to stop her, then, realizing Anne was watching him, stroked the donkey's nose. As he helped her down from the carriage, she made him promise to be good to Millie, certain Charlotte and Ellen weren't amused when she told him she would haunt him if he wasn't.

"You've worn yourself out caring more for that donkey than yourself," Charlotte said softly, sadly.

Anne assured all she needed was to rest and a dose of Mrs. Jefferson's dandelion coffee. "I have my heart set on a stroll along Cliff Bridge before sunset."

Ellen put a hand on Charlotte's arm and, although she whispered, Anne was certain she heard, "This evening, tomorrow, and however many days after are your sister's to be foolish with."

A few hours later they were walking the gusty roadway over the steep descent between St Nicholas Cliff and the Spa, Charlotte and Ellen holding onto their bonnets and each other, stopping to see where Anne was.

"Take my hand," Charlotte begged of her sister, "or I'm afraid I'll lose you like a feather in this wind."

"Don't worry. I'll meet you at the other side." Anne knew it would take more than words to persuade them to move on. She stepped to the bridge's seaward railing, looking east, the darkness slowly coming towards and over her, not ominously but illuminating as God was, turning her around in the direction of his promise.

Anne reached up and lifted the veil between her and what was meant to take her breath away.

AFTERWORD

Anne Brontë died in Scarborough on Monday, May 28, 1849 at about two in the afternoon. Charlotte and Ellen Nussey were at her bedside in Wood's Lodgings where the Grand Hotel now stands. Charlotte made the decision to have her youngest sister buried "where the flower had fallen" rather than transport her body back to Haworth. Besides Charlotte and Ellen, the only other mourner at Anne's Christ Church funeral was their former Roe Head mistress, Miss Wooler, who owned a house on the North Bay. Anne was interred in St. Mary's churchyard on Castle Hill overlooking the sea.

> *I longed to view that bliss divine,*
> *Which eye hath never seen;*
> *To see the glories of his face*
> *Without the veil between.*
> ~ from Anne Brontë's poem, *In Memory of a Happy Day in February*

READING THE BRONTËS

Merry Christmas from Aunt Renee, 1943. When my mother was fourteen she received a book that fed her appetite for novels and offered an escape from her own complicated narrative. Published by Random House, New York, it was wider and "taller" than it was thick, bound in dark blue-green with a slightly gullied joint and gold lettering on a strong spine, front and back boards illustrated by the work of Fritz Eichenberg, more of his moodily magnificent wood engravings within. Monotype Bodoni with long descenders and double-columns presented its text, chapters running on without pause, like the brave and breathless mind and spirit that filled it with one of the most mercilessly compelling, passionate, earthy unearthly stories ever told.

Over twenty years later this classic hardcover edition of *Wuthering Heights* was re-gifted to me and my reading the Brontës began with Emily. She immediately and irrevocably enticed me out of 1960s suburban America, away from fenced-in yards, narrow sidewalks, and managed nature, into the wilderness of her West Yorkshire world, inexhaustible imagination and uncompromising soul. I had never before read a novel as descriptive and dramatic, bold and mesmerizing, as validating of my own mystic inclinations. Of course, I hadn't. I was only twelve.

I believe I can credit reading Emily with the early maturing of my literary preferences. Her poetry soon followed and I felt even more akin to her: introverted but intense, a homebody with wanderlust, quiet with much "to say", my fantasies my salvation.

Wuthering Heights led to *Jane Eyre*, also at my adolescent fingertips. My mother owned the matching 1943 edition originally boxed as a set with *Wuthering Heights*. Lent to a reckless relative, it came to me a little battered and begged to be handled devotedly. Soon I was occupied by the reticence, resilience, and quiet and artistic sensibility of Jane, and entertained by the romance, mystery and maneuverings of her journey. If in my younger days I didn't feel the empathy with Charlotte I did with Emily, later, much later I found myself identifying with Charlotte's struggles and strength, even her stubbornness, certainly her conflicted ambition. Earlier and later I couldn't help appreciate and aspire to

Charlotte's mastery at storytelling.

Unfortunately, neither of Anne's novels were included in the Eichenberg illustrated collection. Still, a treasured copy of *Agnes Grey* also found its way to me through my mother: a 3 ¼ by 5 ¼ hardcover edition she had purchased from a second-hand book store in Oxford on a visit while I was living in England. It was part of the Oxford University World Classics range, first published in 1907 and reprinted numerous times up until the 1970s, which included all four of Charlotte's novels, *Wuthering Heights*, and, also, Anne's *The Tenant of Wildfell Hall*. Despite the diminutive dimensions of this edition of *Agnes Grey*, the front of its burnt-sienna dust jacket had space for a Leonard Rosoman black and white illustration of governess Agnes. Its text was tiny, reminiscent of the Brontë juvenilia, requiring youthful eyes or a magnifying glass.

From the multitude of documentaries about the Brontës, and movies, even pop music, inspired by Charlotte's and Emily's books, it was all too easy to neglect Anne's presence and influence in her family and literature. As an English major in college, those "in charge" of my education barely mentioned her if at all. They might have been directing my edification as they thought necessary, but not my curiosity more piqued by the neglected than celebrated.

In the mid-1990s while organizing book shelves I happened upon my minature *Agnes Grey*. Flipping through it I stopped at Chapter XXIV, *The Sands*. I was reminded of my first and only visit to Scarborough, North Yorkshire in March 1974 when sightseeing took me up to the medieval Fortress on the town's northern headland. Back down Castle Road I detoured into the yard of the little church—St. Mary's—where, a month or so earlier, when at last I made it to Haworth, I had learned Anne was buried. If walking through the cold, rolling fog behind the Brontë parsonage unable to resist calling out "Heathcliff" was surreal, standing at the small wind-and-salt weathered monument to Anne's courageous self-determination opened a new chapter in my Brontë reading. Finding her interred apart from her family, away from the place name and environment that, for me as for so many others, she and her siblings were inevitably associated with, my first thoughts on "why?" were intuitive rather than informed.

I could understand Anne wanting to be near Scarborough's curve of headlands, beaches, and watery outlook to "somewhere foreign and, therefore, appealing." I found myself in her reasons to value those rare moments in sight and sound and smell of the sea. I identified with her relief and exhilaration when she was out-of-sight of all whose assumptions had for too long defined and restricted her.

Even when all I had to go on was a hunch, I suspected Anne Brontë was something of a rebel, not in defiance but for discovery.

Scarborough had lured Anne to move from mortality to eternity because she couldn't ignore her need for a way all her own. The only thing in error regarding her burial away from Haworth was the inscription on the stone noting her age when she died. Symbolically that chiseled "typo" took away the year of Anne's greatest accomplishment, forewarning Charlotte literally doing so when she refused a posthumous reprinting of *The Tenant of Wildfell Hall.*

I'll admit I didn't read Anne's second novel until I decided to write one about her and wondered—and soon recognized—why it had taken me over half a century to do both.

Sometimes the closest thing to ourselves takes a long time to reach. My mother made it to Haworth in 1975. For reasons that seemed important at the time and now I can only regret, I wasn't with her as she walked up the hill, heard her steps on the cobblestones and voices of the dead, inhaled the mist, saw the parsonage and windswept trees and moors, and, perhaps, if silently, did a little Heathcliff calling of her own to turn the pages back. I didn't see if her eyes sparkled, but like to think they did.

NOTES: QUOTED POETRY AND PROSE

PART ONE

Chapter One

1) "a gentleman with a little dark speck of a dog running after him"
   From *Agnes Grey* by Anne Brontë, Chapter XXIV

Chapter Two

1) *unto her spirit given*
   From fifth verse of *In Memory of a Happy Day in February* by Anne Brontë
   It was a glimpse of truth divine
   Unto my spirit given
   Illumined by a ray of light
   That shone direct from heaven!

2) *The lightest heart I have ever known, the kindest I shall ever know*
   From second verse of *A Reminiscence* by Anne Brontë
   May stand upon the cold, damp stone,
   And think that, frozen, lies below
   The lightest heart that I have known,
   The kindest I shall ever know.

Chapter Three

1) *Oh let me be alone a while, no human form is nigh. And I may sing and muse aloud, no mortal ear is by*
   From first verse of *Retirement* by Anne Brontë
   O, let me be alone a while,
   No human form is nigh.
   And may I sing and muse aloud,
   No mortal ear is by.

Away! ye dreams of earthly bliss,
Ye earthly cares begone:
Depart! ye restless wandering thoughts,
And let me be alone!

2) *Oh, dear God, let his memory stay with me and never pass away*
From first verse of *In Memory of a Happy Day in February* by
Anne Brontë
Blessed be Thou for all the joy
My soul has felt today!
O let its memory stay with me
And never pass away!
I was alone, for those I loved
Were far away from me,
The sun shone on the withered grass,
The wind blew fresh and free.

Chapter Six

1) "'In the dungeon-crypts idly did I stray, reckless of the lives
wasting there away; Draw the ponderous bars! open, Warder
stern! and He dared not say me nay—the hinges harshly turn.'"
From first verse of *The Prisoner A Fragment* by Emily Brontë
In the dungeon-crypts idly did I stray,
Reckless of the lives wasting there away;
"Draw the ponderous bars! open, Warder stern!"
He dared not say me nay—the hinges harshly turn.

3) "'The captive raised her face; it was as soft and mild as a sculptured marble saint, or slumbering unwean'd child; it was so
soft and mild, it was so sweet and fair, pain could not trace a
line, nor grief a shadow there!'"

From fourth verse of *The Prisoner A Fragment* by Emily Brontë
The captive raised her face; it was as soft and mild
As sculptured marble saint, or slumbering unwean'd child;
It was so soft and mild, it was so sweet and fair,
Pain could not trace a line, nor grief a shadow there!

2) "'I have gone backward in the work, the labor has not sped; drowsy and dark my spirit lies, heavy and dull as lead.'"
From first verse of *Despondency* by Anne Brontë
I have gone backward in the work,
The labour has not sped,
Drowsy and dark my spirit lies,
Heavy and dull as lead.
How can I rouse my sinking soul
From such a lethargy?
How can I break these iron chains,
And set my spirit free?

3) "'How can I rouse my sinking soul from such a lethargy? How can I break those iron chains and set my spirit free?'"
See #2

PART TWO

Chapter Eight

1) "'What though the Sun had left my sky—'"
From first verse of *Fluctuations* by Anne Brontë
What though the sun had left my sky;
To save me from despair
The blessed moon arose on high,
And shone serenely there.
I watched her, with a tearful gaze,

Rise slowly o'er the hill,
While through the dim horizon's haze
Her light gleamed faint and chill.

2) "'To save me from despair the blessed Moon arose on high,
    and shone serenely there.'"
    See #1

3) "'I thought such wan and lifeless beams could ne'er my heart
    repay, for the bright sun's most transient gleams that cheered
    me through the day. But as above that mist's control she rose
    and brighter shone—I felt a light upon my soul!'"
    From second and third verses of *Fluctuations* by Anne Brontë
    I thought such wan and lifeless beams
    Could ne'er my heart repay,
    For the bright sun's most transient gleams
    That cheered me through the day:

    But as above that mist's control
    She rose, and brighter shone,
    I felt her light upon my soul;
    But now—that light is gone!

Chapter Nine

1) "'God. If this indeed be all that Life can show to me; if on my
    aching brow may fall no freshening dew from Thee; if no
    brighter light than this the lamp of hope may glow, and I may
    only dream of bliss and wake to weary woe—'"
    From first verse of *If This Be All* by Anne Brontë
    God! if this indeed be all
    That Life can show to me;
    If on my aching brow may fall
    No freshening dew from Thee,—
    If with no brighter light than this
    The lamp of hope may glow,

And I may only dream of bliss,
And wake to weary woe;

2) "'If friendship's solace must decay, when other joys are gone,
   and love must keep so far away—'"
   From second verse of *If This Be All* by Anne Brontë
   If friendship's solace must decay,
   When other joys are gone,
   And love must keep so far away,
   While I go wandering on,

Chapter Ten

1) "'Music, when soft voices die, vibrates in the memory.'"
   From first verse of *Music, When Soft Voices Die* by Percy Bysshe
   Shelly
   Music, when soft voices die,
   Vibrates in the memory -
   Odours, when sweet violets sicken,
   Live within the sense they quicken.

2) "'Come, chase that starting tear away, ere mine to meet it
   springs; to-night, at least, to-night be gay, whate'er to-morrow
   brings. Like sunset gleams, that linger late when all is
   darkening fast, are hours like these we snatch from Fate—the
   brightest, and the last.'"
   From refrain of *Come, Chase that Starting Tear Away*, French Air
   by Thomas Moore
   Come, chase that starting tear away,
   Ere mine to meet it springs;
   To-night, at least, to-night be gay,
   Whate'er to-morrow brings.
   Like sunset gleams, that linger late
   When all is darkening fast,
   Are hours like these we snatch from Fate--
   The brightest, and the last.

Then, chase that starting tear, etc.

3) "'To gild the deepening gloom, if Heaven but one bright hour allow, oh think that one bright hour is given in all its splendor now!'"

    From verse of *Come, Chase that Starting Tear Away*, French Air by Thomas Moore

    To gild our dark'ning life, if Heaven

    But one bright hour allow,

    Oh! think that one bright hour is given,

    In all its splendour, now!

    Let's live it out -- then sink in night

    Like waves that from the shore

    One minute swell -- are touched with light --

    Then lost for evermore.

PART THREE

Chapter Thirteen

1) ... composed musings out of *sorrows or anxieties* to acknowledge in a resilient way all those *powerful feelings* that could never be *wholly crushed* and for which solace from *any living creature* shouldn't be sought or expected.

    Italic words/phrases from *Agnes Grey* by Anne Brontë, Chapter XVIII

2) *The ties that bind us to life are tougher than you imagine, or than anyone can who has not felt how roughly they may be pulled without breaking.*

    From *Agnes Grey* by Anne Brontë, Chapter XIII

Chapter Fourteen

1) Again exalted voices: "'*Sei getreu bis in den Tod, so will ich dir die Ktone des Lebens geben. Fürche dich nicht, ich bin bei dir.*'"
Emily understood German better than Anne and didn't need to refer as often to the English translation of the libretto they shared.
Be faithful unto death, as I want to give you the crown of life. Fear not, I am with you.
"'*Sie weinten und sprachen. Schone doch deiner selbst. Das widerfahre dir nur nicht*'".
They wept and said. Save yourself. That shall not happen to you.
As the Oratorio's drama neared its end, Anne saw she wasn't the only one wiping away tears as well as sweat. "'*Er hat den Lauf vollendet, er hat Glauben gehalten.*'" *He has finished the course, he has kept the faith*
Original German and English translation from the Oratorio *Paulus* by Felix Mendelsohn

Chapter Fifteen

1) "'A younger boy was with me there, his hand upon my shoulder leant; his heart, like mine, was free from care.'"
From *Z---------'s Dream* by Anne Brontë

2) "'They had learnt from length of strife—of civil war and anarchy—to laugh at death and look on life with somewhat lighter sympathy.'"
From *Why Ask To Know The Date—The Clime?* by Emily Brontë

3) "'We had wandered far that day o'er that forbidden ground away—ground, to our rebel feet how dear. Danger and freedom both were there—'"
From *Z---------'s Dream* by Anne Brontë

4) "'It was the autumn of the year; the time to laboring peasants,

dear: week after week, from noon to noon, September shone as bright as June.'"
From *Why Ask To Know The Date—The Clime?* by Emily Brontë

5) "'He bade me pause and breathe a while, but spoke it with a happy smile. His lips were parted to inhale the breeze that swept the ferny dale, and chased the clouds across the sky …'"
From *Z---------'s Dream* by Anne Brontë

6) *I know that ghosts have wandered on earth. Be with me always—take any form—drive me mad!*
From *Wuthering Heights* by Emily Brontë, Chapter XVI

7) *First study; then approve; then love*
From *The Tenant of Wildfell Hall* by Anne Brontë, Chapter XVI

Chapter Sixteen

1) *upon the wintry breezes borne*
From first verse of *Music on Christmas Morning* by Anne Brontë
Music I love - but never strain
Could kindle raptures so divine,
So grief assuage, so conquer pain,
And rouse this pensive heart of mine -
As that we hear on Christmas morn,
Upon the wintry breezes borne.

PART FOUR

Chapter Nineteen

1) *My nature was not originally calm … I have learned to appear so by dint of hard lessons and many repeated efforts.*
From *The Tenant of Wildfell Hall* by Anne Brontë, Chapter XXXVIII

Chapter Twenty-two

1) *O let me suffer and not sin, be tortured yet resigned.*
From first verse of *Last Lines* by Anne Brontë
A dreadful darkness closes in
On my bewildered mind;
O let me suffer and not sin,
Be tortured yet resigned.

2) *Still let me look to Thee, and give me courage to resist the Tempter till he flee.*
From second verse of *Last Lines* by Anne Brontë
Through all this world of whelming mist
Still let me look to Thee,
And give me courage to resist
The Tempter till he flee

3) *Thus let me serve Thee from my heart, whatever be my written fate.*
From fourteenth verse of *Last Lines* by Anne Brontë
Thus let me serve Thee from my heart
Whatever be my written fate,
Whether thus early to depart
Or yet awhile to wait.

4) *secret labor to sustain with humble patience every blow, to gather fortitude from pain, and hope and holiness from woe,*
From thirteenth verse of *Last Lines* by Anne Brontë
That secret labour to sustain
With humble patience every blow,
To gather fortitude from pain
And hope and holiness from woe.

5) *crushed with sorrow, worn with pain,*
From eleventh verse of *Last Lines* by Anne Brontë
Weak and weary though I lie,
Crushed with sorrow, worn with pain,

Still I may lift to Heaven mine eyes
And strive and labour not in vain,

6) *For Thou hast taken my delight and hope of life away.*
From seventh verse of *Last Lines* by Anne Brontë
For Thou hast taken my delight
And hope of life away,
And bid me watch the painful night
And wait the weary day.

7) *I said so with my bleeding heart when first the anguish fell.*
From sixth verse of *Last Lines* by Anne Brontë
But Thou hast fixed another part,
And Thou hast fixed it well;
I said so with my bleeding heart
When first the anguish fell.

8) *more humble, more wise, more strengthened for strife, more apt to*
lean
From fifteenth verse of *Last Lines* by Anne Brontë
If Thou shouldst bring me back to life
More humbled I should be;
More wise, more strengthened for the strife,
More apt to lean on Thee.

9) *a dreadful darkness* and *bewildered mind*
From first verse of *Last Lines* by Anne Brontë
A dreadful darkness closes in
On my bewildered mind;
O let me suffer and not sin,
Be tortured yet resigned.

About the Author

A native of Western New York, DM Denton finds her voice in poetry and prose, truth and imagination. Through observation and study, inspired by music, art, classic literature, nature, and the contradictions of the creative and human spirit, she loves to wander into the past to discover stories of interest and meaning for the present, writing from her love of language and a fascination with what has been left in the shadows.

Her educational journey took her from a theater and communication major at SUNY Brockport to an English literature and history curriculum at Rosary Hill College (now known as Daemen College), Amherst, NY and Wroxton College, Oxfordshire, England. She stayed in the UK for sixteen years in a yellow-stoned village with thatched cottages, duck pond, and twelfth century church and an abbey turned Jacobean manor house (now Fairleigh Dickinson University Wroxton College), surrounded by the beautiful hills, woods and fields of the Oxfordshire countryside—a life-changing experience that resonates in her personal and professional endeavors to this day.

Always writing and creating, DM Denton's day jobs have included gardening, retail, administration, and volunteer coordinating at WNED Public Broadcasting. She currently works as clerk for the Zoning and Codes Administration of the small rural Western New York town where she resides in a cozy log cabin along with her mother and a multitude of cats.

DM Denton is also an artist who has illustrated the covers and interiors of her own and others' books.

Previous publications by DM Denton released by All Things That Matter Press are: *A House Near Luccoli*, its sequel *To A Strange Somewhere Fled* and two Kindle shorts, *The Snow White Gift* and *The Library Next Door*. She has also published an illustrated journal, *A Friendship with Flowers*.

Please visit DM Denton's website: http://www.dmdenton-author-artist.com and blog: http://bardessdmdenton.wordpress. You can also find her on Facebook, Twitter, Goodreads, Pinterest, Google Plus, LinkedIn and Instagram.

ALL THINGS THAT MATTER PRESS

FOR MORE INFORMATION ON TITLES AVAILABLE FROM
ALL THINGS THAT MATTER PRESS, GO TO
http://allthingsthatmatterpress.com
or contact us at
allthingsthatmatterpress@gmail.com

54797970R00124

Made in the USA
Columbia, SC
06 April 2019